Praise for R

Good Neighbors

"Connor's ability to richly develop each character and plot thread is fascinating even when the horror is reserved... the constricting pressure as the dread piles on makes this book hard to put down and even harder to go to sleep after reading. This is a great novel..."

-David J. Sharp, *Horror Underground*

Second Unit

"Intricately plotted and vividly layered with suspense, emotional intensity and strategic violence."

-Michael Price, *Fort Worth Business Press*

"Drips with eeriness...an enjoyable book by a promising author."

-Kyle White, *The Harrow Fantasy and Horror Journal*

Finding Misery

"Major-league action, car chases, subterfuge, plot twists, with a smear of rough sex on top. Sublime."

-Arianne "Tex" Thompson, author of *Medicine for the Dead* and *One Night in Sixes*

The Jackal Man

"Connor delivers a brisk, action-packed tale that explores the dark forests of the human--and inhuman--heart. Sure to thrill creature fans everywhere."

-Scott Nicholson, author of *They Hunger* and *The Red Church*

Also by Russell C. Connor

Novels
Race the Night*
The Jackal Man
Whitney
Finding Misery*
Sargasso*
Good Neighbors
Between
Predator

Collections
Howling Days*
Killing Time*

The Box Office of Terror Trilogy
Second Unit*
Director's Cut

The Dark Filament Ephemeris
Volume I: Through the Deep Forest
Volume II: On the Shores of Tay-ho
Volume III: Sands of the Prophet
Volume IV: The Halls of Moambati

eBook Format Novellas and Shorts
Outside the Lines*
Dark World
Talent Scout
Endless
Mr. Buggins
The Playground

*Indicates Dark Filament Ephemeris supplementary connection

BETWEEN

Russell C. Connor

Visit us online at

DarkFilament.com

Contact the author at
facebook.com/russellcconnor
Or follow on Twitter @russellcconnor

Cover Art by SaberCore23 Artwork Studio
For commissions, visit sabercore23art.com

ISBN:
978-0-9864431-6-9

First Edition: 2017

ONE

Roberta spotted the man in the white coat first, as he stumbled through the shaggy grass lining the edge of Country Road 407 with his back to them. She turned down the sweet sounds of George Strait crooning on the radio, jabbed a blunt finger at the windshield, and asked, "Honey, who is that?"

JD Miller squinted over the Tahoe's steering wheel. Beyond the blazing cones of the truck's headlights, the slivered October moon dusted the land with a cold glaze. Just enough to crisp the outline of the sparsely wooded fields as they rolled past without giving any real definition to anything beyond the glass. The darkness allowed a billion stars to glow overhead, but he didn't know how his wife could possibly see—

Wait. *There*. The shape of a long, square-shouldered jacket floated through the gloom on the right side of the road ahead, visible only because of the night's contrast against its glaring white surface. The figure's dark head and hands and lower half blended in with the surroundings, making it look like the Invisible Man out for a stroll.

"Don't know," JD answered, "but that looks like some sorta hospital getup."

"*Hospital getup?*"

"You know, like a doctor coat."

"Oh. Well, maybe it's Doc then."

JD shook his head. If it'd been the veterinarian whose property bordered the tail end of CR 407, they would've recognized him, even from this distance. The man weighed over 300 pounds; his backside would've been as broad as a blimp. "Nope. Prob'ly just an escaped mental patient. Gonna sneak in your window tonight and get a li'l nookie." He put a hand on the wide thigh of her jeans and squeezed.

"Oh goody! Let's see if *he* can get the job done without fallin asleep halfway through." She gave him a teasing smirk and slapped his hand away, then leaned forward to peer through the windshield again. "Who'd be out here in the dark without even a flashlight?"

JD shrugged. Couldn't be that much of a mystery. 407 was a dead-end road, branching off of Bear Creek Parkway far behind them. The only traffic this hidden slice of heaven ever saw came from those fortunate enough to live on it. At this point in its long, winding course, the closest house was the Austin's split level ranch about a quarter mile back, but they'd already shuttered it for the winter and lit out for their home in Phoenix. Ahead, empty Corp of Engineering land stretched for a few acres before you hit the last run of properties and the empty Texas hill country beyond.

So, more than likely, the person coming up on the shoulder was one of their neighbors, out walking in the dark while wearing a knee-length, butcher-style coat for some reason. Heck, maybe he was even heading to the same place as them.

Just a neighbor. A familiar face.

All the same, an uneasy worm inched its way up JD's spine.

As they approached, their headlights finally washed over the figure, giving his backside more detail. A scrawny build, maybe a buck-fifty on weight, if that. Gray pants of some rough weave, black loafers, short brown hair. He took small, halting steps along the right side of the road with shoulders hunched, one arm wrapped around his middle and the other hanging limp. Their headlights threw the man's shadow out long in front of him, but he gave no reaction.

JD still didn't recognize the guy, but, then again, he didn't make a habit of memorizing what his neighbors looked like from behind. As George Strait gave way to Willie Nelson on the radio, he slowed the truck and swung far over to the left, until the driver's side tires departed the loose gravel of the narrow road and rolled through the grass.

"What are you doin?" Roberta asked.

"What's it look like? I'm goin around him."

"Hold on, he might need help!"

Roberta Miller, ever the philanthropist. She must be sponsoring a dozen Ethiopian children these days, feeding them all for just pennies per day. "I'm sure he's fine, Berta."

"I don't know, he looks hurt. We can't just leave him without checking!"

JD glanced at the dashboard clock. 7:12. She'd delayed him a half hour by taking so long to get ready, and now she wanted to play Good Samaritan. "We're late enough as it is. I promised Mitch we would be there."

She flapped a dismissive hand. "Mitch is a big boy. He became president of the HOA all by himself, and he can handle one meeting without you there."

"Yeah, but you know what's on the agenda tonight. He needs all the support he can get."

Roberta looked at him in the dark truck cab with eyes narrowed and jaw set. "John Delbert, you pull up next to this man so I can talk to him. Go on now, it'll only take a sec."

JD sighed and pressed the brake as they came abreast of the figure on the roadside. The white garment definitely looked like a doctor coat, but now that they were so close, he could see that ragged holes and dirt stains covered the back. No, not dirt; they were too black for that. In fact, they looked more like...

Scorch marks.

The worm moved again, up his neck and onto his scalp, making the hair bristle.

Roberta either didn't notice, or remained unfazed. She pressed the button to roll down her window and poked her head out. "Excuse me, sir, are you all r—"

The figure's head came up and slowly swiveled to face them.

JD's wife gave a tiny screech and jerked back inside the truck.

The entire left side of the man's face was a burned, melted ruin, the flesh mottled red and boil-ridden, the nose charred, the hair along his temple singed. One eyelid looked seared shut; the other widened when it registered their presence. His mouth opened—the lips peeling back to reveal blackened gums—and he garbled something that was lost under the growl of the engine. He raised the arm wrapped around his midsection and clutched at the open window. Flakes of cooked skin stuck to the door wherever he made contact.

Roberta screamed long and loud this time.

JD's foot came off the brake for only a moment—more from shock than an attempt to flee—but it caused them to lurch forward. The man beside the vehicle was yanked off his feet and fell out of sight. JD's knuckles whitened on the steering wheel as he waited to see if he would get back up.

"Oh my Lord. Oh sweet heavens." Roberta's hand fluttered at her chest between her massive breasts.

"Where..." JD stopped, swallowed a hard lump of saliva. "Where'd he go? Did we run him over?"

"I don't know..."

"Well *look*, woman!"

It took her several seconds to work up the nerve, but then she eased her head out once more and stared downward. Finally, she declared, "I don't think you hit him, but he's ain't movin!"

JD threw the truck into park and remembered to flip on the hazards as he opened his door and jumped from the cab. The cool October night slapped him in the face after the warmth inside the Tahoe. His breath left a contrail as he ran around the front of the vehicle, where clouds of road dust swirled through the headlights. He slowed as he reached the passenger side and eased cautiously around the bumper.

The man in the white coat lay face down beside the truck, sprawled half across the gravel and half in the grass. They hadn't run him over, but it was a close thing. If they'd rolled so much as another foot forward, they'd have been washing brains out of the Tahoe's rear tire treads.

"Buddy? You, um...you all right?" JD approached as gingerly as he would a wild animal. When the man gave no response, JD knelt, grabbed one shoulder, and rolled him over gently, out of the way of the truck's wheel. Even through the man's burnt jacket and the collared blue shirt beneath, JD could feel the flesh crinkle and crunch under his hand, like the charred shell of a roasted marshmallow. He wiped his palm on the leg of his jeans.

From above him, Roberta asked, "Is…is he…?"

"He's alive. I think." The man's good eye was now also closed, but his chest rose and fell, the breaths too shallow to crystallize in the chilly air. Hard to tell with all the damage to his face, but JD didn't think he was one of their neighbors after all. Those scorch marks were all over his clothing, and wispy tendrils of smoke still rose from a few of them. The smell of burnt hair and well-done meat made JD's gorge rise. He noticed a rectangle of plastic clipped to the breast pocket of the lab coat, but couldn't read it in the dark. "Get my phone. Call 911."

Roberta turned in her seat and rummaged through the center console. JD stayed hunkered beside the prone figure, wanting to try rousing the man again but unable to bring himself to touch that blistered flesh. Jesus, what could have done so much damage to him?

A high chittering sound from behind tore his attention away.

He rose and spun. Just a few yards from the edge of the road lay the wire fence that formed the boundary of the Corp land. Beyond that, the grass grew tall and wild for a short stretch before turning into dense woodland. The boughs of the first oaks and ash trees—still full from this year's mild autumn temperatures—were visible only as vague silhouettes against the stars. JD peered into the night, whose darkness now seemed less comforting and more ominous.

The noise came again from the left, closer this time, a grinding chirp. Almost angry-sounding. It could've been a squirrel or chipmunk, except such critters were already sheltered for the night, hiding from owls and snakes on the hunt. JD took a step forward, squinting into the grass, and then the hip-high weeds on the other side of the fence rattled and shook as something bolted through them, making for the tree line.

JD gasped and stepped away, bumping into the body behind him. It'd been a hell of a lot bigger than a squirrel, huge enough for him to hear its footfalls. JD couldn't think of any animal around here big enough to make a racket like that.

He didn't realize how creeped out he'd become until Roberta grabbed his arm, sending an electric bolt of shock through him.

"It's not working," she said, squeezing her wide shoulders through the truck window.

"What's not?"

"Your damn phone. It just keeps beepin."

"Then you're doin somethin wrong, woman." JD took the device from her and looked at the screen. Full signal bars showed in the corner; they never had any problem with reception, even way out here. He dialed 9-1-1 and hit send, but his phone just gave a series of rapid tones before disconnecting.

"Told you." Roberta sounded reproachful, but her eyes looked large and glassy in the dimness. "Whatta we do?"

JD looked both ways up 407, hoping to see approaching headlights. Someone else that could offer an opinion. But they were still alone. "C'mon," he finally said. "Grab his feet and help me lift him into the back of the truck."

"I'm not touchin him!" Horror swept over his wife's face. Apparently it was all right to be Mother Theresa as long as the lepers weren't too gross.

"Fine." He went to open the tailgate. "You can stay here with him while I go get help."

She glared at him again but reluctantly got out of the truck. JD let her grab the man's ankles while he slid arms under his shoulders. Together, they managed to get him off the ground and onto the truck's bed. He moaned once but didn't stir.

"You wanna drive him all the way to town?"

JD shook his head as he raised the tailgate. "It'd take us an hour. Can't let him rattle and roll in the truck bed that long, especially not with it this cold out. Community center's just ten minutes further. We can use someone else's phone to call for help. And maybe Gladys can do something for him until we can get an ambulance."

And, of course, Mitch would be there. He would know what to do. Always had, ever since they were in high school. The world just made sense to JD when Mitchell Flynn was in charge of it.

Roberta climbed back inside the truck on the passenger side. JD went to his door, but spared one last glance at the dark Corp land before ducking into the cab. As he popped the transmission into drive and steered them along the meandering path of 407 once again, he noticed an interesting thing.

The radio, still turned low, now played only the hiss of static.

TWO

From his seat on the tiny stage, Mitch Flynn studied the audience for the monthly Homeowner Association meeting while his vice president finished giving a report on the trash dumping situation along Bear Creek Parkway. The small community center was crammed to capacity tonight, so many folks in attendance they'd brought out every folding chair in the building, and a few people were still forced to stand near the back. In reality, he figured it was probably only about half the overall membership—everyone who lived here year round, in other words, the rest having fled to warmer climes for the winter season—but it still felt like an ocean of eyeballs when they focused on you. Mitch had been president of the HOA for ten months now, and all the other meetings consisted of him and the three members of his board reading the financial report to a few old codgers that attended just to make sure the bylaws were obeyed to the letter.

Of course, the reason for tonight's unusually high attendance wasn't hard to figure out.

Like ringside wrestling spectators, they came to see some blood.

As he scanned the crowd, cataloguing familiar and unfamiliar faces, Mitch's eyes accidentally locked with Lena's. She sat next to the middle aisle in the very last row, as close to the entrance of the building as possible. He saw her narrow nostrils flare before quickly moving his gaze away.

"So, to recap." Mitch's VP, Porter Staubs, used one delicate finger to push his horn-rimmed glasses up on his nose. He was the only person here in business attire, a gray tweed double-breast with black tie that made him look like he'd time-travelled here straight from the Depression. "There will be more prominent signage erected by the end of next week, and the county has agreed to put our stretch of Bear Creek Parkway on the community service assignment list."

"*Grrreat,*" Denny Carson muttered audibly from his seat front and center in the audience. The top of his mulleted head towered over most of his seated neighbors. Beside him, Joy Carson cringed at the snarky tone of her husband's voice, but his trio of hunting buddies sneered from the second row. "Now we'll have a buncha criminals hangin around our homes. Might as well give 'em copies of our keys too, make it real easy for 'em to come and go as they please."

Porter paused, cleared his throat, and glanced down at Mitch from the podium situated at the end of the board table. The officious little bald man was a retired real estate attorney; great with details and contracts, but his time arguing in an actual courtroom had been limited.

Mitch gestured to Gladys on his left, sitting hunched over a steno pad behind the 'Secretary' placard, as she had at every meeting since the HOA's inception more than two decades ago. "Denny, do you have something you'd like added to the official minutes of the meeting?"

The construction foreman held up a callused, thick-knuckled hand. "No, Your Honor, just thinkin out loud."

"As I've told you several times, I'm not a judge."

"Sorry, I just get confused when you start bangin that pretty little gavel." More snickers from the peanut gallery behind him.

Mitch sighed. He didn't know Denny Carson all that well, so he couldn't say if the man didn't like him, or if he just had a problem with authority in general. Probably the latter; Denny seemed like the type who believed the world only existed for his smirking amusement. A guy who would put sugar in your gas tank and then get upset when you didn't laugh about it with him.

Porter thanked the audience and returned to his seat next to Mitch, who got up and crossed the upraised stage toward the podium. As he passed the Treasurer position, Arthur raised one bushy eyebrow and gave him a surreptitious thumbs-up.

Mitch could feel the attention of the audience sharpen as he stood in front of them, people looking up from phones or books and leaning forward in anticipation. This is what they'd come for, after word spread about the ridiculous mediation item he'd been forced to put on the agenda. And really, he couldn't blame them. At 43, Mitch was one of the younger residents of 407, and the majority didn't even come within a decade of his age. The development was nothing more than a white-collar retirement community, mostly city-bred couples who flocked to the countryside when their children left home. Tonight would undoubtedly be the most excitement his AARP-registered neighbors would get all year, and they intended to enjoy the hell out of it.

"The last item on the agenda," he began, "deals with a complaint about outdoor lighting recently installed on lot 17. The board has reviewed these complaints and come to the conclusion that the lighting in question, is, in fact, in violation of the bylaws."

"Hallelujah!" Denny called out, slinging an arm around Joy Carson's shoulders. His bicep swallowed her tiny frame. With his other hand, he gave a high-five to Bo Coleridge, sitting behind him in a camouflage trucker hat.

Mitch ignored him and kept going; better to push through this all at once. "It's the decision of the board—"

"Excuse me!"

The outraged cry drifted up from the back of the room. Mitch pretended not to hear it.

"—that these lights be taken down immediately—"

"Excuse me!"

"—no later than two weeks from today—"

"Excuse me! May I speak? *May I speak?*"

He couldn't talk over the gravelly shriek any longer, not to mention the fact that its owner was now on her feet and making her way to the front of the room. Lena Henning stopped at the edge of the first aisle and demanded, "Are you going to let a poor old woman defend herself, or would you rather your persecution go unchallenged?"

Mitch stopped himself from performing an eye roll so deep, it probably would've left him permanently staring at the inside of his own skull. For starters, the woman in question could hardly be classified in the same 'old' category as the majority of the room. Her face was heavily creased, every muscle lined with dry, leathery flesh, and she sported doughy bags under her eyes and jowls that sagged off her cheekbones like wet sheets flapping on a clothesline, but all of that was just premature aging from the same endless chain of cigarettes that had given her the voice of a eunuch toad. He pegged her in the mid-to-late-fifties, with an awkwardly lanky body. Her brown-and-gray-flecked hair resembled a helmet around her head. She stomped her way toward the podium in a pair of black combat-style boots and a thick brown housecoat whose lapels she clutched in white-knuckled bunches.

Several months back, right around the time she'd finished building her house, JD referred to her as 'Olive Oyl's less attractive sister' while they were out fishing. Mitch laughed until he'd damned near fallen out of the boat.

"Let the record show, the floor is ceded to Lena Henning," Mitch said reluctantly. "Let's try to keep things civil, Miss Henning."

"Don't you tell *me* about civil!" She planted her feet in front of the podium and crooked a finger at him while still holding on to her ratty housecoat. "I'm the civil one who moved here and did nothing but mind my own business! *You* people are the ones trying to dictate what I can and cannot do on my own property! What right do you have? What right, I ask!"

"As I told you over the phone when I first made you aware of the complaint, the bylaws give us the right. Which you signed before you were ever allowed to buy property anywhere along CR 407."

"I can provide copies of that, if needed," Porter added helpfully.

Lena scowled at him, then turned back to Mitch. "And which of these 'bylaws' have I broken, hm?" She made the word sound like something with as much basis in reality as fairies or unicorns.

"For starters, you installed lighting too close to Mr. Carson's property."

"Oh, how would you even know that?"

"Because we measured." As renewed fury spread over her harsh features, Mitch rushed to clarify. "It was fully authorized by the sheriff's office in Fallon and we were accompanied by deputies. Not only did we find the lights are too close, but the wattage on the bulbs are far above the allowable threshold."

"That is absolute bologna!"

"You kiddin me?" Denny called out from just behind her. "That shit's so bright, you could land planes in your yard in the middle of the night! I woke up at three AM yesterday and thought the goddamn woods were on fire!"

"And what about *you*?" Lena asked over her shoulder. "Shooting guns and...and driving your little carts around all day! You don't think that disturbs us?"

"What're you talkin about? Bein able to shoot guns and ride ATV's is the whole reason you move someplace unincorporated!"

"But you're just doing it to bother us!"

"Bitch, I don't spare you so much as a fuckin thought unless your lights are givin me a sunburn!"

"All right, that's enough, both of you," Mitch barked. "Denny, we can handle this."

"Sorry, Your Honor."

Another reason to dislike Lena Henning: she'd forced Mitch into a position where he actually sided with Denny Carson.

A hot, sickly pressure beat at his temples. Mitch squeezed the sides of the podium, waiting to see if it would blossom into one of the full-on migraines that had plagued him for the last year, and tried to recall how, exactly, he'd ended up here. He'd given up the auto shop, sold his house, and moved here with the intention of *removing* complications from his life. It'd been JD and Doc's brilliant idea for him to run for HOA president, the former to get him out of his cabin, the latter, he suspected, so that the vet himself wouldn't have to do it. He even ran unopposed, which should've been his first clue. Now, here he was, moderating between a brash moron and a woman who desperately wanted to throw herself a pity party, when all he wanted to do was go home, have a beer, feed his dog, and watch cable until he fell asleep.

And space out for a few hours. Don't forget that vital part of the nightly ritual.

"Miss Henning, if you're having a problem with Mr. Carson, submit a complaint to the HOA the same way he did and we'll investigate it. The matter we're addressing now is your lighting."

"But we *need* that light," Lena declared, stamping one of her thick-soled boots on the floor like an angry kindergartener. "We are a couple of frightened women living alone in the middle of the woods! Why would you want to deprive of us our peace of mind?"

"We don't—"

"Anything could happen to us!" Her throaty voice sounded comical as it spiraled higher. "We could be robbed and murdered! Or *raped*!"

"Huh. Not likely on that last one," Denny muttered with a smirk, and elbowed Joy in the side hard enough to make her jump. Behind him, his buddy Bo and another named Ned Thompson guffawed. The third—Mitch believed the snaggle-toothed man's name was Claude—clapped him on the back.

"I'm very sorry you're scared to live here," Mitch said. "Maybe you shouldn't have moved to the country if you're so afraid of the woods. But it doesn't give you the right to disturb your neighbors. People come here to get away from bright lights. The bylaws are in place for a reason, and you'll have to take the lighting down or face legal action."

"*Hear, hear!*" Surprisingly, this didn't come from Denny, but several others in the audience. Maybe she'd made more enemies than just Denny in the short time she'd lived here.

Lena stood frozen in front of him, eyes slitted until he could see no more than a black glimmer in the community center fluorescents. "I know what this is *really* about," she growled. "You can cover it up with your speeches and your...your bylaws all you want, but I know. Yes, I do." She turned to face the crowd now, and swept hooked fingers across them. "You all were out to get us since the day we bought land here. All because you simply *cannot* stand to have lesbians bringing down your precious property values!"

The room exploded in outrage. These people came to watch a feud, not get dragged into one.

"That's right," Lena shouted over them. "A couple of gen-u-ine rug munchers, right here in your midst! Oh, what *will* the rest of the world think?"

Several people yelled back in response to the taunts, others brandished their fists, a few got up and made for the door, shaking their heads in disgust. The Whitakers, sitting in the center of the small auditorium, clasped each other's hands and began praying furiously.

"Quiet down!" Mitch called. He banged on the podium with the cheap plastic gavel given to him upon assuming his new post. "Quiet down and come to order!"

The woman spun back to face the podium, a self-satisfied grin on her lips from the chaos she'd created. "You see? You see how they feel about us? This is what we put up with every day from people like you. My darling Cynthia couldn't bear to come here and face such discrimination. She's not as strong as I am, you know."

At this, Samuel Whitaker shot to his feet. Even across the room, Mitch could see the glittering gold cross dangling from his neck as he shouted, "*You are an abomination before God!*"

Lena Henning's smile grew even bigger. She closed her eyes, as though savoring a bite of a gourmet meal.

This is exactly what she wants, Mitch thought. *This isn't about lights or being afraid to live in the woods. She's just one of these people that thrive on being hated.*

"Miss Henning," he began again, speaking patiently and deliberately. That pressure at his temples thudded in tune with his heartbeat. "I can't speak for your neighbors, but neither this board, nor myself, cares in the slightest about your sexual preferences. We're here to uphold the bylaws, which you are currently in breach of. You have two weeks to take down the lighting or we'll be forced to begin legal proceedings. There really isn't much more to say. I'm considering this matter closed, and, unless there are any objections from anyone else, this meeting is adjourned."

"You won't get away with this!" Lena screeched. "I'll sue, I'll sue every last one of you! I'll go to the media and tell them all about how you're persecuting two elderly lesbians! I'll—!"

But whatever else she intended to do was cut off as the glass door behind the last row of chairs crashed open, and Mitch's best friend came running into the community center.

THREE

"Call 911!" JD shouted, waving his arms in the air like a drowning man. His face was flushed, the tops of his freckled cheeks apple red. He halted just behind the last row as every face turned to him.

"Why, what's wrong?" someone in the crowd asked.

"I got a hurt man outside!"

Madeline Springwell—queen of the 407 busybodies and, Mitch figured, the one most likely responsible for the abundant attendance this evening—called out eagerly, "What happened? Did you run him over?"

JD tossed his hands up again in frustration. "Would you just call for help already?"

Mitch stepped off the tiny stage and hurried down the center aisle. Lena watched him with those angry, glittering eyes and drew away as he passed, pulling her housecoat tight around her waist, as though he might attempt to cop a feel of her non-existent breasts. All over the room, men pulled cell phones from pockets while women dug in purses, a race to be the person who got to summon help and be part of the story. The emergency dispatch in Fallon—the closest town to 407—was about to get slammed with calls.

When he reached JD, Mitch asked softly, "Who is it?"

"I don't know, never seen him before. Berta and me found him by the side of the road on the way here." He swallowed with some difficulty, and ran a hand through his thinning hair. "Jesus, he's burnt all to hell, Mitch."

"*Burned?*"

From behind them, a creaky female voice called out, "I can't get a signal!"

"Me neither!"

"Huh. My phone ain't workin," Bill Hamilton remarked from a few feet away, frowning at the screen in his hands.

"Goddamn piece of shit!" Denny exclaimed, whapping his own device against his palm, as though that would somehow fix its malfunction.

The same sentiment repeated across the crowd. Mitch held up his hands to get their attention. "Folks, wait a minute. Can *anybody* make a call?"

All over the room, heads turned to him and shook negatives. Except for Lena, who continued scowling in his direction, and Gladys, who wouldn't know how to use a cell phone with an instruction manual. Mitch pulled his own phone from the back pocket of his jeans, but, when he tried to dial a number, it just gave a series of recalcitrant beeps and returned to the home screen to sulk.

"What in hell's going on?" he murmured to himself.

Standing up at the board table, Arthur declared, "Must be a cell tower out somewhere, don't you think?"

"If so, it ain't just cell," JD told them. "I couldn't get the truck radio to pick up any stations on the way here, either." He looked to Mitch. "Figured it was just me, but maybe there's some kinda...I don't know...outage or somethin."

Mitch nodded. Whatever the cause, without cells, they were out of luck on the phone front. The community center—which consisted of only the open main room and stage, one restroom, a long coat closet, and a bare-bones kitchen—was only used for monthly board meetings and the occasional birthday party or potluck. There had never been a need to install a landline. Hell, Mitch didn't even have a landline at his cabin.

He headed for the door. "C'mon, let's take a look at your guy."

Outside, the night was crisp and blessedly quiet. Mitch didn't realized just how stuffy the inside of the center had become in the midst of the arguing. The front door opened onto a short gravel turnoff from 407, and a weedy field that served as a parking lot, lit by a few buzzing electrical lamps on wooden poles and floodlights mounted to the exterior awning of the community center. Vehicles sat in haphazard clusters in the meadow. JD's burgundy Tahoe waited in front of them all, just a few feet beyond the awning, in the turnoff from 407. Roberta stood beside the rear passenger tire, rubbing up and down her doughy arms to stay warm.

"Hey Mitch," she greeted him.

"Roberta. Where is he?"

She pointed into the truck bed and then moved aside quickly, relieved to pass the responsibility on to someone else. Mitch stepped to the rear panel and looked over the side.

The form stretched out in the back of his friend's pickup reminded Mitch of Two-Face, the Batman villain with half his features sizzled away by acid. This man's burns weren't quite as severe as those of the fictional character, but bad enough to make Mitch wince. Some of the wounded parts of his flesh looked red and wet, oozing with clear pus or some kind of glistening run-off, while others were crispy black. His clothes were singed and one of his hands looked just about burned down to the bone.

"Where'd you say you found him?"

Roberta said, "Just up the road a piece, by the Austins' place."

"Close to where the Corps land runs up against the road," JD clarified.

"Lying on the ground?"

"No, he was up and moving when we got to him."

"He say anything?"

JD shook his head. "Tried to grab at Berta through the window, but I think he was just desperate to get help." He dug his hands into his pockets and looked at the ground sheepishly. "Then he sorta...just...keeled over. Been out ever since. I woulda driven him straight to town, but I didn't want him rolling around in the truck bed in the cold for an hour."

"Probably better, in case they wanna send a CareFlite out of Waco. I don't know what they could do for him in town anyway."

Mitch leaned over the truck bed and held his breath to keep it from pluming. The man's white coat had a square of plastic clipped to the lapel. He turned it toward the lights from the building.

An ID card with a small picture in the top left corner of a non-descript white guy with glasses and a neatly groomed goatee, presumably their mystery man before his face got seared off. Next to that were two lines of script in bold type: 'MORGAN, T.' on top, and 'LAB 4H' beneath. The entire bottom of the card contained one long barcode.

That was all, on either side. No address, no company name. Perhaps Mr. Morgan possessed a wallet that could tell them more.

"Wooo-*eeee*," another voice said beside Mitch. Denny stood hunched over the tailgate of the truck, looking in at the unconscious passenger. "Looks like somebody left that one on the griddle a li'l too long, huh?" His big nostrils flared. "Smells like it, too."

"All right, that's enough. Stand back." Mitch felt like a crossing guard as he waved the other man away. The rest of the meeting attendees were creeping outside or gathering behind the glass door so they could gawk as well.

"Relax, I'm just takin a look." Denny stood his ground until Mitch stepped between him and the truck.

"Okay, you looked. No need to turn him into a zoo exhibit."

"Whatever you say, *Your Honor*." Definite reproach in the title this time. He sauntered back to where the others waited, but took his time doing it.

"All right, whose place is closest?" Mitch asked the crowd. He had yet to memorize the map of residences that came with his gavel when he took the presidency. "*And* has a landline?"

After a moment of debate, Madeline Springwell's husband—Jerry, if Mitch remembered correctly—raised his hand. "That'd prob'ly be us, hoss."

"How fast can you get there?"

Jeremiah gestured to the east, back toward the open end of 407, where the unpaved road eventually met Bear Creek Parkway a little over ten miles away, as the crow flies but not as the road twists. Beyond that, civilization was non-existent for a good eighty miles. "Eight or nine minutes, tops."

Mitch breathed an internal sigh of relief. "Get home, call 911, and see what they wanna do. If they need us to start driving him somewhere to meet an ambulance, we can put him in someone else's car. Oh, and better tell them to send Sheriff Detwiler, too."

"Will do." Jeremiah tried to take his wife's hand, but she pulled free.

"You go on, sugar," she said, her eyes never leaving JD's truck. She was a curvaceous woman with a beehive of unnaturally black hair, dressed in skintight jeans and a purple blouse that put her liver-spotted cleavage on display. Mitch could practically see the rumors she could start dancing in her head. "I'll...I'll just stay here in case they need any help."

From behind Mitch, Roberta harrumphed. "And just what's she gonna do that the rest of us can't?"

The Springwells didn't appear to notice. "All right, I'll be back as soon as I know somethin." Jeremiah gave his wife a peck on the cheek that she barely noticed and hurried across the tiny lot to his own truck. Mitch waited for him to pull out onto the road amid a cloud of stirred dust before speaking again.

"I have no idea what to do for him in the meantime."

"I thought Gladys might be able to help," JD told him.

Feeling stupid for not having thought of it himself, Mitch looked up and searched the crowd for the board secretary's tightly coiled nest of snow-white hair. "Gladys, where are you?"

"Right here, Mitchy." The octogenarian elbowed her way through the throng and then wobbled toward him on bird legs whose pantyhose bagged around the ankles just beneath the hem of her long plaid skirt. Gladys Grimsby had been a nurse in the Korean War, told stories about it often, but after the conflict she married a stock broker (whom she outlived by a good fifteen years) and spent her life raising his children, now scattered across the country. Mitch had no idea how much medical training she could possibly have retained, but it would have to do.

"Should we get him some ice for these burns?" he asked.

Gladys patted him on the cheek and then gave him a gentle shove aside with her bulbous rump. "You're pretty Mitchy, but ya ain't terribly bright. You pack him in ice, you'll just give him hypothermia and frostbite. What we need are towels soaked in cool water." She peered over the edge of the truck bed, seeing her patient for the first time. "Ordinarily, I would say not to move him any more than we already have, but we can't leave him out here in case the temperature keeps dropping."

"All right. Arthur, JD, could you gimme a hand?"

Arthur McIntyre lumbered forward with the grace of a sasquatch. The sixty-three-year-old stood just as tall and broad-shouldered as Denny, with a bristle of silver hair and a wiry mustache to match. He sounded like Teddy Roosevelt and looked like he should be playing rugby or tossing cabers, but he'd once been the district manager for a chain of retail electronic stores. He climbed into the bed of JD's truck, worked his hands under the unconscious man's shoulders without hesitation, and said, "You lads each grab a leg and we'll have him out in a jiff."

They did so, walking backward toward the doors with the body slung between them. The crowd stood in their way, eager for a closer look, until Porter and Bill jumped forward to clear a path.

"Where d'you want him?" Arthur grunted once they were inside.

Mitch nodded toward the stage area around the board table. "There."

They got him to the front of the room, the audience following every step of the way, and Porter moved the podium aside so they could stretch him out along the upraised platform. His jaw fell open, allowing his tongue to loll out, a surprisingly pink lump of flesh against his blackened lips, but otherwise, he didn't move throughout the entire operation. Mitch ran his hands down the man's sides and across the front and back pockets of his tweed pants, a cursory pat-down. No keys, no wallet, no cell phone, nothing to identify him except the ID badge.

"Anybody recognize him?" Mitch asked.

A chorus of no's. A hefty woman Mitch didn't recognize demanded, "How'd he get burned like 'at?"

"Car accident," Denny proclaimed confidently, and Mitch couldn't keep from flinching at those two little words. "Probably been drinkin, had hisself a mother-of-a-dustup with a guardrail out on Bear Creek, then crawled outta the wreckage. I'm tellin you. Wait and see."

Several others expressed their agreement. Samuel and Deborah Whitaker were the only ones not in the crowd pressing in around them. The couple had moved to an empty space in the aisle so they could kneel and pray.

"How about those towels?" Gladys asked.

"I'm on it," Bill declared. The handyman ran for the kitchen on his scarecrow legs.

Gladys lifted the huge lenses of her glasses away from her eyes and perched them in her hair as she leaned over Morgan. She gently took his chin and turned his head back and forth, examining his burns, but she let go in a hurry when his torso suddenly convulsed. He coughed up brownish, watery fluid that spattered across the base of the podium and dribbled down onto the stage. Several ladies squealed and backed away.

Mitch noticed Arthur standing off to the side and discreetly beckoning with one finger. He got up and slipped through the crowd, who pressed in closer to watch Gladys work as Bill returned with towels. JD and Porter joined them a moment later.

"If I were a betting man—which I most assuredly am—I would not lay odds on that poor fellow surviving too long without help," Arthur said, his deep voice hushed. "He must be in terrible shock."

Mitch chewed the inside of his lip. That horrible pulsing slid behind his eyeballs; he would have to do something about it soon. "He's breathing and he's not bleeding out. Gladys is making him comfortable, so I don't see what else we can do for him."

"We should've taken him into town ourselves." Porter's Adam's apple bulged against the tight knot of his tie. "If he dies and we didn't do everything in our power to help him, they could hold us legally responsible."

"Oh shiiiit," JD moaned. "Mitch, I didn't say anything before, but I...well, I got scared when he grabbed at Berta and...and I let the engine slip...just for a second!...and the truck sorta knocked him to the ground pretty hard and he hasn't woken up since." He grimaced. "You don't think they'll get me for that, do ya?"

"Just relax, all of you," Mitch told them. Porter's legal background made him believe everything would lead to a lawsuit, and JD's tendency to panic caused him to fail more than a few tests when they were in school. "You didn't murder him, JD. He's just a guy that was in an accident."

"That's another thing," Arthur said. "I don't put much stock in *that* being the result of a car accident either. He doesn't appear to have any injuries but burns. You'd think any crash bad enough to cause a fire that severe would've banged him up at least a little. Broken bones, torn skin, bloody..." He trailed as he realized what he'd said and then blurted, "Oh, oh Mitch, I'm sorry, I didn't mean to—"

"It's fine." Mitch played off the apology with a wave of his hand, but, in reality, the words knifed through him with brutal efficiency. The pain in his temples ratcheted up another notch. "Even so, I still think an accident is most likely."

Porter shook his head. "Then where's his car? You're telling me he wrecked on Bear Creek and then tried to find help by walking across the Corps land? That doesn't make any sense."

"He could've come up 407," Mitch pointed out.

"Then why wouldn't he have stopped at any of the houses along the way?"

"Because nobody's home." Mitch nodded around at the full community center. "Or maybe he's just out of his mind with pain. What else could've done that to him?"

"An explosion." Arthur's answer came immediately. "He could be a surveyor or contractor from the Corps of Engineers who had some dynamite go off in his face."

"Don't you think we would've heard it blow? And he's not dressed like any surveyor I've ever seen. He looks like he just stepped out of a lab full of test tubes and beakers."

"*Oh!* Oh shit, you know what it could be?" JD's brow shot up on his forehead with excitement. "I just thought of it! He coulda come from a *meth* lab! Those things explode all the time!"

Porter snorted. Mitch hid a grin by shaking his head.

"Meth labs are usually a little too informal for white coats and laminated ID cards, JD."

"They wore them on that one TV show!"

"Yeah, well, until we're sure he's Walter White, let's just keep that theory to ourselves."

"Nevertheless." Arthur stroked his broad jaw thoughtfully. "There could be something untoward about all this. Someone could very well have done it *to* him. Maybe we should try to keep everyone here until the authorities arrive. They may want to speak to as many residents as possible."

Mitch turned back to look at the group. He couldn't help wondering why this all fell to him. The meeting had ended, he was no longer president of anything. Then he saw their neighbors crowded in lynch-mob close around Gladys and the injured man now, burying the little old lady in a forest of bodies. Madeline even had her phone out, trying to record video over people's heads.

You're in charge because no one else is going to be, he thought. He walked back toward them, flanked by JD and Arthur.

"Okay, everyone back off, give him some room to breathe." They went willingly, some plopping back down into chairs, but most remained standing so they could still get the best view. Mitch used the opportunity to try and take a quick headcount.

"What're you doin that for?" Denny stood with his bare arms crossed, watching from a few feet away. A faded snake tattoo coiled around one bicep.

"I just want a number to give the sheriff, in case he needs it."

"Why would he want *that*?"

"I don't know, Denny. Maybe he won't. I'm just trying to be thorough."

The foreman nodded, rubbed one hand across the scruff on his upper lip, and muttered something behind his palm that Mitch didn't catch.

At the same time, a couple at the back of the crowd turned and started toward the doors.

"Folks? Where you going?" Mitch asked.

The man, dressed in dark slacks and a cream blazer over a black turtleneck, made a half turn without stopping and raised a hand in farewell. "Home to bed. This is enough excitement for one night. Madeline, let us know how it turns out."

"I'll call you first thing in the morning, Tony!" she assured him.

"Hold on, just...hold on," Mitch told them. Tony and his wife both turned around. "I think it would be better if everyone just stayed put, at least until the police arrive."

A brief pause came as this information was digested before the shouting began.

"I have to get home—!"

"Why should we—?"

"You can't make us—!"

Mitch sighed. Most of these people would've been content to stay all night to watch the proceedings. Tell them they *had* to stay, and they fought you tooth and nail. "Look, I'm not giving anyone orders here. Stay or go, do what you like."

"Are we in danger?" Roberta's voice rose up from the edge of the crowd. "Is that it, do you think we're in danger?"

"No, no, not at all. But if this man was involved in—or the victim of—some sort of crime, the sheriff may want to talk to us."

"Gimme a break," Denny groaned. "You think someone here is gonna crack the case? We already told you, we don't know the dude."

Mitch squirmed, searching for a diplomatic response. "That doesn't mean you might not've seen or heard something. You might not even realize it's important until you're asked about it."

"Yeah, and if we turn off all the lights, maybe one of us will get bumped off by the *real* killer." Denny snorted laughter. "Come on Joy, let's go."

He put a hand on his wife's shoulder as he turned toward the door, but she stayed in place. "No. I think he's right. We should stay."

Denny froze as though the words slapped him across the face. He looked at his wife with his jaw jutted forward and the tendons in his neck standing stiff against the skin. Mitch saw the blunt tips of his fingers sink deeper into the bare flesh of her shoulders. "Babe..."

"*No.*" Joy shook her blond head adamantly but wouldn't meet her husband's eyes. She looked like she'd probably been a stunner once upon a time. How she'd ended up married to a roughneck like Denny was a mystery. "You can go if you want. I'm staying."

Denny glanced up at Mitch, then back at his wife. The tension suddenly drained out of him; or rather, he *forced* it out. He plopped back down in his seat on the front row. "Fine. I'll stay till the goddamned sheriff gets here. Everyone happy?"

"Well, if *they're* staying, *I'm* not." This came from Lena, speaking for the first time since the meeting ended. She pushed her way through the crowd, marching toward the exit which Tony and his wife had reluctantly moved away from.

Mitch walked after her. "Miss Henning, please, if you'll just—"

"You have no authority over me, sir," she declared haughtily without turning. "No, not a bit. My Cynthia needs me at home. And I won't sit here in a room full of people that hate me. I can feel the...the *disgust*...just oozing from you all. If the sheriff needs me, he can come to my home. He obviously knows where that is."

"Okay," Mitch conceded, "but, please, just be careful. Drive straight home and don't stop for anyone."

Lena paused with one elbow against the metal bar that ran across the glass door and told him, "Not that it's any of your business, but I didn't drive my car. There's no reason to waste good gasoline when I can just as easily walk."

With that, she shoved through the door and walked out.

FOUR

"Damn it," Mitch muttered, as he watched Lena leave through the glass.

Bill sidled up next to him. "Her fear of bein *alone in the woods* sure comes and goes whenever it's convenient, don't it?"

"My fault. I should've known better than to ask her to do anything. But we can't just let her walk home by herself."

Mitch tried to keep his voice low, but the rest of the room remained too quiet in the wake of Lena's dramatic exit. "Why the hell not?" Denny called out, twisting around in his chair. "She walked here by herself, didn't she? Let the old clam digger get home the same way."

"That 'clam digger' is one of your neighbors. She might be unpleasant, but that doesn't mean she deserves to have anything happen to her."

"For chrissake, *nothin is gonna happen to her!* Quit makin the situation sound worse just so you can play the big man in front of everybody."

Anger bubbled up in Mitch's chest, shooting his internal thermometer right into the red and causing that pain behind his eyes to spike, but before he could say something he would regret, Porter raised one hand timidly on the stage, as though scared to get between the two men. "I'll make sure she gets home, Mitch."

"You sure?"

"Yeah, I don't mind. In fact, if you think it's okay, I'll go on a little further and let Bitsy know what's happening before I head back, just so she doesn't worry."

Mitch slowly nodded. Porter was probably one of the few married people here whose spouse was absent; of course the woman would be worried when she didn't hear from him. He remembered what that was like, having someone who cared whether you lived or died. "That's probably a good idea, Port. You might try calling town from your phone, too."

"Oh, so now *he* gets to leave?" Denny turned away and shook his head. "Unbe-fuckin-lieveable."

Porter hurried down the aisle in his impeccable, antiquated suit, passing by Bill. Mitch stepped outside and held the door for him. Roberta had moved JD's truck to the front edge of the parking lot, and the short turnoff leading to 407 was empty. When the little bald man stepped out from under the awning, the motion sensor floodlights blazed on overhead, chasing away the night.

"Listen Port," Mitch said. "Just...be careful. Keep your eyes peeled for..."

For what? Mitch didn't know how to finish that sentence. As he'd told Roberta, there was no reason to think any of them were in danger.

And yet...something felt very strange about all this.

As if to emphasize his unease, a bird squawked somewhere off to the west, a high, startled noise. The shrill blast repeated twice and then abruptly cut off on the third.

Porter seemed to understand what he meant. "No problem. I'll be back as quick as I can. Try not to kill Denny while I'm gone."

"All right. I'll wait till you get back to do it."

The other man grinned and set off across the dirt lot, hurrying through the cars after Lena's bobbing flashlight, which moved parallel to the road. Mitch watched until the darkness swallowed up his VP and then went back inside the community center.

The rest of the gathering had finally lost interest in Morgan. They'd broken up into smaller cells, which calmed the mood in the auditorium. Madeline stood in the middle of a group of women, chattering so fast she never seemed to breathe, bobbing her head like a bird as she spoke. Denny still sat with Joy beside him, but he was twisted around in his chair again so he could talk to Claude, Bo, Ned, and a few other folks that included Tony and his wife. The Whitakers remained deep in murmured prayer; Mitch didn't know their denomination, but he would hate to see how long their services lasted. Gladys still sat hunched over Morgan-Comma-T, with Bill, Arthur, JD, and Roberta hovering nearby. Mitch went up the aisle to them, trying his cell phone again to no avail. His burgeoning migraine made each footfall feel like miniature explosion in his brain.

Gladys looked up when he got close. "I've done everything I can think to do, Mitchy." Her patient now lay covered in a patchwork quilt of damp dish towels. Concealing the burns made him look a little more normal, a little more *human*, and the tense coil of Mitch's guts began to loosen. "Doc could probably do better, if he were here."

"Let's just try to keep him comfortable. Jerry should've gotten to a phone by now. Hopefully help is already on its way."

JD sidled closer and put a hand on his shoulder. "Sorry we missed the meeting, buddy. Sounds like things got a little dicey."

"To say the least."

"Actually, I thought Mitch handled the situation admirably," Arthur said.

"It was a disaster," Mitch countered. "Lena more or less called us all intolerant bigots. Of course, Denny and the Whitakers didn't do much to convince her otherwise. She thinks we all want nothing more than to send her and Cynthia packing."

One side of Arthur's bushy mustache lifted in a lopsided grin. "Which she's right about, just for the wrong reasons."

Roberta chuckled and slapped him on the arm, but Mitch gave a quick glance around the room. No one paid them any attention except Joy Carson, whose eyes met his for a split second before she quickly looked away. "For god's sake, Art, don't let anybody hear you say that."

"Sorry Mitch. I have my foot firmly wedged in my mouth tonight. Didn't mean to sound as uncouth as Denny."

"It's not that. I'm just worried because, I can guarantee you, she's not gonna take those lights down. We're gonna find ourselves in court with her sooner or later, and, if she's right about anything, it's that the media would just love to use the headline, 'HOA Board Bullies Elderly Lesbian Couple.'"

Bill removed his worn John Deere cap and rolled the brim between his spindly hands. Beneath it, tangles of wispy gray hair lay across his thinning pate. "People like that," he began, "go through their whole lives just knowin everybody is out to get 'em. They live or work some place until they tie up in a fight with somebody, then they go someplace else and do it all over again. My sister was the same way. And she always went on and on about how everybody else was the problem, everybody else was to blame, never once stoppin for a second to realize *she* was the common denominator."

"Damn, Bill." JD whistled through his teeth. "That's deep."

Mitch nodded. "Sure, she'll always be a thorn in someone's side, but right now she's firmly lodged in mine. And if she brings a case against the HOA for discrimination, I don't want it to be under my administration. Next year it'll be somebody else's problem and you make all the cracks you want."

"Truth be told, I'm afraid it's worse than that, Mitchy." Gladys shifted on the stage beside the unconscious man, turning her egg-shaped lower half to sit level, adjusted her huge glasses on the end of her nose, and then folded her veiny hands primly in the middle of her pleated skirt. "I watched her while she yammered on tonight, and that woman...she just has this *look* in her eye. A dangerous sort of look. Something tells me when she gets pushed too far, she won't bother with lawsuits and the like. Oh no, bankrupting someone is far too impersonal for her brand of revenge. She's the type that gets madder and madder and works herself into a tizzy until she just *snaps*, and cuts off her husband's willy in the middle of the night." She gave a girlish titter. "Lucky for you boys, she prefers innies to outies."

JD, Bill, and Roberta all stared at her, dumbfounded, but Arthur barked laughter and threw an arm around her shoulders. "Gladys, you feisty ol' tart, how did your husband ever keep up with you?"

"Who's to say he did? The man's been dead a decade and a half."

Mitch found himself chuckling also, despite what it did to the throbbing in his head. "Okay, if we're done painting Lena as the boogeyman, maybe we should—"

Without warning, the man on the stage sat up and began screaming.

They all leapt away in surprise. Bill made a valiant attempt to catch Gladys as she tumbled forward off the stage, but the elderly woman slipped through his hands to sprawl painfully in the floor. Morgan sat bolt upright now, shrieking one long, continuous note like a fire whistle as his hands went to his face and ripped away the damp towels covering his burns. His fingers explored the charred flesh roughly, causing blackened flakes to rain down on his white coat. The contact caused his cries to renew, but he continued to claw at the wounds. Mitch ran to him and grabbed his wrists before he could damage himself any further.

"Calm down! Sir, *calm down!*" Mitch shouted.

"*Cwa!*" he gasped into Mitch's face. His breath smelled like a well-done steak, a fact Mitch could've gone his whole life without knowing. That one good eye rolled wildly in its socket. "*Cwa-cwa-cwar...!*"

"What?" The repeated syllable sounded like the call of a riled crow. I don't underst—"

"*Cwa-cwar-quarantine!*" the man finally choked out. And then, as if the word got his tongue to work again, "Have to...s-seal up area! The d-doors...anything could come through! Call Cybil, t-tell them..." Before he could get out the rest, a spasm ran through him. He opened his mouth and spewed more of the brown bile all over the front of Mitch's shirt. Then his good eye rolled back in his head and his body went slack again, falling backward so fast that Mitch couldn't stop the back of his head from cracking against the stage. Mitch might've thought him dead if not for the labored rise and fall of his chest.

"What did he say?" Madeline demanded. "Did he say 'quarantine?'"

"Oh Christ, he's sick with somethin!" Ned Thompson exclaimed, slapping a cupped hand over his mouth and nose. The comment sent a nervous murmur through the crowd as people started to back away.

"Nobody panic." Mitch let go of Morgan's arms, picked up one of the towels he'd cast aside, and used it to wipe at the vomit all over his shirt. It took considerable effort to remain calm while doing so. "He's delirious. That's just gibberish."

"You don't know that!" Madeline screeched, one hand clutching at the pile of raven black hair on top of her head, as though it might slide off at any moment. "It could be a disease! It could be *Ebola!*"

Everyone in the room took another step backward in perfect unison.

"Oh, come now," Arthur chided. "Do you honestly think Ebola burned him to a cinder?"

"I don't know! Who knows what Ebola does?" She shook her head adamantly and crossed her arms over her exposed cleavage. "I'm sorry, I just can't take the chance. I have kids!"

"Your kids are thirty and live in Houston!" Roberta snapped from behind Mitch.

"So?" Madeline's upper lip curled defensively. "That doesn't change the fact that we could've been exposed to whatever he has!"

"That's all the more reason we should stay here until the authorities arrive," Mitch told her.

"Says the man who just got puked on by Patient Zero." Denny stood up from his chair and stepped into the aisle. His beer-gutted cronies followed suit, looking like a pack of roving gorillas. "C'mon Joy, let's go," he called to his wife, but she again stayed put, glancing uncomfortably around the room, as if waiting for someone to help her. "I said, *let's go!*"

"Uh, Mitch, we got a problem here!" JD called.

Mitch turned from the crowd, tired of playing babysitter, not caring any more if they stayed or went. Bill and JD were crouched down beside Gladys in the floor, trying to help the old woman up. She tucked her left arm awkwardly against her chest.

"It's a break," JD said as Mitch reached them. "Pretty bad one."

"Oh, phooey! I'm fine," Gladys said.

Mitch gently took her hand and uncurled the limb from her body. The movement caused a moan to escape her. A spot of maroon stained her long sleeve just below the underside of her wrist. He undid the cuff, folded it back, and winced at the sight of a white bone shard protruding from her papery skin.

"Better make sure that ambulance is big enough for two," Bill said over his shoulder.

"Ooooh," Gladys groaned. The humungous lenses of her glasses magnified the tears leaking from her eyes. "Eighty-two years, never broken one bone. Figured it would be my hip that finally did the honors."

Arthur crouched down beside Mitch to see for himself. "We really need Doc."

Mitch considered this, then turned back to the rest of the room. Most of the group had retreated as far as the exit, but then halted to see what was happening with Gladys. Apparently not even fear of death could stop a good gawking.

He took a deep breath. This would be bitter, but it was the only thing he could think of that might get the situation back under control.

"Denny," he said. "We need your help. Would you mind driving down to the end of the road with JD to see if you can convince Doc to come back here?"

It took a moment for this request to filter through the other man's mullet to get to his brain, but then a grin twitched the corners of his mouth. Denny's spine straightened and his chest puffed out as he said, "Yeah. No problem. That's what I was thinkin, too."

"Great. And will the rest of you stay, at least until Doc can get here and tell us what he thinks?"

"It's okay," Denny added, granting his permission. "I'll be back in no time."

The assurance seemed enough for most of his fellow mutineers, but Madeline declared, "I'll stay, but I'm not sitting in here with that man for another second! I don't even want *you* near me, Mitch!"

"Then whoever wants to can wait outside in the parking lot."

The whole room became a bustle of motion as people gathered up belongings and hurried outside, many of them trying their cell phones again. Bill volunteered to go with Denny and JD, to which Mitch shrugged and threw up his hands in surrender. If this really did turn out to be some kind of disease, quarantine would be a real bitch.

Denny gave his wife a stiff pat on the back, then said to Mitch. "We'll get the fatso back here before you know it."

Mitch swallowed the bile collecting in his mouth and said, "If you happen to see Porter, let him know what's happening. He might wanna wait to see Bitsy until we know if there's really any danger."

Denny sketched him a sarcastic salute and started out of the building. JD clapped Mitch on the back as he followed.

"See you in a bit, man."

"Do me a favor," Mitch told him. "I left Sergeant in the kennel. Don't let it hold you up from getting back here, but would you just run by and make sure he's all right?"

"Yeah, no problem. You keep an eye on Berta for me. She's pretty freaked out."

And maybe she should be, Mitch couldn't help thinking.

The trio left, and the rest of the group filed out behind them, leaving Mitch, Gladys, Arthur, and Roberta with the unconscious Morgan.

FIVE

Porter Staubs kept his distance from Lena Henning as she made her way home. The woman was so uptight, even her gait reminded him of a crisp Nazi goosestep, her booted feet stomping and arms swinging with stiff mechanical chops that sent the beam of her flashlight in sweeping arcs. He tried to leave enough of a cushion to be inconspicuous, but it made no difference. They were barely out of sight of the community center before she halted in the middle of the road and turned back to shout at him, "*I know what you're doing, following me like this, but it won't work! You can't intimidate me!*"

"Miss Henning, my place is just past yours, remember?" he called back. "I'm walking home also!" Which was, when you got down to it, the absolute truth. Sure, he'd volunteered to make sure this hate-filled harpy arrived home safely, but there had been nothing generous about it. Secretly, he'd wanted any excuse to get free of that mess at the community center so he could check on his wife of twenty-seven years. Bitsy Staubs wasn't the type to start planning his funeral if he didn't arrive home on the dot, but that combined with the fact that none of the cell phones were working might be enough to get her nervous.

Besides, this whole situation felt very wrong to him. The burned man's arrival seemed like a prelude to something worse. The tip of an iceberg whose bulk remained hidden beneath dark, chilly waters. He was very glad to be away from it all.

And, judging from Mitch's last comment to him, Porter wasn't the only one unsettled.

"*You don't fool me!*" Lena screeched, shaking a fist in the air. "*You don't need to walk, you have that big, fancy Cadillac, I saw it in the lot! So you just toddle on back to your leader and tell him you failed at your mission!*"

Porter sighed, shook his head, and kept walking.

Afterward, she continued to yell back every few minutes, taunts that grew increasingly more antagonistic and delusional, but he didn't take the bait. He couldn't help wondering, however, if she actually believed the nonsense that came out of her mouth, or if she just spewed vitriol intended to make people despise her. Even though they lived within a stone's throw of one another, Porter and Bitsy never had any issues with the woman and her...girlfriend? wife? partner? Porter was never clear on what terminology they preferred... in the six months they'd lived here, unlike so many of CR 407's other residents. Nevertheless, they told one another—on numerous occasions and only in private—how thankful they were that Lena didn't buy the open acreage which abutted their land to build her permanent residence. Let her stay Denny Carson's problem.

Lena continued the barrage, and Porter tried to ignore her and just enjoy the exercise. Moonlight made the gravel of the road glow a ghostly pale white, but otherwise, a blanket of cloying darkness lay across the land. Thick trees on an undeveloped plot lined the left edge of this bit of 407; on the right, an open field stretched out for a short distance to the south before rolling into more woods. The air nipped at his exposed face and hands, yet he found himself sweating beneath the thick layers of his woolen suit.

Bitsy told him not to wear it, just as she did every month. He knew the ensemble looked a bit formal for the HOA meeting—where most of the attendees dressed in jeans and even shorts during the summer—but he'd worn garments like this every day at his practice for close to forty years (had been dubbed the 'Great Gatsby' by his closest colleagues because of them, a title he missed dearly in retirement), and it was a hard habit to break. He reached up now and loosened the knot of the tie as another bird gave an upset squawk somewhere in the night.

And then Lena broke away from the road ahead of him and bolted into the open field to their right.

Porter stopped and stared after her in confusion, watching as she sprinted through the thick grasses, the tail of her housecoat flapping. With heart thumping, he scanned the night, looking for whatever frightened her. His imagination insisted a mountain cat or bear must've lumbered out of the trees. Neither were common in the area, despite the name of the closest major road, but you never knew what could wander into the area from the hills to the north.

And then the truth dawned on him.

She was trying to lose him. Like a secret agent in a bad spy movie.

Fine. She was a grown woman. Let her go pelting off into the dark wilderness, and good riddance. With the way 407 twisted and turned, she would actually get home a lot faster if she cut straight through the woods.

That's if she doesn't get lost, or sprain her damn ankle in a rabbit hole.

So what? If that happened, it would be her own fault. Certainly not his responsibility. He had Bitsy to think of.

Yes, except you told Mitch you would make sure she got home. He trusted you to get it done. How will it look if she ends up dead in a ditch somewhere? A pause came before the voice in his head added, *You could even be found* liable *for it.*

Liable. That was the magic word for Porter Staubs. In his career as a real estate attorney, he saw clients sued for some outrageous reasons. The courts awarded settlements for just about anything these days. With lawsuits and insurance claim scenarios playing out in his head, Porter bit the inside of his cheek in frustration and then reluctantly started across the field.

"*Miss Henning, wait!*" he called, breaking into a cautious jog. "*Don't go that way! You could get hurt!*" She gave no notice that she heard, just kept pelting away from him like...well, like a madwoman, to call a spade a spade.

Once he left the white gravel of the road, visibility along the ground narrowed to a few feet. At least it was dry; during the spring rains, this area would've harbored hidden mud pits everywhere. Porter squinted his eyes as he ran, searching for obstacles in the calf-high grass. Ahead, he could make out only the beam of her flashlight, wavering wildly across the grassy plain, and angled to follow. She was actually pretty spry for a woman in her mid-fifties. Porter himself would be sixty in the spring, and already wheezing by the time he'd crossed three-quarters of the distance to the tree line, but at least he'd gained a little ground.

Lena didn't hesitate for a moment when she reached the woods, just plunged between the trees and kept running. Porter arrived just a few steps behind her, but paused before entering.

These woods only got bigger to the south, eventually becoming untamed Corp land. To reach the Henning house from here, one only needed to cross a narrow wedge of dense trees that sprang from the main body. As long as they didn't meander from a northeasterly course, they would be in and out in minutes.

But the darkness contained by the dense oak boughs was murky and absolute. Once he went in there, he would be all but blind.

"To hell with this," he muttered. He pulled a handkerchief from his breast pocket and mopped at the sweat collecting beneath his heavy collar. Part of him knew he was only giving her what she wanted, reinforcing the narrative she'd built up in her mind that he—and the HOA, and the residents of 407, *and* the entire world—were out to get her. Good Lord, by now, she'd probably painted him as a serial killer in her twisted delusions.

There was utterly no good reason to keep chasing her in the dark.

But he just couldn't quit. Porter Staubs didn't survive law school, raise three children, and build a successful real estate firm by rejecting the task at hand. Even before that, his days in the Boy Scouts instilled the same never-say-die values. This was no different than helping an old woman across the street, a task he still held a merit badge for.

Even though this particular old woman wanted to push him into traffic.

So Porter slid into the woods, stepping carefully over exposed roots and thorny brush. He moved laboriously from tree trunk to tree trunk, holding on to each as tightly as a life preserver. The thick undergrowth clutched at his polished wingtips and tore his suit pants. Within seconds, he became disoriented, all sense of direction gone. This had been a stupid idea, one he regretted more with each passing second. At least Lena appeared to have slowed as well; her flashlight flickered with much less urgency through the trees in the distance. Since it was his the only point of reference, Porter kept his eye on the glow and prayed that Lena knew the way.

Something snuffled in the darkness at his feet.

Porter halted and looked down. A seething cauldron of shadows covered the woodland floor. He couldn't even see his own legs below the knee. But he held his breath and peered into the gloom anyway.

The noise came again—a sort of piggy snorting—from somewhere in front of him. Sounded like an animal, but damned if he knew what. Were there boars in these woods? Before he could get a fix on it, Porter sensed movement to his left.

He turned his head to find an odd shimmer filtering between the trees. The shifting illumination was so dim and ephemeral that he couldn't judge its distance, just a vague, colorless twinkling that hung in the air, like a cloud of fireflies. Porter might've believed it a trick of the eyes, if not for the silhouette of a low shape standing atop a shattered tree stump just a few yards away. He caught only the barest glimpse of the thing before it leapt down into the darkness and out of sight.

It had been small, the size of one of Bitsy's Pomeranians, and walked on four legs. But its back appeared to have a hideously hunched spine that thrust up in crooked knots. Some sort of rodent. Maybe even a nutria rat. Must be.

Another snort drifted up from his right, followed by a hiss behind him.

Whatever they were, they had him surrounded.

"Uh, Miss Henning?" Porter shouted, unable to keep a sudden surge of fear from his voice. "Miss Henning, please, wait for me!" He started moving again, faster now, leaving the strange glimmer behind and stumbling through the woods toward the distant glow of her flashlight. The bushes all around him shook and rattled as the creatures paced his movements. The air filled with angry snorts and snarls and growls, a chorus like feeding time at the zoo. Porter went even faster, running through the pitch black woods. Now he could see another, brighter light through the trees ahead, a blinding white glow, and realized it was the lights Lena Henning put up at the edges of her property, the very ones the HOA demanded she take down. Well, maybe he would just speak up in her defense, because Porter didn't think he'd ever seen anything so beautiful in all his—

Something slammed into his leg, hard enough to knock him off balance. He threw his hands out, grasping at the darkness to save him, then sprawled full body atop the damp earth, knocking his glasses askew. He scrambled immediately onto all fours, in a panic to get off the ground.

Teeth sank into his ankle.

The pain was bright and instantaneous. Porter cried out and jerked his leg free, then kicked at his attacker. His foot connected with something hard and lumpy that latched on to his loafer like a playful terrier and bit him again, higher up. At the same time, more of the creatures swarmed in on him from both sides, nipping at his calves, thighs and hips. A sudden weight landed atop his back, and, a split second later, needle-sharp fangs dug into his left butt cheek. An image popped into Porter's head, visible even through the pain: hundreds of piranha crowding in to devour a South American cow.

He jumped to his feet, thrashing and flailing. The creatures dropped away from him and hit the ground with heavy thumps. Before they could come at him again, he ran, hurtling through the trees once more. A scant second later he bounded onto the meticulously mowed grass that represented the border of the Henning property. Those blazing lights poured down on him from atop high poles arranged in a rough semicircle around the house, as bright as daylight, dazzling his eyes after so long in the dark.

Gasping for breath, Porter spun and looked behind him.

The gigantic lamps scorched the lawn, like spotlights from a prison tower. They turned his shadow into a long-limbed freak and revealed every blade of grass in stark detail all the way back to the tree line.

Nothing followed him out of the woods. He squinted at the trees, but could find no sign of the creatures that just mauled him.

Porter looked down at his body, assessing his injuries. He bled from at least half a dozen tiny wounds where the little beasts bit right through his thick suit pants and into the flesh beneath. None of them looked severe, but he would have to get checked out for rabies first thing in the morning.

What on earth were they? They'd looked like some sort of deformed beavers. He'd been utterly terrified in the moment, but now he wondered how much danger he'd actually been in. Surely creatures that small couldn't have killed him...right?

A keening wail split the night behind him.

He spun. His eyes adjusted to the enormous floodlights and he could see the Henning residence now, a two-story deck house with a triangular chimney and a gorgeous second-floor veranda. It lay just twenty yards away, at the top of a short rise.

Porter started toward it, circling around toward the front, panting as he ran up the hill. The lights angled outward, creating a barrier of cool darkness around the residence. He reached the house seconds later and saw that the front door hung open.

No, not *open*.

The entrance to Lena Henning's home had once been a decorative slab of solid ash, adorned with carved angels and sporting three deadbolts as big around as his thumb, undoubtedly to keep out all the rapists and robbers that stalked County Road 407. As he approached, Porter found that it wasn't left open, but *bashed apart*. The upper half still clung to the frame by the hinges, but the bottom ended in a splintery edge, with chunks scattered across the tile floor beyond. It looked like a rhino had charged right through it.

Porter leaned through the busted frame and timidly called out, "*Miss Henning? Are you all right?*"

From within, the unmistakable sound of weeping drifted out to him.

Porter stepped into the house, careful not to tread on the wood shards. The wide entryway led past a half-bath on the left and then into a darkened living room with the feel of a cozy ski lodge, complete with dying embers in the fireplace and beautiful Victorian furniture. He remembered hearing that the lesbian couple made their living reconditioning antiques; some of their pieces were supposed to be in quite high demand in the northeast. A pump-action shotgun sat on the fireplace mantle, vital home protection for the paranoid Lena Henning. Porter could see a hallway leading deeper into the house on the far side of the room, but the soft cries drifted down a staircase that stood at the edge of the entry tile.

He ascended, thinking about the battered door and the things in the woods. His feet felt leaden and impossibly heavy as he reached the top of the stairs and a narrow hallway, but still he couldn't turn back. Light spilled out through an open door at the far end, which is also where the crying seemed to come from.

"Miss Henning? L-Lena? Do you need help?" His voice came out a choked whisper this time. He eased down the hall to the door, noted the ragged scratches across its faux wood surface and the broken latch in the floor, then stuck his head through.

And gasped.

On the other side of the door was a bedroom with the same rustic décor as the rest of the house. A cheerful brass lamp burned on a bedside table beside a huge, four-post bed positioned in the center of the room. The light illuminated the entire space, giving Porter a generous view of the carnage that lay within.

Blood splattered the walls and carpet in swirls and loops like a gruesome art display, most of it fresh enough to still be runny. But it looked like a gore-filled bomb had exploded on the bed. The rumpled, twisted bedclothes were literally soaked with blood, so much that it stood atop the navy blue comforter in shining puddles.

In the middle of this nightmare sat Lena Henning, cradling a spherical lump of bloody, gnawed flesh in her lap and weeping copiously.

It took Porter several seconds to understand she held a human head.

Cynthia Nolan was so nice the one time he and Bitsy met

her, soft-spoken and shy, leaving them to marvel at the most mismatched couple since Oscar and Felix. She'd been pretty, with wide blue eyes, chestnut hair cut in a page boy bob, and a petite body just as flat and featureless as Lena's, yet carried with far more feminine poise.

Now her ravaged head lay on her lover's thighs, short hair matted with clots and chunks, patches of skin chewed away to reveal muscle and even bone in some places. Porter spotted an arm hanging off the side of the bed and realized the rest of her must be sprawled somewhere in the tangle of blood-soaked blankets and sheets.

A ream of yellowish, acrid vomit punched its way out of his mouth. There was no warning, no tightening of the stomach or flexing of the throat muscles; one second he stared in horror, the next he laid down a line of puke across the wooden floor of the bedroom.

"J-Jesus. Jesus Christ," he muttered, wiping drool from his chin with the back of one shaking hand. He stepped further into the room. "Lena...what happened? Who did this?"

On the bed, Lena Henning's teary eyes rose from her partner's severed head and zeroed in on Porter with a hatred he could feel against his skin.

"*You*," she hissed through clenched teeth. "*You* did this. You and all the others."

"What? Lena, we didn't—"

"*You DID!*"

Before he could react, she picked up Cynthia's severed head by the hair and lobbed it across the room at him. The gory wrecking ball smashed into his chest with a wet *thunk* and then rebounded into the floor, leaving a Rorschach crimson blotch across his Gatsby duds. He recoiled in disgust as the head rolled beneath the coverlet and out of sight.

"This is what you wanted, isn't it? *Isn't it?*" she demanded, more tears spilling down her leathery cheeks. "To purge us from your precious neighborhood. *Oh, look at the scary lesbians, they might infect us with gay!* That's what you all thought. You and that caveman Denny Carson and Mr. My-Poo-Doesn't-Stink-HOA-President." Lena slid off the bed, leaving a trail through the red swamp on the covers, and stood with her maroon-coated hands bunched in front of her face as though ready to box. Blood dribbled and dripped from her in sticky strings. She looked deranged, like some Hollywood screenwriter's version of Lizzie Borden after going axe-happy.

Porter held up his own hands, but left them open and flat. The coppery smell in here made him want to throw up all over again. "Lena...please listen to me. The police are already on their way, but we have to let them know to come here also. Where's your phone?"

She turned to the bedside table, slid open a drawer beneath the lamp, and drew out a kitchen carving knife as long as her forearm. He didn't know if she'd snatched it on the way in or if she just kept weapons stashed all over this house, ready to grab whenever she felt threatened.

"We won't need the police," she snarled.

Porter turned and fled, out of the bedroom and back down the hall. You couldn't argue with that level of insanity; one look at her holding the knife assured him of that. He'd reached the top of the staircase when the blade stabbed into his upper back. He screamed and turned to defend himself, but she placed her hands on his side and shoved. The world tilted. Porter tumbled all the way down the steps in a whirlwind of limbs.

The pain came from so many different places on his body, he couldn't even catalog it all. He lay on the tile at the bottom of the stairs for a full ten seconds before trying to move. His right leg was surely shattered, along with his left wrist. Something in his chest felt tight and hot, and each breath proved harder to draw than the one before it. But when he heard heavy footsteps descending the stairs, he rose up on his elbows and attempted to crawl toward the open door.

"You distracted me with your silly meeting and then, while I was gone, you people broke into my home and murdered my poor, sweet Cynthia." The tears were all gone. She sounded in control again, almost happy. While Porter dragged himself toward the door, he heard her walk across the room, then come back. One booted foot pressed against his back, forcing him to the floor. "And then Mr. President sent you to do the same thing to me. Didn't he? Go on, admit it."

"*N-no...I swear...*" He could barely get the words out. Porter turned his head to look up at her, and found himself staring down the barrel of the shotgun from the mantel.

"That's all right. Be stubborn. I know the truth. But you can't get rid of Lena Henning this easily. Oh no, you'll have to do much better than that."

"*Please,*" Porter wheezed.

"It's time for you to pay the piper," she said primly. "For all your bigotry. And then, do you know what? It's *their* turn."

She pulled the trigger, and a mist of brains and skull ruined Porter Staubs' fancy suit.

SIX

"Oh shit, the look on that bitch's face was priceless, wadn't it?" Denny threw an elbow into Bill Hamilton's ribs as he asked this question.

JD saw Bill—crammed in between the other two men on the truck's bench seat—grimace and rub at the spot where he'd been poked. Denny's ride was a monstrous F-350, big enough to comfortably seat five adults, but overflowing toolboxes took up the back seat, along with an extra-long, fully loaded gun rack mounted to the back window, full of hunting rifles, shotguns, and what appeared to be an actual AK-47. The arrangement forced one person to ride squashed in the middle, and the lanky Mr. Hamilton had gotten the honor. If they couldn't convince Doc to drive his own car to the community center, either he or JD—or more likely both, considering the vet's girth—would have to ride in the truck bed on the way back.

"I'm tellin you, you missed the whole show, Miller," Denny mused. "Flynn told her to shove those goddamn nuclear searchlights up her ass and she just about shit a cat right there in front of everyone."

"Funny, I don't remember Mitch phrasing it quite that way." Bill's brow drew together in a stiff line beneath his John Deere cap. JD had always liked the handyman, who did work up and down 407 and accepted whatever payment his neighbors deemed necessary. Mitch hired him to help build the dog kennel attached to his back porch, but he'd ended up accepting only a case of beer for the job, which he, Mitch and JD drank while they worked.

Denny twirled both hands in the air as if to dismiss the semantics, leaving the steering wheel unmanned for a few heartbeats as they careened down the twisting path of 407. "Justice was served tonight, boys. Yessir, that old lesbo'll think twice before fuckin with me again."

They were coming up on the home of the 'old lesbo' in question now. The mounted lights that marked the side and rear boundaries of her property were visible from the end of her gravel driveway even through a screen of trees. JD had to admit, those jobbers were so bright, it looked like the distant glow of a baseball stadium nestled into her property. As they roared by, Denny turned loose of the wheel again to stretch his arm across the truck cab. His hairy-knuckled hand floated right in JD's face as he shot Lena's house the bird through the passenger window.

JD ignored him and craned his head around to study the Henning house, but caught only a glimpse among the trees. He couldn't be sure with those lights glaring back at him, but it looked like the front door stood open. They'd seen no sign of either Lena or Porter on the road as they drove. They must've at least made it as far as Lena's place, although JD couldn't imagine the woman inviting Porter in for coffee.

As he studied the house, a burst of bright light flashed from inside that open doorway, accompanied by a distant boom that the truck engine all but drowned out. Then the property swept out of view as they followed another drastic curve of CR 407.

"Hey, did you guys see—?"

Bill shoved Denny's arm out of his face, cutting off JD's question with one of his own. "Would you grow up?"

Denny guffawed obnoxiously. His own dwelling came up quickly on the lot next door, just at the edge of that blazing light pouring off Lena's property. Casa Carson—as he called it—was a beautiful pine lodge painted multiples shades of camouflage green. A bit ironic, since he'd clear cut the rest of his acreage, leaving only an open, overgrown field for it to hide in. A long metal shed that looked like a shipping container sat on one back corner of the lot. The property also featured a pump water well, an ATV parked under a carport adjoined to the house, and both an American and a rebel flag hanging from a pole beside the entrance, lorded over by an arch with a buck skull mounted on top.

A regular redneck paradise.

JD was still contemplating that flash of light inside Lena Henning's house when Denny leaned forward to look around Bill and asked abruptly, "So what's with your boy?"

"My...boy?" JD's mind went to his son, Aaron. His and Roberta's only child was a junior at A&M this year, and called home only when he needed more money.

"Yeah, you know. Flynn. Your little butt buddy." Denny snorted laughter.

JD bristled. "What about him?"

"Why's he actin like this is the end of the world, and he's King Jack of Shit Hill?"

"He's just tryin to do what he thinks is best," JD answered irritably. Why that included sending Denny on this mission, JD would never understand. "I think he's right to keep us all together 'til the sheriff can get here."

"I'm sure you do," Denny muttered, then raised his voice quickly to add, "Flynn's pretty weird anyway, if ya ask me. Moves way out here, lives by hisself in that tiny cabin, hardly ever leaves. Kinda thought he might be a serial killer when he first moved in."

"His wife died, you asshole."

"Hey!" Denny barked. "No need to get all defensive 'bout your boyfriend. Just makin an observation." His lips pulled back into a hard sneer. "'Ya know, if it turns out that burned fella *does* have some sorta disease, Flynn's gonna get sued so hard, he'll prob'ly have to move in with you and Roberta. Bet that idea gets your panties pretty wet, don't it?"

JD kept his mouth shut this time. His father used to say, when you got into an argument with someone full of shit, you only ended up soiling your shoes. Better to just clam up until they lost interest.

Which is exactly what happened. They rode the rest of the way in blessed silence, passing homes that were mostly shuttered for the winter season. Even Porter's house looked dark and empty as they sped by, although Bitsy's vehicle sat in the carport.

It took another eight or nine minutes to reach the dead end of 407. Here the gravel petered out into an overgrown morass for a short distance before transitioning to woods so dense they might as well be jungle. This continued for miles to the north and west, all wild Texas hill country.

The last two occupied lots sat on the left side of the road, in close proximity to one another but none of the other developed properties. Mitch's place came first, a one-bedroom, one-bath cabin with only a single acre of land around it, the tiniest home in the entire community. The original owner built it as a weekend fishing retreat, never intending for anyone to live there full time. Mitch could barely finance even that much after selling his shop and liquidating his assets. With no lights on, they could see only the barest outline of the dwelling a hundred yards or so away.

Doc's home, on the other hand, dwarfed his neighbor from its seat at the tail of 407. It started life as a modest cottage in the 80's, but now, after extensive refurbishing and add-ons, the wealthy veterinarian turned it into a sprawling postmodern lodge, sporting an entirely glass-fronted living room, fully enclosed garage, in-deck hot tub, and small horse stable in the rear for his overnight clients. A warm glow exuded from the porch and the clear wall that curved around the entire left end of the house, a welcoming beacon in the darkness.

Denny pulled to a stop by the side of the road. As soon as he cut the engine, the barking of a dog rolled out of the night, the sound ferocious and frenzied.

"That's Sergeant," JD said. "Sounds like he's mighty pissed off about somethin."

"Maybe he thinks his owner's a self-righteous dick, too," Denny offered. When he saw this wouldn't get a response either, he shrugged. "Whatever, go collect the fat man and let's get back. I'd like to go home at some point this year."

"Hold on, lemme run next door. I told Mitch I'd check on the dog."

"I'm goin with you," Bill said quickly, reaching to unfasten his seatbelt.

Denny groaned. "You two maybe wanna make dinner for him, too? Turn down his sheets? Fluff his pillow? Fer fuck's sake, I thought we were supposed to be in a hurry."

"It'll just take a sec." JD pulled the handle and swung open the truck's enormous door. "Why don't you go get Doc while we do this? Divide and conquer."

"Pass." Denny fiddled with the radio controls on the steering wheel, but each station held only static. "Me and the Doc don't get along too well. He didn't take too kindly to me putting down a few of the stray cats on my property with an AR."

"Imagine that," Bill said, scooting across the seat to climb down behind JD.

"You boys go right ahead. I'll wait here. But I ain't waitin all night." Denny popped a disc into his stereo just as JD closed the door. Heavy metal music thumped inside the cab-in.

"C'mon." JD went behind the truck and started down the long rutted dirt track that served as Mitch's driveway. The cold air cut through his sweater; he didn't plan to be outside tonight, so he hadn't bothered to grab a jacket before he and Roberta left home.

Bill hurried to catch up, his gangly legs scissoring. "Christ on a cracker, that guy has gotta be the most ignorant, arro-gant sumbitch I've ever met."

"You're preachin to the choir on that one, buddy."

"Sounds like he's got it out for Mitch as bad as he does that Henning woman."

"Yeah, well, he just automatically don't like anybody who can give him orders. And Mitch don't put up with shit from *anybody*." JD heard the pride in his own voice. He'd always been thrilled to call Mitchell Flynn his best friend, ever since they'd started hanging out in junior high. "Hell, Denny better watch his step anyway. That shed of his ain't any more up to code than Lena's lights."

Bill chuckled softly. "That information prob'ly needs to find its way to her."

The dirt track curved through the middle of the field toward the dark cabin. Denny's music faded with each step they took. Off to their right, the lights from Doc's house shone through the skeletal branches of a birch stand. Otherwise, the night was as barren and empty as frozen Arctic tundra.

"So, Mitch is a widower?" Bill made a solemn *tsk*ing noise between his teeth. "Had no idea. He's never said a word."

"Yeah, and he won't, so don't ask. But I'll tell you, it pretty much destroyed him. After it happened, I convinced him to move out here. Told him he could start over and decide what happens next, but mostly I just wanted to keep an eye on him. He's gotten a lot better, but..." He stopped just short of telling Bill about those weird headaches Mitch thought no one knew about, the ones that caused him to wince whenever he got frustrated or stressed out. JD believed these quick-onset migraines to be no more than phantoms, imaginary aches brought on by whatever sickness of the soul ate away at his friend.

That thought was bad, enough to crush JD's heart, but he was far more concerned about the empty bottles of aspirin, acetaminophen and various other painkillers that constantly showed up in Mitch's bathroom garbage can.

And then there were the several times when JD dropped by to find him sitting on his porch, staring into the distance, a can of Bud forgotten in his hand, hardly blinking, hardly even *breathing*, so far in his own head that you just about needed to slap his cheek to get him out of it. The blank expression on his face during these episodes made JD feel even colder than the late autumn wind ever could.

Bill must have sensed that the conversation had reached private waters. He remained respectfully silent as they pressed on down the driveway.

They could finally see details of the cabin at the halfway point, the tiny front porch with fishing rods leaned against the wooden railing and lawn chairs beside them. The back door opened right into the dog run on the back patio, a rectangular chain-link enclosure several yards long, just big enough for the German Shepherd to stretch his legs. Those deep, angry barks still drifted up from the rear of the house. As JD and Bill approached the head of the driveway, the barks abruptly cut off, replaced by distressed whining.

"Shit." JD broke into a run. Bill did the same. They rounded the corner of the cabin, ran along the side, then stumbled to a halt next to the kennel, both of them gasping for breath.

Sergeant sat inside, cowering in the corner at their feet with his back to them. His head, however, was up and alert, turned toward the opposite end of the enclosure. He shivered continually, hard enough to rattle the fence. A steady stream of whimpers issued from his long, dark muzzle.

"Sarge, boy, what's wrong?" JD knelt beside the dog, who curled up in his lap whenever he came over to watch a game with Mitch. He poked his fingers through the chain link to stroke the animal's pointed ears. Sarge glanced at him gratefully but then his attention drew right back to the other side of the kennel. He pressed himself even farther into the corner, until the metal fence dug into his dark fur.

"Somethin's sure got 'im spooked," Bill whispered.

"He acts like he sees somethin..." JD scanned the entire enclosure. Just three chain link walls, the fourth made from the rear of the cabin itself. The only entrances were through the back door of the house, and the outer gate set into the stretch of fence across from it. Besides the dog, only bowls of kibble and water sat inside.

He looked beyond, into the field around the house, searching for whatever had the dog so frightened. That uneasy worm returned, gnawing through his gut with cold, anxious teeth. And then, as he turned his head, he caught a silver glint from the corner of one eye.

JD looked straight ahead once more, down the length of the dog run, but saw nothing. It wasn't until he turned his head again, slowly and deliberately, that he could recreate the flash and keep it in view this time.

Something hung in the air just inside the chain link on the far end. Something shimmery and translucent, almost invisible, that reflected the moonlight in watery waves. He stared at it sidelong without moving, trying to make sense of it.

"What the hell is that?" Bill whispered from behind him. JD felt some relief knowing that the other man could see it too.

"Hold on." Still squatting, JD reached in the kangaroo pocket of his sweater and pulled out his phone. The device still got no signal, he'd checked it on the way there, but he didn't intend to call anyone. Instead, he found the app for his flashlight and clicked it on. The bulb—meant for the flash on his camera—produced more of a glow than a beam. He aimed it between the chain links and across the enclosure.

For a moment, JD thought something must have gotten into his eye. Or that he was hallucinating. Because what he saw now just...just made *no sense*. It reminded him of a peyote trip he took with three others guys back in his twenties, during which the sky bled on him and the trees appeared to be melting.

The opposite side of the kennel was obscured by some kind of milky white...*curtain*, was the word his mind clung to. The light from his phone reached just far enough to brighten it, but it remained hazy and indefinite, the fence behind it visible only as undulating lines. The effect was like the headlights of a car reflected in heavy fog, except this fog appeared to have a perfectly smooth surface. And clearly defined edges, too; they formed a ragged oval about a yard in diameter and two high.

All in all, it could've been a sheet of soapy glass hovering in the air several inches above the dog's food and water bowls.

Bill moved out from behind him, slowly edging around the corner of the dog run. He inched outward from the house in a wide arc, circling around so he could look at the object from all angles. "Looks the same over here, but it's so thin you can't even see it from the side!" he reported, pushing up the brim of his hat to scratch his long forehead.

JD wanted to laugh at the awed sound of Bill's voice, but the unreality of the thing made him a little dizzy, like staring at one of those optical illusions where the design appears to be moving. Without looking away, he reached down between his knees and snagged a pebble off the ground. He rolled it between his fingers for a moment, considering, then reared back and lobbed it at the shimmery circle. His first attempt hit the chain link in front of him and ricocheted away. The second slid through one of the gaps, sailed through the air, struck the object...

And vanished.

"Whoa! Holeee shit!" Bill came running back, almost bowling over JD when he reached the kennel. "Did you see that? *Did* you? It just...disappeared! What *is* that thing? I mean...what the hell *is* it?"

"I don't know and I don't care," JD answered numbly. The other man might not have been able to see it from his angle, but the pebble actually appeared to go *through* the faintly glowing curtain. In fact, as it breached the boundary, the translucence cleared and, for just a split second, JD could've sworn that darkness filled the floating window. A deep, rich black that the light from his flashlight could not penetrate. Then the rock (*crossed over*) vanished, and the reflective shine returned.

For some reason, his mind went back to that chittering noise he'd heard, standing outside the truck with the burned man while Roberta tried to reach someone on the phone.

What should they do? Get Doc? Tell the police? Call *Guinness Book of World Records*?

At his feet, Sergeant gave another terrified whine.

That decided him. He shoved the phone back in his pocket, then stood up and started down the side of the dog run, toward the gate in the middle.

"Hey, what're you doin?" Bill demanded. "Don't go in there!"

"I'm not. I'm gettin Sergeant and then we're gettin the hell outta here."

No lock on the gate, just a flip-down catch. JD worked it up and pulled the barrier open, the hinges giving a rusted squall that made him wince. He stood in the opening and looked from the dog on his right to the shimmering patch just a few feet to his left. This close, he could see it even without the flashlight. The moonlight lent its surface a pearlescent sheen. Not only that, but his skin prickled, as though static electricity coursed across it. Every hair on his body strained in the direction of the thing.

JD tore his eyes away with some difficulty. He patted his leg and said, "C'mon Sarge. I'll take you to Mitch."

The dog looked at the gate longingly and whimpered.

"Go on!" Bill gave him an encouraging nudge through the fence. Sergeant feinted toward the exit, then changed his mind. He didn't like being trapped in there with the shimmery curtain, but he certainly didn't want to get any closer to it. He drew back into the corner with his ears down, ashamed of his cowardice.

JD knelt and held his arms out, glancing warily over his shoulder at the hovering circle. "C'mon, boy! You can do it! Let's go already!"

Sergeant slunk along the fence, each step deliberate as he worked up the nerve, then suddenly bolted toward JD.

The curtain flickered.

"Look out!" Bill shouted.

JD swiveled in time to see a long, thick cylinder with a spiked tip come shooting out of that shimmering surface. It punctured Sergeant's side as he tried to dart through the gate, impaling him in a heartbeat and pinning him to the ground. Something warm and wet splashed across JD's face. He fell backward in shock as the dog shrieked and writhed, trying to free himself.

The object that speared the animal was several inches thick, three feet long, segmented, and made of some rough blackish-brown material. As JD watched, it moved, the swollen joints flexing, the entire rod curving inward to drag Sergeant back toward the (*hole, dear God, it's a hole*) curtain, which was again impossibly black.

And something else stirred in that darkness. Another object emerged, slower than the spike, cautiously, this one an ovoid shape that looked like a deformed, pitted watermelon. It swiveled back and forth, swinging stiff filaments that jutted from its top.

Then, as the spike pulled Sergeant directly under it, the

bottom third of that oblong swung open, revealing twisted rows of tiny yellowish triangles skewering in all directions, and JD understood.

It was the head of some giant, hideous creature, complete with antennae and a jaw full of razor sharp teeth. The rest of it must still be on the other side of this shimmering hole in midair, but the spike was some kind of appendage it used to catch its prey. As he watched, disgusted and horrified in equal measure, more of the creature emerged, the head attached to a slithery, segmented body at least a foot wide, and lined with countless squirming legs, like a centipede. The longer protuberances—like the one that speared Sergeant—grew from the front of each row. The thing lowered its upper end and buried those craggy teeth in the German Shepherd's throat, tearing away a chunk of flesh that stopped Sergeant's feeble thrashing for good.

"C'mon, get up!" Bill cried. The man had somehow gotten behind him, and hauled at his arms. "JD, *let's go!*"

But he couldn't move. He couldn't look away from the terrible sight of the thing tearing at Sergeant's body. It didn't even appear to be eating the dog, just using its spiky appendages to mangle the corpse and play in the intestines. The loose, out-of-body feeling of being on a peyote trip came back stronger than ever.

The giant, misshapen centipede swung in their direction next, flicking the dog away as it did. The body tumbled away and smashed into the far end of the kennel.

That broke the spell. JD climbed to his feet only with Bill's help. They ran back around the cabin. Bill loped toward Denny's truck, but JD stopped him.

"Doc's place is closer." He pointed toward the welcoming light, and they angled toward it.

SEVEN

They splinted Gladys' arm as best they could with broom handles, to keep the protruding bone from moving too much. Roberta had a couple of pain pills in her purse, leftovers from an ankle surgery the year before, and made the elderly woman take two. When she wasn't looking, Mitch snagged a third for himself. Gladys wanted to lie down when they kicked in, but the floor proved too hard for her old bones. Arthur said a fold-up cot could be found in the back of the coat closet. Sure enough, there it was, along with a set of golf clubs and a portable humidifier, all items left behind by a former HOA president—now deceased—who occasionally slept in the center to escape his nagging wife. Gladys wanted to stretch out in the closet where she could sleep in peace without anyone goggling at her, and Roberta agreed to stay within shouting distance.

Everyone else milled outside in the parking lot, safe from the horrible disease Morgan, T. brought into their midst. Mitch knew Madeline's fears weren't completely insane. He replayed the burned man's frantic words over and over as he scrubbed the vomit from his shirt in the kitchen sink, but could make no sense of them. *Quarantine*; he definitely used that word. But if he'd been talking about a disease, how did he get fried to a crisp? He's mentioned something about doors and someone named Cybil, too. None of it made any sense.

Mitch paced around the nearly empty community center while he waited for the pill to dampen the painful jabs of lightning that lanced behind his eyeballs every few seconds. When that did nothing, he left Arthur to keep a watch on Morgan while he grabbed his coat and ducked out the back door of the center beside the stage. A bare concrete stoop lead down to a stretch of open field before the woods took over. He lowered himself onto the third stair and studied the chilly night as his breath plumed in the air.

Thankfully, it was quiet and dark and lonely back here, three qualities he'd discovered he liked quite a bit since moving to the ass end of nowhere. They were also the only alleviation he'd found for these skull-splittingly bad headaches. Lately, he'd started imagining them as two granite stones positioned on either side of his brain, squeezing the gray, pulpy mass with unrelenting brutality. Mitch spent a large chunk of his time these days sitting outside with Sergeant at his feet, enjoying the absence of electricity and traffic and, most importantly, people. He listened to the wind sigh through the trees while his mind entered a sort of perfectly blank standby mode that not even an entire bottle of Wild Turkey could induce. Like floating in a sea of comforting darkness, a makeshift womb where none of life's general overall shittiness could get to him. Where he didn't have to think or feel...or grieve. These fully awake but completely oblivious trances had slowly gotten longer (last week he'd stared at the night sky for close to two hours before Sergeant's whining brought him back) but they appeased the headaches. For a while, anyway.

And just what do you think any psychiatrist in the world would have to say about that mental dead air, Mitchell? They have a word for what you're doing, how you're living, and it's called avoidance.

Yeah, well, I think the Buddhists have a word for it too: nirvana.

Mitch had grown very tired of this argument. Right now, an empty head was the only thing that helped, the only way to get out from between those two stones. And, in three months, when his time in the president's seat ended, he would give up this failed attempt to reenter society and devote himself entirely to his newfound version of meditation.

You know that's not what she's feeling...don't you? that voice in his head asked tentatively. *Allie doesn't feel anything at all anymore. And you spacing out until you go comatose isn't gonna get you any closer to her.*

Another spike of pain hammered through his brain, so deep it reached all the way into his nasal cavity. With it came a roiling nausea in the pit of his stomach. Mitch groaned, kneading at his brow with his fingertips, and then found a random spot in the woods behind the community center to focus on. If he stared hard enough, eventually he would drift away into that dark sea and forget about all of this.

And then a shape burst from the tree line and bolted across the meadow at him. Mitch jumped before recognizing the willowy outline of a fawn. Before he'd gotten Sergeant trained, the dog loved to bark and startle them into flight. Their long limbs barely touched the ground as they bounded away.

But this one was nowhere near as graceful. It moved in drunken hops and lurches, bleating with its head thrown back and mouth wide open, trumpeting an endless squeal toward the moon. The awful noise twisted Mitch's guts into a bigger knot.

Even with its awkward gait, the animal still moved at a good pace. It covered most of the distance to the building in seconds, and showed no sign of slowing. For a moment, he thought the damn thing would barrel right into him, but then it abruptly changed direction just a few yards away.

An acrid stench hit his nostrils, the smell of burned meat.

His mind shot immediately to Morgan's injuries.

Mitch caught a glimpse of the animal's flank as it fled along the rear of the community center, still moving with those disoriented leaps. He couldn't be sure in the dark, but there appeared to be a large, blackened patch on its chestnut fur, running all the way down its hind leg.

And then the fawn leapt into the brush along the south side of the building. He heard its awful cry for another few seconds before even that faded away.

Mitch stared at the spot where it disappeared, headache pulsing. A thousand tiny needles pricked at his scalp.

The door swung open behind him, nudging him in the back and scaring him halfway to a heart attack. He turned, expecting to see Arthur or Roberta, but instead, Joy Carson slipped her narrow frame through the exit and pushed the door shut behind her.

"Heeeey," she said uncertainly, drawing the word out, standing with hands tucked in the back pockets of her jeans. She wore a frizzy green sweater with half-sleeves that looked like it might've been made for a twelve-year-old, and black hiking boots. Her eyes skimmed across his face quickly, on their way somewhere else, but then they returned in a hurry. She frowned down at him, cocked her head to the side, and asked, "You okay?"

"Uh...yeah. Yeah." Mitch ran a hand down his face, trying to smooth away whatever she'd seen there. For a heartbeat, he actually considered telling her about the deer. Just to hear how it sounded coming out of his mouth, if nothing else. But already the encounter seemed unreal, more like something he'd dreamed. "Did you...need something?"

Joy looked away from him again, focusing on the toe of one boot. She opened her mouth, let it hang for the span of a breath, then closed it again. Her tiny frame shifted back and forth, as though preparing to flee at any minute. Finally, she bit her bottom lip and flapped a hand at the stoop. "All right if I sit?"

No, no. No way could he hold up a conversation right now, especially if she wanted to needle him about the meeting. Still, he tried to sound affable as he said, "I don't know. Aren't you scared of catching Ebola or black plague or whatever else Madeline's convinced them of by now?"

She grinned at the ground and shook her head, causing a curl of short, sandy blond hair to fall over one eye. "Nah. I don't believe that guy has any disease. And she's upgraded it to super space rabies. Much more dangerous."

Mitch grunted, caught off guard by the humor. He slid over to give her room, the shift causing another aching lurch behind his forehead. She sat down on the step above him, leaned back on her hands, and let her legs sprawl down the stoop. Then she shifted, letting one leg dangle off the side. Then drew them back up and wrapped her arms around her midsection. She bristled with nervous energy, like static electricity.

"I just wanted to say I'm sorry," she finally told him, her hands moving in quick, compulsive strokes down the legs of her jeans, as if smoothing invisible wrinkles. "About Denny. About...the way he acted. "

He shrugged nonchalantly, but the simple statement was a far cry from what he'd expected. Mitch realized he'd never spoken to this woman directly, only as part of a couple. And even those times, he'd really been addressing Denny. She was just sort of...an accessory. "You don't have to apologize for him. You didn't do anything."

"I know. But when you're married to a guy like Denny, that's all you do is apologize." She sighed and leaned over until her forehead rested on top of one knee. "God, he's *such* an asshole sometimes."

At her exasperated tone, a sharp bark of real laughter escaped Mitch. He couldn't help it; she sounded like a sitcom wife after the oafish husband drives his car through the garage door. "Well, no argument there. But I should probably thank you for backing me up in there. Things could've gone a lot worse if you'd left."

She muttered something under her breath that sounded like, "Yeah, that one's gonna cost me." Then she sat up and fished a pack of crumpled cigarettes from one pocket of her tight jeans. "You mind?"

He shrugged and watched while she shook one out. Thin moonlight painted her face with somber, glowing brushstrokes. The thought occurred to him again that she'd probably been beauty queen caliber in her teens and twenties. Even now, at the tail end of her forties, she was certainly easy on the eyes. Full lips, cute little button-of-a-nose, and emerald green eyes that she tried to hide beneath that chaotic mop of blond curls. She was narrow above the waist, perhaps even a tad on the scrawny side, but her hips filled out the seat of her jeans nicely.

Joy took a drag, savored it, and then let loose a stream of smoke that mixed with Mitch's frozen breaths. The action soothed her jitters. She leaned back again, considered the cigarette, and said, "Have to suck these things down whenever I get the chance. Denny doesn't like women who smoke. Doesn't like them to have tattoos, too much jewelry, or opinions either."

Now Mitch shifted uncomfortably on the step. You didn't talk about a man with his wife; it was one of the hard and fast precepts of his personal moral code.

Then again, the man in question *was* Denny Carson, and *she* was the one doing all the talking.

Joy's gaze wandered the cold October stars, but she seemed to be waiting for him to say something. He finally mumbled, "I know the type."

She snorted. "Yeah, me too. One right after the other. Trust me, if I hadn't married Denny, it would've just been some carbon copy. Except with him, I get the added bonus of living out my golden years in the middle of the most godforsaken stretch of woods on the planet."

He frowned. "What's wrong with 407?"

"Sorry. That didn't come out like I meant it. I loved it out here. At first. I was a suburban girl my whole life, so when Denny and I got married, the great outdoors, they were actually an adventure." She spoke fast, hands fluttering, the orange tip of the cigarette leaving contrails in the darkness. "I went along on all his camping trips, stayed inside and made myself useful—you know, cooked like a good little wifey while the men went hunting. Even six or seven years ago, when he announced out of the blue, 'Hey, I wanna retire early, sell the house, build my own hunting lodge,' it sounded fantastic. But it gets old real fast. There's only so many times a girl can eat freshly killed venison three meals a day before regret creeps in. You know what I mean?"

Mitch wasn't sure he did. "I like it out here," he said simply.

She moved abruptly, scooting down a step right next to him, overbearingly close, and turned to face him for the first time. "No offense intended. Really. I get it. Probably your lifelong dream to live someplace like this, huh?"

"No. Not at all. Three years ago I owned a house in Dallas that I loved. I ran a semi-successful auto body shop, and all I wanted in the world was to leave it to my son one day."

She flashed him that grin again, shy and somehow aggressive at the same time. "Yeah? And what happened there? Let me guess, he told you he wanted to be a liberal arts major or something?"

Mitch chuckled. "No, he...well, he died. Him, and my wife."

"Oh shit." The smile melted, and a look of absolute and total horror passed over Joy Carson's pretty features. She shrank into herself. "God, I am so, so sorry—"

He waved the familiar apology away before it could get started. "It's okay. You didn't know."

She fumbled, searching for something to say, just as most people did at this point in the conversation. Yet another benefit reaped by stepping out of his old life like a pair of dirty underwear: he didn't have to go through this a hundred times a day anymore, as in the days after the funeral. But, because of those experiences, he knew what her next question would be. "H-how did they...I mean, if you don't mind me asking..."

Mitch shook his head, even though he did mind. Quite a bit. "Allie—my wife—she was three months pregnant. At our age, we knew a baby was a risk, but you couldn't tell her no about anything. We worried constantly about miscarriages and birth defects. Preeclampsia. Ectopic pregnancy. The doctors were always throwing some new medical gibberish at us." A grim smile worked its way onto his lips. "All that shit used to give me these nightmares about the baby turning into some kind of hideous freak and ripping its way out of her. I lived in terror that it would hurt her. But in the end, all it took was a rainy night and a bad stretch of road on her way home from work."

It never stopped shocking him how bad it hurt to say, to admit to himself that Allison Flynn had left this world once and for all, taking their unborn and unnamed child with her. Not many people even knew the latter part, including JD. He had no idea why he'd told this stranger.

"After that...nothing really seemed worth the effort anymore. My mind felt muddled all the time. Like I was... *trapped*, I guess. Between the life I planned, and the life I suddenly found myself in, and I just couldn't deal with it."

Mitch stopped, and the silence that followed wasn't the comforting kind that he loved so much. It was bitter and thick and hungry. He'd never put his agony into words like that, not even to himself.

And yet he was pleasantly surprised to realize that his headache had faded to a distant roar at some point while they were talking.

Joy put a tentative hand on his shoulder. Five minutes ago, he probably would've stiffened, maybe even shrugged it off, but, all of a sudden, he found himself craving human contact. "I can't even imagine—"

"No, you couldn't," he cut her off. Not unkindly, but as a mercy that, he'd found, most people greatly appreciated. "You couldn't imagine, and you don't want to. Do you have any kids?"

"No. Denny didn't want them. Which is just as well. He would've been a shitty father." She ground out her cigarette and flicked it out into the night. "You know, I think I've intruded on you enough for one lifetime. I'll go back and see if..."

Her words halted midstream. Mitch looked over at her. She stared hard into the meadow in front of them with eyes narrowed. "Do you see that?"

He snapped his head up, sure that he would find another injured deer hurtling out of the woods, this one charred to a crisp and still smoking. "See what?"

She laid a hand on his forearm, then pointed with her free hand. "Out there. That...that glow. Do you see it?"

Mitch leaned forward and squinted. After a few seconds, he spotted what she meant. It wasn't really a glow as much as a murky gleam, a watery reflection of moonlight about halfway between them and the trees, maybe twenty-five or thirty yards away. "I see it. It looks like...a patch of ground mist or something."

Joy stood up. "Let go have a look."

His heart gave a brief hiccup at the thought of going out there where the deer came from. "No thanks."

She leaned over him, their faces uncomfortably close. "Oh, c'mon. Be a gentleman and don't make a lady go into the dark alone."

Before he could answer, the door at the top of the stairs opened again. This time, Arthur stuck his head out, took in their positions, and mumbled, "Oh, uh, sorry to interrupt—"

"You're not," Mitch said quickly, spinning away from her and jumping to his feet.

"—but it looks like several of the people out front are getting ready to leave."

Mitch sighed. "Oh well. Let 'em go. I'm tired of trying to talk sense into them."

"But if they're dead set on going, they should probably stay at home and not interact with anyone else, don't you think? At least until we know for sure about our friend in here."

"Then why don't *you* go tell them that?"

"Because it sounds so much better coming from someone who has 'president' in their title."

"Jesus." Mitch's head dropped in defeat. "You can be a real pain in the ass, Art."

"This is just incidental. You should see me when I'm actually trying."

"All right, fine. I'll see what I can do." Rather than go back through the community center, Mitch hopped off the stoop and started around the building.

Joy caught up with him as he rounded the corner. He shot her a questioning look.

"Maybe it'll help if I back you up again."

"Couldn't hurt, I guess."

He expected to find people milling all over the dirt parking lot, but instead, everyone clustered in one huge group beneath the buzzing light poles. Madeline stood in the center, her dark beehive towering above the rest. She gestured wildly at the road as she jabbered. The Whitakers were the only ones not involved in the discussion; they huddled together a short distance away with their heads bowed, murmuring in prayer or conversation.

"What's happening, folks?" Mitch asked loudly as he and Joy approached.

The entire crowd gave a guilty jump. They all turned to face him. Madeline's eyes flicked back and forth between Mitch and Joy behind her tortoiseshell glasses. One sculpted brow shot up her forehead and a knowing smirk tugged at the corners of her thin mouth as she proclaimed, "We're leaving."

"Look, I know everyone's tired and scared. But I think if you'll just give Denny a chance to get back with Doc, he'll be able to tell you there's nothing to worry about."

"*No*," she barked, a childish negation that, he felt sure, would've been just as forceful in the face of any logic. "This has gone on long enough. Do you realize it's been more than an hour since Jeremiah left to call the sheriff?"

Mitch looked at his watch and was amazed to find the time nearing nine o'clock. Still too soon for the authorities to have arrived, but Madeline's husband would've had time to *walk* home and back by now, much less drive. For that matter, even Porter should've returned, unless he'd hitched a ride with JD's group on their errand. "No one's heard from him?"

"How?" This came from Tony, the man who tried to leave earlier. He stood with Claude, Bo, and Ned just behind Madeline. "All the cell phones are still down."

"He was supposed to come right back for me," Madeline continued, primping at her beehive in agitation. "So where is he?"

Mitch walked a few steps further. "I don't know, but we can—"

"*Stay back!*" she screamed, holding out one hand to ward him off. "Do not come any closer! You are contaminated with whatever that man has!"

He halted and held up his hands. "Madeline, please—"

"The lady said no." Claude stepped protectively in front of her, as though he expected Mitch to suddenly charge like a rhino. He was an oddly proportioned man, with arms too-long for his height and a beer gut that hung cartoonishly low on his hips, but he looked thick enough to put Mitch on the ground if he wanted. "Tony's givin her a ride home. The rest of us are leavin, too." Bo and Ned voiced their agreement.

Joy spoke up from behind Mitch. "Denny said to stay put."

"So?" Claude lifted one shoulder in a gesture that, in conjunction with his dangling arms, made him look like a puzzled orangutan. "Denny ain't the boss of me no more'n this guy is." He glared at Mitch, daring him to say otherwise. "Now, we're gonna go, and I don't want anyone tryin ta stop us."

"And if anything happened to my husband, I'm holding *you* personally responsible!" Madeline screeched, jabbing one finger over Claude's shoulder.

"All right." Mitch retreated with his hands still up. "Just...please get home and stay put, until you hear otherwise."

No one answered as the group split apart and headed toward their vehicles. Tony got behind the wheel of a Jeep Grand Cherokee parked near the front of the lot with his wife beside him and Madeline in the back seat. Mitch saw him turning the key in the ignition, but only a sickly rumble came from the engine. He said something that looked like a curse and pounded a fist on the steering wheel. Then his door opened and he climbed back out, pausing to bend and release the hood latch under the console. The engine covering popped up a few inches, and Mitch thought he saw a dim glow leaking out between it and the vehicle frame.

"Goddamn it," the man mumbled, as he came around the front of the vehicle.

"You need a jump, Tony?" Claude called across the lot, standing in front of his own pickup.

Tony waved a hand. "I don't know, hold on a sec."

"I can give you a hand with that," Mitch offered.

"No, just stay back." Tony slid his fingers into the gap and lifted the hood.

And then fell away as a flood of flying, screeching nightmares came boiling out of his engine compartment.

EIGHT

Denny sat in his idling truck with the stereo blasting Megadeth, and thought about his wife.

Or, more specifically, how she dared to embarrass him in front of the entire goddamn neighborhood.

He still couldn't believe it happened. When they'd first met, Joy had been a headstrong, bar-hopping, chain-smoking 22-year-old, defiant to the core, always ready for an argument. Which is the reason he'd been attracted to her. Not for the character trait itself (the last thing any man needed was a female yapping at him all the way into the grave, and Denny didn't understand those weak-willed pussies who let it happen), but because of the challenge it represented. For Denny Carson, who spent most of his childhood on his uncle's horse ranch, taming a good woman shouldn't be too different than taming a wild bronco. You wanted them to have a little spirit, a little fire, a little fight, so that, when you finally broke them, you could redirect that fire where you wanted it—mostly into the bedroom—and extinguish it where you didn't.

Of course, a man could use a variety of techniques to get them to this point, depending on the woman. Some responded to gentleness. Some to mere words. But, just as with a horse, you couldn't be afraid to bring out the whip once in a while to make sure the lessons took root.

Denny long believed Joy to be as tamed as any woman could get. She knew her place in his kingdom, and generally let him determine the course of their lives. Sure, her personality occasionally slipped—just as any tamed horse might one day buck and bolt for no reason—but these slips were always in private, behind closed doors.

And, when they happened, he remained ready to dole out a reminder on just who the master was in their relationship.

Back there though, in the meeting…she defied him in *public*. In front of their neighbors. In front of his friends. Worst of all, in front of those he considered his enemies. Before tonight, that list consisted mainly of Butchy McMuffdiver, but now El Presidente had worked his way onto it. For just a moment, the sheer emasculation had made him so furious, he wanted to pick his wife up and put her through the nearest wall head first, like a goddamn tavern dart. Then he managed to calm himself, and play off the whole thing to save face.

But as soon as he got her alone again…oooh boy, you better *believe* the whip would come out. He would have to keep her hidden in the house for a month so the damn bruises had time to heal.

A shout from outside interrupted the daydream. He muted the stereo and looked across the field toward Flynn's shitty little cabin. There were two shadows out there, hurrying toward Doc's palace next door.

"Morons better hurry the fuck up," he muttered. "I got a wife to retrain."

He reached to turn back up the music as a loud thud came from outside the truck.

"What the hell…?" It sounded like something bashed against the bottom of the driver's door. Denny peered through the window beside him with his forehead against the glass, looking down at the ground as far as the angle allowed, but could see nothing that might've caused the noise.

The thump came again, further back, close to the rear tire.

"Goddamn it!" He turned on the dome light, jabbed the button to roll down his window, and poked his head out to look along the length of the truck.

Nothing but gravel and the weed littered gutter that ran alongside the road.

"*Hey!*" he shouted into the night. Had to be an animal, and he wanted to make sure he scared it off. "*I'm gonna bust your head open if you scratch my paint job!*"

Something struck the underside of the vehicle with a resounding clang. Right below his feet, from the sound of it. This time, the Ford rocked back and forth on its springs.

"Shit." Now Denny's voice was nothing but a whisper. He'd hunted every species in these woods over the last five years, and he couldn't think of a single one small enough to fit under the truck and yet still strong enough to hit it so hard. Or one that would even *want* to; even the big predators—mountain lions and the occasional coyote—went out of their way to avoid human beings. An uncomfortable tingle took up residence in his bowels, one he had trouble identifying because he'd so rarely experienced it: cool, creeping dread. He rolled back up his window and reached to shift the vehicle into gear, his hands moving slow and calm, so as not to give that uncomfortable tingle anything to work with.

Whatever was beneath the Ford launched a savage attack on the undercarriage, scratching and pounding at the frame. A horrible squealing gibberish drifted up through the floorboard, the sound of turkeys gobbling in hell. The vehicle shuddered and jumped. Its front wheels lifted off the ground and slammed back down, the motion so violent Denny bounced around the seat like the saddle on a rodeo bull. He clutched at the door handle to steady himself and again reached for the shifter, intending to floor the gas and peel out.

A series of quick, muffled pops stopped him.

The son of a bitch just popped all four of his tires, one right after the other. The cabin of the pickup sank as the tubes deflated.

He heard a scrabbling in front of him, from inside the engine compartment. Thin reams of smoke squirted from the sides of the hood. A moment later, the dome light and his dashboard gauges flickered out. The engine died with a rattling whine, leaving him in strained silence. Denny sat perfectly still, waiting with breath held, no longer able to deny the caustic fear pumping through his veins.

Without warning, the floor between his feet bulged upward before giving way with a shriek of ripping metal. The carpet and rubber floor mat tore open in a ragged hole. A brown, scaly arm reached into the truck, one with three knotty digits at the end that sported two-inch long claws. It groped at his leg.

A scream erupted from Denny so girlish, he never would've lived it down if it'd been heard by another living soul. He jerked his legs up, but not before the claws on that deformed appendage shredded his jeans from knee to cuff. He pressed himself into the corner with his boots up on the steering wheel, his body folded so deeply he could just about give himself a bj. The hand slashed around in manic circles, tearing chunks from the bottom of the leather seat. Still screaming, Denny lunged across the center console and wormed between the seats until his upper half hung over the rear of the cabin. He reached for the rack of guns mounted in the middle, just a tiny sampling of the arsenal back in the survival shed on his property. He grabbed the first one his fingers touched.

His Remington 12-gauge. A flood of relief hit him as soon as his hand curled around that sweet metal tube; guns had a way of making him feel invincible. Now he could bag the shitstain that tore through his truck like tissue paper and have a new head for his gate arch.

He kept all of his weapons fully loaded. Still jammed between the seats, he awkwardly pumped a shell into the breach and then squirmed around to face the front.

The arm was still there, ripping at the wires beneath his steering column. Denny pointed the barrel at it and pulled the trigger.

In the closed truck cabin, the roar of the shot was all-consuming, a concussive blow to the head. The muzzle flash momentarily blinded him. When his eyes cleared, he saw the basketball-sized hole he'd just blown in his own dashboard, along with a shredded stump of flesh that lay wriggling in the floor in a puddle of some dark, tarry substance.

Through the hole in the bottom of the truck came a high, piteous moan that he could barely hear over the dizzy ringing in his ears.

"*Yeah!*" Denny shouted hoarsely. "*Didn't like the taste of* that, *did you, motherfucker?*"

In response, the world began to shift.

For a few precious seconds, Denny thought his punch drunk head was playing tricks on him. Then gravity tilted, tugging him toward the driver's door. In the back seat, his toolboxes tilted and fell over with a tremendous clatter. He realized the passenger side of the Ford was rising as the entire goddamn truck rolled onto its side. Denny slid down the seat until he stood on the door panel in the now sideways cabin. Next to his feet, the driver's side window shattered from the truck's weight crushing it against the ground. A long crack raced across the length of the front windshield. He stood still, fingers clinched around the shotgun, trying to decide what to do.

With a triumphant squeal, his assailant shoved the vehicle the rest of the way over.

Denny pitched forward, hit the roof of the truck hard on his stomach. A monsoon of heavy steel tools pelted his body. The butt of one of his hunting rifles struck him in the chin, coming close to dislocating his jaw. Blackness crowded his vision, invited him to sleep, but he fought against it, forced his limbs to work, and rose shakily until he knelt in the upside-down cabin.

Somehow, he'd managed to hold on to the shotgun. His thoughts were syrupy, but he jacked another shell into the chamber as he looked for a way out of the vehicle. The passenger door latch in front of him wouldn't budge.

The windshield sat to his right, slanted inward so as to give a sweeping view of the shallow ditch the Ford now lay in. He spun and sat on his rear with his back against the upside-down seats, then raised one boot and kicked at the glass. The crack widened, but the windshield held.

Denny raised his foot to give it another blow when a dark form landed in front of him with a heavy thud. It rushed at the glass in a blur of speed. He got only a vague sense of disjointed limbs and claws and impossibly long teeth before he lowered the shotgun and opened fire.

This time, the blast struck his aching head like a sledgehammer. The windshield blew outward in a spray of chunky glass. The thing on the other side fell backward in the ditch, shrieking and writhing in agony. Head spinning, Denny crawled forward, under the dashboard, and slid out through the windshield. As he emerged, he took care to stay out of range of the creature's many flailing appendages. The ringing in his ears sounded as loud as a passing locomotive. It took him three tries to stand up without falling back over, but then he cocked the shotgun again and pumped another round into the fucker. It finally stopped moving.

He inched forward to examine his quarry. It was about the size of a newborn foal, with a deformed body that looked like several different pieces stuck together and an outer coating more like rough shell than flesh. Hadn't been a match for the shotgun though; he could see where his rounds shredded the outer coating, the holes weeping blackish oil. Six twisted, lumpy limbs grew from its bulbous midsection. Well, five and a half, since the one he'd blown off was no more than a nub. Several of them still twitched, and all of them had those clawed, hand-like extremities. He circled warily around to its lumpy head. He could see no eyes, just a huge, gaping maw. The teeth jutting from it were a multitude of sizes and shapes, no two even pointing the same directions, a piecemeal collection of fangs.

A new species. Holy motherfucking Christ. He'd discovered—and killed—a new species. Denny stared at it in amazement. Pride replaced his fear, a pride so sharp and radiant he needed to express it, and he did so the only way he knew how: by snorting a thick wad of phlegm into his mouth and letting it fly onto the creature's corpse before he finally turned away.

Doc's house sat just a hundred yards from the road. Denny left his prize kill and his overturned truck and stumbled toward it.

Behind him, an alien screech warbled across the cold night.

NINE

JD leapt up onto Doc's wraparound porch a half second ahead of Bill. The wooden boards were firmly set with no gaps, glossed and polished to a bowling lane gleam. Coupled with the high-end, wrought iron patio furniture, they always made JD feel like he just walked onto the deck of a cruise ship. Beyond the row of chaise loungers sat the floor-to-ceiling wall of curved glass that encircled three-quarters of the vet's swanky living room. It put the entire room on display, like a circular aquarium. The man himself was passed out in a double-wide leather recliner with his feet up and his glasses still on, a roaring fire in the fireplace behind him and *It's the Great Pumpkin, Charlie Brown* playing on a huge flat screen television in the middle of the room. Aside from the TV, the whole image resembled a scene from *Masterpiece Theater*, complete with an overflowing bookshelf behind the leather sofa on the far side of the room.

"*Doc! Doc, wake up!*" JD reached the glass and pounded against it with the bottom of his fist. Bill took up the cry beside him.

In his recliner, Doc jolted awake and raised his head. He looked around the room blearily until his eyes landed on the two figures on his porch. His voice didn't carry through the glass, but the words were readable on his lips as he frowned and asked, "JD? Izzat you?"

"*Yes, Doc, it's me! Come to the door and let us in! Hurry!*"

Steven Q. Vintner, DVM, struggled to get himself upright in the recliner and pop the lever to lower his stumpy legs to the floor. The man was pushing 63 years and 300 pounds, most of the latter in his pork-barrel-of-a-torso. He wore a Hawaiian-themed robe that strained at the belt holding it closed, and a pair of boxer shorts adorned with puppies from which his pudgy ankles and bloated feet emerged. After heaving himself to a standing position, he paused long enough to step into a pair of worn slippers beside his chair and then waddled out of sight into the hall that led to his front door. JD and Bill followed the curve of the glass wall around to the point where the house became brick and waited at the double doors of the entrance. When he heard the bolts slide open, JD shoved the entrance into Doc's belly and squeezed through. Bill did the same, then slammed the doors closed and leaned against them.

"Shit on toast, boys, I have a goddamn doorbell, you know!" Doc squeezed the flabby dough at the base of his grizzled neck before the hand slipped down to his chest and rubbed at the area over his heart. "Jeeeesus, my ticker can't take a shock like that! We'll be lucky if you don't have to get the horse defibrillator after me! I don't..." He trailed as he got a good look at JD's face and adjusted the tiny, round-framed glasses on his bulbous nose. "You okay, son? You've got blood on you."

JD swiped a hand across his cheeks. It came away sticky and red. Bile rose in his throat. "Somethin killed Sergeant!" he exclaimed.

The bags around Doc's eyes stretched open wide. "What are you talking about? Where's Mitch?"

"At the community center for the HOA meeting! He sent us here to get you!"

"What was Sergeant doing at the HOA meeting?"

"No, no, this was at Mitch's place!" JD pointed through the wide opening to the living room. The night beyond the glass wall looked infinitely darker from the inside, beneath the warm tract lighting.

Doc frowned in confusion. "Then how did Mitch know to send you for me?"

"Wait, no, just...just hold on." The story had gotten all muddled. JD's hands fluttered in front of him as he worked to put his tumbling thoughts into some sort of logical order. When he spoke again, he forced himself to remain calm. "On the way to the meeting, me and Roberta, we found a man in the road, all burned up, and took him to the community center. We sent for help from town, but this guy started upchuckin and screamin about quarantines and Gladys broke her arm and Mitch thought maybe you could help until the ambulance gets there, so he sent us to get you."

"Well hell, why didn't he just call me?"

"Cause all the cell phones are down."

Doc raised a sausage-fingered hand. "Now hold on, you ain't making a lick of sense. If the phones're down, then how'd you send for help?"

"We got Jerry Springwell to call from his landline! But that don't matter!" The vet's lightning-quick intellect frustrated JD. He rushed to get out the rest before he could be interrupted again. "We came here, went to Mitch's place first to check on the dog, and while we were over there—"

"Some kinda giant centipede killed Sergeant!" Bill finished for him, still standing with his back against the door, as though holding it shut. "It just appeared outta nowhere, like...like it was crawlin through a hole in midair!"

JD doubted he could've described the horror they'd seen any more skillfully, but still, he winced at the insane way it sounded when spoken aloud. Doc confirmed this a moment later when he turned slowly from Bill to JD and asked, "What in Jesus-jumped-up-Christ is he talkin about?"

"Doc...you know that old black-and-white movie where the giant ants kill everybody?" JD asked quietly. "That's what this thing looked like. Some sorta big, lumpy insect. Had deely-bobbers on top of its head and everything." He shivered with revulsion as he recalled the creature's plated skin and huge mouth, which really hadn't looked like an ant's mandibles at all, but he couldn't think of a closer comparison. "It came outta this shimmery fog and skewered Sergeant like a goddamned shish-ka-bob."

"It's true!" Bill confirmed.

Doc stood for a long moment, eyes searching JD's face. They'd both lived on CR 407 for years, but JD hadn't considered the man a friend until Mitch moved in, and since then they'd gone on several fishing expeditions aboard the vet's fully loaded pontoon boat. Yet the other man took a tiny, shuffling step backward now as he asked, "So what have you two taken tonight, huh? Wacky tobacky? Maybe laced with a li'l LSD?"

JD shook his head, trying not to feel stung. "I know how it sounds."

"I sincerely wonder if you do."

"If you'll just—"

A distant boom interrupted his plea. In the silence that followed, they could hear Sally screaming at Linus on the television about missing trick-or-treating.

"Gunshot," JD declared softly.

"Oh shit! Denny!" Bill exclaimed. "We just left him out there!"

"Denny Carson is here too?" Amazingly, Doc sounded even more bewildered at this than the idea of giant bugs coming through glowing holes in reality.

JD went through the doorway into the vet's living room and stepped up to the section of glass wall that looked out toward the road. With his eyes adjusted to the light, he could barely see beyond the edge of the porch, much less all the way out to the truck. But, as he watched, another gunshot came, followed by a third several long moments later, both marked by distant flashes. "Doc, you got any guns in here?"

Both the vet and Bill took up positions on either side of JD, the former pressing his chubby cheeks against the glass and cupping his hands around his face to cut down the room's glare. "Not a one. I fish, not hunt. You know that."

"Any weapons? Anything at all?"

"Just the aforementioned horse defib. And various kitchen knives." The vet grabbed his arm. "JD...what's going on? What is this?"

"I got no idea. But whatever it is, I think it's gettin worse."

Bill jabbed a finger against the clear glass. "I see somethin!"

JD peered through the glass until he caught sight of a shambling shadow approaching the house. "It's Denny! Get the door open!"

Doc hurried toward the front door again as fast as his ill-supported girth could carry him. A moment later, he returned with Denny in tow. The man cradled a shotgun to his chest like a newborn baby. Bloody scratches and bruises covered him, the worst of which was a purplish lump across the left side of his jaw. Splatters of some black substance that glistened like tar decorated the front of his t-shirt, and one leg of his jeans hung in tatters. A glazed, distant look dulled his eyes as Doc led him into the room and forced him onto the couch, then ran to get a brown leather satchel sitting on an empty shelf of his bookcase.

"I got it. I got that sumbitch," Denny mumbled, as Doc knelt in the floor beside him and set about examining his injuries. "Fuckin thing'll think twice before it comes at me again."

"Denny…Jesus, are you okay?" JD asked.

The other man stared at him without recognition, eyes wobbling a bit in their sockets, but they came into focus quickly when Doc's fingers brushed his bruised jaw. "Watch it, tubbo, that hurts!"

"Not enough," Doc grumbled.

JD jumped in, eager for answers. "What happened?"

"Huh? Speak up, I damn near deafened myself out there." JD repeated the question, and Denny exclaimed, "This big ol' bug-lookin thing tore my truck to shit, then tried to do the same to me!"

"Oh god," Bill moaned, pulling the brim of his hat down until it covered his eyes, then shoving it back up again. "Where'd it go? What happened to it?"

"Let's just say it didn't get along too well with Mr. 12-Gauge." Denny patted the barrel of the shotgun.

"So you killed it?" A flood of relief warmed JD, only to be shoved aside by an awful thought that followed right on its heels. "What'd it look like? Big head fulla teeth, hundreds of little legs and two long ones in front?"

"You got most of it right, 'cept it only had six legs."

"Six? You sure?"

"*You think I don't know how to count to six?*" Denny roared, but the anger faded from his eyes quickly, leaving him pale and haunted. He looked down at his chest, at the oily stain on his shirt. "Each one of 'em had a goddamn *hand* at the end..."

That convinced JD. He looked over at Doc, who eased his bulk up onto the couch beside Denny. "There's more'n one of these things out there."

"More than one of *what?*" the vet demanded. "I still have no goddamn clue what's going on!"

JD tried to figure out how to answer that, but Bill cried, "Holy hell, look at that!"

They turned and looked where he pointed now.

On the porch, just about where JD and Bill stood minutes before, a tiny creature barely a foot tall waited in the ring of illumination that stretched through the transparent living room wall. Without exchanging a word, all four men drifted slowly toward it—Denny and Doc rising from the couch as though entranced—and crowded around the inside of the glass just in front of it. JD felt like he was outside the primate exhibit at the zoo as he leaned forward to examine their visitor.

At a glance, it would be easy to mistake the ugly thing for a chicken, if not for the pitted brown shell that covered its entire body in place of feathers. Two muscular, reverse-hinged legs ending in twisted talons supported a torso which stretched up to a cylindrical head no bigger than a tennis ball. The surface held lots of lumps and shallow cavities, but at its peak formed an upraised ridge, like a Mohawk. It came to such a sharp point that the thing's entire skull resembled an axe. As with the monster that killed Sergeant, there were no eyes, just two saucer-shaped horns jutting from the sides of its head. While the four of them peered out at it, the creature turned its head from side to side, swiveling those strange growths across each of them. A tiny jaw on the underside of its head dropped open, giving them a look at its needle-like teeth. It emitted a high mewl, barely audible through the glass.

"Doc," JD began, then paused long enough to eliminate the tremor from his voice, "what is that thing?"

"How in hell should I know?" the other man responded vacantly, without taking his eyes from the creature.

"You're a vet, ain't ya?"

"I treat horses and cows, jackass. I didn't memorize a list of every animal in the world."

"I know, but...look at it, it's gotta be some kinda insect, right?"

"That big? If so, it would probably be a record holder."

Bill gave a soft, derisive sigh. "You shoulda seen the one we ran into."

"I mean, it's possible," Doc continued. "It's...well, I guess it could very well be a—"

"New species," Denny finished for him. They all turned to look at him. One corner of his lip curled up in an angry snarl as he stared out at the little thing, but his swollen jaw pulled the whole expression out of alignment. His hands methodically squeezed the length of the shotgun.

"You're telling me something like that killed Mitch's dog?" Doc asked.

JD nodded. "Only much, much uglier."

"Yeah, this one's actually kinda cute," Bill said. It certainly wasn't how JD would've described it. The handyman reached down and tapped the glass just in front of the scaly chicken. "Hey little buddy."

The creature had been studying Doc, but its head jerked around and honed in on the source of the new noise. Once he had its attention, Bill moved his hand up and down and then around in a circle, dragging his fingertip across the glass. The thing followed him the whole way, those cones on the sides of its head twitching.

"Uh Bill, maybe you shouldn't do that," JD cautioned.

The words were barely out of his mouth before the creature lowered its head and darted at the glass.

TEN

To Mitch, the monstrosities that boiled out of Tony's engine compartment looked like a colony of disturbed bats exiting the mouth of a cave. In the buzzing lamps over the community center parking lot, he received an impression of fist-sized brown bodies propelled by leathery wings, but they moved far too fast for him to tell much else. Most of them hurtled straight into the air in a flurry of flapping appendages and angry shrieks—a mass of what must be hundreds, far more than could have fit inside the tight space beneath the hood; a fact his mechanically-inclined brain couldn't help registering—but a good ten or so wrapped their membranous wings around Tony's face, neck and chest as though trying to smother him. He screamed and bashed at himself as everyone else milling in the parking lot watched, dumbfounded and frozen in place.

"Tony? *Tony!*" His wife flung her door open and leapt out of the vehicle, leaving Madeline behind in the back seat. Mitch thought about calling out for her to stay back, but before the woman could cross half the distance to her husband, he stumbled away from the car and fell to the ground, then rolled back and forth in crazed agony, like a dog driven insane by fleas.

The flood of winged nightmares from the Jeep's engine had run out, but the cloud of chittering forms circled just over the field. Mitch craned his head back to look up at them. Joy did the same beside him. The swarm was lost against the dark sky, nothing but the barest sensation of movement in front of the pale moon.

But their squeals grew louder as they descended again.

Claude raised a finger to the heavens in a way that made Mitch think of the old Superman serials, just before they started yelling about birds and planes. "Look out, they're comin back!"

A dense wave swooped down from the sky and then spread out across the parking lot, moving from the northeast corner toward the building. Mitch saw the...whatever-they-weres...gliding in like fighter pilots on a strafing run, their wingspans close to two feet. They latched on to several other people, enfolding their victims in triangular, near-transparent wings. Tony's wife became so thoroughly covered, the poor woman looked like a scabrous papier-maché sculpture. As she writhed helplessly, unable to move arms or legs, Madeline scrambled over the seat in the couples' Jeep, grabbed the door that the other woman left open, and yanked it closed.

Everyone else screamed and ran around the dirt parking lot in a blind panic, waving their arms to swat at the creatures.

"*This way! Get inside!*" Mitch shouted. The people closest to the center heeded him, ducking their heads and heading toward the door, a few hobbling on elderly hips and at least one leaning on a cane. Some of the others scrambled to unlock their own cars and seek safety within. Mitch grabbed

Joy's shoulder and pushed her toward the building just as the air around them filled with fluttering movement.

The front door of the community center couldn't be more than ten yards away. He could see Roberta in the opening, holding the glass door open and beckoning to them frantically.

Something dry and rough brushed against his ear.

Mitch yelped and flailed away. His hand connected with a shape like a cucumber wrapped in large grain sandpaper. Razor sharp pain sliced across his temple. He renewed his speed, bending ninety degrees at the waist to stay beneath the screeching cloud.

Ahead of him, Joy screamed. She had one of the damn things wrapped around the back of her head, tangled in her mop of blond locks, playing Guess Who with its tattered wingtips over her eyes. She kept running as she beat at the thing, but veered off course from the building. She made it a few strides toward the road before she tripped and sprawled full out.

He reached her a split second later. Dropped to his knees beside her. Joy flopped against the ground in absolute terror as the creature raised a misshapen head the size of a half dollar. In the floodlights, Mitch could see that it was no bat, but more like something a paleontologist would study. Its features were a garbled mess of scales, antennae, and other unidentifiable parts, but there was no mistaking the inch-long fangs it sank into Joy's scalp.

"*Hold still!*" he ordered. She stopped thrashing, but a muffled whimper escaped her as the thing reared back and bit her again, higher up, chewing into the flesh.

Mitch took hold of the creature's wings on either side of her head. Their texture reminded him of well-done bacon; he didn't see how they could possibly keep the thing airborne. It raised its head and snapped at him, but he stayed out of range of those jagged teeth. He pulled in either direction, expecting the thin membranes to uncurl or tear apart entirely, but they were clamped around Joy's head like a bear trap. The muscles in his arms screamed as he tried to pry them apart.

People bustled past them now as they fled the parking lot. Mitch threw out a hand and pleaded, "*Someone help me!*" Samuel Whitaker caught his eye, but kept right on moving past him.

And then Arthur materialized from the crowd, pushing his way out of the door against the stream of people. He dodged one of the creatures as it dive-bombed him and landed on his knees across from Mitch.

"*Just like a wishbone!*" the big man shouted. They each grabbed a wing and hauled in opposite directions.

This time, with both men focusing on one side, the wings came loose from around Joy's head. They lifted the ugly little monster off her. She wiggled out from between them with the back of her scalp trickling blood. Unfortunately, this also left them holding the creature like a tug-of-war rope. It struggled in their grasp, straining to bite either of them, its alien face twisted with rage. Mitch hesitated to let his side go for fear it would roll up onto Arthur's hand.

Joy solved this problem. She popped up and cried, "*You son of a bitch!*" Before Mitch could stop her, she grabbed the horrid thing by its head and squeezed. A burst of black fluid squirted between her fingers. The wing went limp in Mitch's hand, making him wish he'd tried that in the first place.

He and Arthur tossed the mangled creature away. Several of its brethren swarmed it in midair, tearing the body to pieces. Mitch, Arthur, and Joy scrambled toward the door of the building on hands and knees.

They were the last ones to make it inside. Roberta pulled the door closed behind him, sealing out the banshee shrieks of the monsters. Arthur shooed everyone back as Mitch and Joy collapsed on the floor and panted for breath.

Scared sobs and shouted questions filled the room, the most common being variations of '*what the hell were those things?*' Mitch could also hear a female voice bawling that this was the end times, that the harbingers of Lucifer were here, and he only needed one guess to figure out the identity of this ball of sunshiny delight.

He turned to Joy, lying beside him on the community center's scuffed tile. "You all right?"

She nodded, but her eyes were too wide, her face a little shell-shocked. She wiped goo from the monster's crushed skull on her jeans and then gently probed at the back of her head.

"Here, let me see." He pulled her upright and made her lean forward. Scarlet stained the blond hair on the back of her skull. Mitch waded through her unruly locks and found two sets of punctures on the back of her scalp, the kind of wounds vampires inflicted in the movies. "It's bleeding a lot and I bet it stings like hell, but it looks superficial. You should be okay."

"Yeah, but who knows what kinda diseases that thing had," she said, looking at her sticky hand again.

"Let's worry about one thing at a time."

Without warning, she met his gaze directly and put a hand high up on his forehead, brushing his hair back. "You're bleeding, too."

He recalled the slice across his temple. "I think one of their wings cut me," Mitch told her, but he let her hand linger there for a few seconds before standing up. The other folks who made it back inside—roughly two-thirds of the original group, he figured—milled in a tight group just a few feet up the main aisle, still talking and arguing in loud, panicked tones.

"Is anyone else hurt?" Mitch asked over them.

Conversation broke off as they looked toward him. Some of them had cuts and scrapes, but most shook their heads, all except Bo and Ned. The duo glowered at him, as though he somehow caused this.

"What happened to everyone else?" someone called out.

"Are those things still out there?"

"They were biting Tony and Patrice!"

"My wife!" a tiny old man slumped in one of the chairs gasped. He sucked air into his frail chest and wheezed, "We got separated! Where is she?"

"I'm gonna take a look right now," Mitch told him. "Just sit tight, everyone."

From the rear of the group, Deborah Whitaker's frizzy black hair was just visible as she declared, "Those things were demons! Sent here by the Devil himself!"

Mitch flapped a hand and turned away. His temples pounded again and there were more pressing matters at hand than arguing the blunter points of religion. He went back to the door, where Roberta still stood looking out, while the rest of the room continued rabbling right where they'd left off.

The buzzing cloud that attacked the parking lot was nowhere to be seen. Even the sky was clear, or as much of it as the awning outside the door allowed him to see. "Where'd they go? Roberta, *where'd they go?*"

"I-I don't know. After you came inside, they all took off toward the road and then..."

"Then *what?*"

She clutched her hands over her bosom and squeezed until he thought she would break her fingers. “They just... disappeared. There was this...this glow way up in the air... and they flew right into it.”

He stared at her for a full five seconds, trying to decide if the woman had lost her mind, then decided, if so, they all had. Certainly not any crazier than the creatures coming out of an engine compartment in the first place.

Except the engine compartment also glowed when Tony first opened it...remember?

“JD,” Roberta said, pulling him away from these thoughts. Her lip trembled. “Do you think he’s all right?”

Mitch put his hands on her plump shoulders. “He’s fine,” he assured her, hoping like hell it was true.

“How can you be sure?”

“I can’t. But he’s gonna have to take care of himself for a while. Right now, we have to see about the people still outside. Why don’t you check on Gladys and try to keep everyone calm.”

She moved away, and Mitch examined the parking lot again, this time focusing on the ground rather than the sky. He’d prepared for injuries, maybe even severe ones, but he was utterly shocked to see bodies lying everywhere in the dirt outside, as casually as trash thrown from a car window. From what he could see, their clothes were shredded and bloody, the exposed flesh ravaged. One man just ten yards from the door appeared to be missing his eyes and have part of his nose torn away. Another woman—perhaps the wife of the old guy behind him—lay halfway beneath an SUV, as though trying to hide under the vehicle. Her face hung in bloody tatters, a lot like Allie when they finally pulled her out of her flattened Honda...

The comparison made him jump. All at once, the cold truth hit him: people had actually *died* here tonight. Human beings with their own spouses and children. Somehow, until this very moment, he never even entertained the idea. They attended an HOA meeting to watch a fight between their neighbors, and instead lost their lives to some kind of psychotic vampire bats. He couldn't get his mind to wrap around the sheer weirdness of that fact and wasn't sure if he wanted to.

There were also living people in vehicles out there, Claude and Madeline among them. Most waved frantically at the building, but Madeline appeared to be screaming angrily from the back seat of Tony's Jeep, her inaudible shouts punctuated every few seconds by a fist pounded on the glass.

"Why aren't they leaving?" Arthur asked quietly as he joined Mitch at the door.

"What do you mean?"

"I mean, why are they all just sitting there? They managed to reach their vehicles, so why didn't even a single one of them make a run for it? It's human nature to get as far from danger as possible."

"Maybe they were worried about the rest of us," Mitch offered, but he thought he saw what his treasurer was getting at.

Arthur made a disappointed clucking noise against the roof of his mouth. "Those people were already set to go home and damn the consequences. Perhaps a couple might've grown a heart, but *Claude?* I'm surprised that beer-gutted troglodyte isn't halfway to Canada by now."

"You don't think their cars are working. Like how Tony's Jeep wouldn't start."

With a tight smile, Arthur touched the end of his reddish nose. "At first, I just figured his wouldn't start because several hundred of those...those *dino-bats* were shoved inside. Now though, I think it's safe to say at least a few of those folks tried their engines at some point and found the same problem. And if that many cars are dead, then it's probably safe to assume..."

"That *all* the cars are dead," Mitch finished for him. "So now we might have no working phones or vehicles. Perfect." He leaned forward to rest his forehead against the glass. "Dear god, what is going on? Have you ever seen anything like that? *Heard* of anything like that?"

"I think if those creatures had ever been seen before, we all would've heard about it, lad. They were like some Martian species from an Edgar Rice Burroughs story."

"So what does that mean? Am I expected to believe these things came down from the red planet, and we just happened to be the first people in history to encounter them?"

Arthur fixed him with a stern gaze. "For all I know, that scenario is just as likely as the one Mrs. Whitaker keeps shouting about."

"Jesus," Mitch said in disgust, to which Arthur just grinned half-heartedly and answered, "Exactly." A hundred other questions and concerns rattled around in Mitch's sore brain, but he focused on the most urgent. "Someone has to go out there. Some of the people on the ground could still be alive."

"I'm game if you are."

Mitch nodded and faced the rest of the room again. "There are still folks outside. We need to get them back in here as quickly as possible."

The reaction to this was a wellspring of vehement denial, summed up neatly by Bo Coleridge, who proclaimed, "I ain't goin back out there!"

"You don't have to. I just need people at every window in

the building, watching to make sure those things don't come back. Arthur and I—"

"And me," Joy said from the floor.

"Arthur, *Joy* and I will go outside and try to get everyone in."

"Did you see my wife?" the codger asked, still gasping for breath.

"I'm not sure," Mitch told him gently. "Go on everyone, find a window and shout if you see anything. Roberta, you stand at the door to relay messages."

The group reluctantly broke apart. Mitch turned and offered Joy a hand, but was grabbed roughly by the arm and spun back around.

"*Do not open that door!*" Deborah Whitaker howled in his face. Her nails dug painfully into his arms as she drove him back toward the wall. The rest of the room stopped to watch. "*You are all in danger unless you repent! Those things are a sign, a sign of the Rapture! We could be battling for our very souls! We have to—!*"

Joy grabbed the woman by her auburn locks, pulled her off Mitch, and gave her a shove that caused her to fall back on her ass. She looked up at them with her mouth a shocked round O.

"Debs, you're gonna be battling for more than your soul if you don't *shut up,*" Joy warned her.

Samuel came to his wife's aid. He helped her up, then wagged a finger at Mitch. "Listen to her, she's right. This is only the beginning. Salvation is our only protection against the things out there."

Mitch pushed through the door of the community center without responding and held it open for his two companions. "If this really is the Rapture," Arthur told them quietly, "let's hope those two nuts get taken first."

ELEVEN

The creature on Doc's porch rammed against the glass wall of his living room, using the sharp ridge along the top of its skull. The impact produced a deep bong that vibrated the entire curved barrier. All four of the men gathered in front of it jumped, but before they could react any further, the thing reared back on its stout little legs and struck the same place again.

Doc grunted. "Damn thing's aggressive."

"You don't think it could bust through, do ya?" Bill asked nervously.

"With that tiny little head? Not a chance. That glass is four inches thick. It'd have to hit that wall a thousand times."

"And if it gets in here, I'm gonna blow the fucker away," Denny muttered.

JD caught only the gist of this conversation. He found himself mesmerized as the creature head-butted the transparent wall over and over again, the action as mechanical as a piston. Despite Doc's reassurance, he found the little critter's tenacity a bit unsettling. Then motion from the edge of the porch caught his attention.

Another of the things hopped up onto the decking and scuttled forward to join its companion. This one was a little taller, its coloring darker, and one of its legs bowed out at an awkward angle, but otherwise identical to the original. The two of them fell into a hammering rhythm even as a third, fourth and fifth lined up to batter at the wall in a constant barrage, like piglets crowding in to suckle. All of them deformed and hideous in their own way, imperfect specimens of a freakish species. Within seconds, chips of glass as fine as sawdust flew in all directions.

JD squinted into the night, trying to see where they were coming from. If he found another one of those glowing holes, he couldn't decide if he should be terrified or just oddly comforted that there was some sort of logic to this insane situation.

What he saw instead caused a lump of cold fear to leap up his throat and threaten to choke him.

More of these creatures emerged from the darkness on Doc's lawn, twenty, fifty, a *hundred* insectile chickens flocking toward the porch in a bizarre stampede.

"*You got enough shots for all of 'em?*" he asked, having to shout over the noise of their pointed heads striking the glass.

"*Not even close!*" Denny answered, backing away.

One long, jagged crack shot up the glass like a bolt of lightning.

"*We gotta get outta here!*" JD yelled, moving away from the wall himself.

"*Doc, where the fuck's your car?*"

The vet waddled after them and gestured toward the hallway ahead. "*In the garage, where do you think?*"

Denny reached the doorway leading into the rest of the house, then halted to wait for them. JD reached him and looked back. Doc had crossed half the room, the tail of his robe flapping as he hurried toward them, but Bill stood frozen beside the glass, transfixed by the creatures now clambering on each other's backs to batter at the wall, like cheerleaders forming a pyramid. Their blows blended together into one long blur of jackhammer noise. Cracks arched across the glass in all directions now, forming a milky spider web.

JD cupped his hand around his mouth and hollered, "*Bill, would you come the fuck o—*"

With a thunderous crash, an entire section of Doc's living room wall shattered. Glass rained down, the tempered glass falling in chunks. They exploded when they struck the floor and scattered in a dazzling array. Some of the jagged bombs landed on the two-legged creatures, crushing them flat.

But there were still plenty left to swarm through the hole they'd created, squealing triumphantly.

Bill flung himself backward when the wall collapsed, falling across Doc's recliner, his trusty John Deere cap knocked off his head. Now the lanky son of a bitch scrambled up and finally turned to run.

Far too late.

The first of the beasts to reach him lowered its head and rammed into his ankle. JD heard a brittle snap from all the way across the living room. Bill yelped and went down on one knee. Blood gushed from his lower leg. Another of the creatures bounced into the air and latched onto his shoulder with its clawed toes, then buried its tiny mouth in the back of his thinning scalp. The handyman swatted at it blindly, but by the time he could knock it away, the rest of the monsters surrounded him. They darted in, ramming and biting and clawing at him. He wailed.

JD started back across the living room toward him.

Denny grabbed his arm. "You can't help that dumb fuck!"

He was right. Bill curled into a fetal ball on the floor and was quickly lost under a pile of the ugly monsters. Even more of them scurried through the hole in the wall. They packed the living room floor and perched on the furniture, like crows on a power line. Several of them zeroed in on the other three men and darted forward.

"Don't be a fool, JD!" Doc told him as he hurried past into the hallway.

"They're coming! Let's go!" Denny shouted.

Reluctantly, JD turned away from Bill's dwindling screams and ran.

In the hall, they went left, away from the front door, and followed Doc toward the back of the house. JD noticed he'd managed to grab his medical satchel off the sofa. The overweight vet huffed and puffed after only a few steps.

Then one of his slippers went out from under him on the tile floor.

JD caught his arm and kept him from going all the way down. As he steadied the other man, he looked back to see a flood of the creatures pour out into the hall. Acidic fear burned the pit of his stomach.

Beside him, Denny spun, aimed the shotgun and fired into the mass. The noise threatened to burst JD's eardrums in the narrow passage, but the entire frontline of the horde shredded into a spray of oily blood. The others raced over their corpses and kept coming, undeterred.

JD shoved Doc to get him moving. This time he ran without looking back.

A right turn at the end of the hall brought them into a long kitchen with a refrigerator big enough to stuff a cow in. Doc plowed through the room, heading toward the door leading out to the garage. Just as he flung it open, the windows over the sink exploded inward. Two more of the creatures landed on the granite countertop and stood hissing. One of them leapt at JD's face.

Denny's shotgun roared, and the thing disintegrated in midair, splattering the wall with gore. He cocked the weapon again and turned the other one into toothpaste, along with a chunk of Doc's countertop.

No time to gloat. The rest of the creatures swarmed into the kitchen. JD and Denny bolted through the door into the garage and found Doc already waiting in his two-door hybrid with the engine purring. The car was so small that the lower rim of the steering wheel dug into his gut.

Both of them attempted to cram themselves through the passenger door at the same time. For a moment, JD sat in the other man's lap until he managed to wedge himself into the microscopic backseat. Denny slammed the door and bellowed, "*Go, go!*"

The garage door made a mechanical rumble as it trundled up. It took an eternity, during which JD got on his knees and peered out the rear window, toward the door they'd just come through. He couldn't see the creatures, but something bashed against the outside of the car. Doc whimpered and put the car in gear. He drove forward, exiting the garage, and they went coasting down his driveway at a leisurely pace. JD watched, but nothing followed them out. The beasts had disappeared as quickly as they came. A moment later, they passed the wreckage of Denny's overturned truck and turned onto 407. The engine in the tiny hybrid made a soothing buzz on the gravel road.

"*Woooo!*" Denny exhaled loudly and ran a shaking hand through his mullet. "Well, that was a trip, huh? Hey, you think you can get this shitbox up to walking speed before those things catch us, Doc?"

"It's not exactly a stock car," the vet grumbled. And then, in a sad, bewildered tone, "I-I-I don't understand a thing that happened back there. Those nasty little beasts…they…they just killed Bill Hamilton in my living room, didn't they?"

"Yeah, and it's a good thing Billy Boy volunteered to became chow mein, or one of us would be ridin on the roof right now."

"Shut up, Denny," JD said as he spun on the rear seat to sit down. He was too exhausted to put much force behind it.

The man twisted around to glare at him. "They'd be shittin you out in a few hours too if not for me. You remember that."

JD just shook his head and looked away.

"What were they?" Doc took a bend in the road fast enough for the hybrid's rear wheels to slip on the loose gravel. "For god's sweet sake, what *were* they? Where did they come from?"

JD wasn't sure if the man really expected an answer, but he gave one anyway. "They came out of holes in the air, just like Bill and I said. Some kind of…I don't know…*portals*." God, but that sounded so stupid.

"Uh, I don't know about any of that," Denny said, "but we need to get to my place. If those things come after us, I got more'n enough toys there to deal with 'em."

"I say we get back to the others."

"Oh, of course you wanna run back and hide behind Flynn, you pussy!"

"Actually, I was thinkin more about my wife," JD said through clenched teeth. "I guess you couldn't care less about yours."

Denny waved a hand. "Joy can take care of herself. 'Sides, the best thing we could do for 'em is to keep those things from ever gettin there. We set up a perimeter, bust out some semi-automatics..."

JD let out a biting, sarcastic laugh. The other man sounded like a kindergartener talking about all the battles his action figures were going to have. "So you, me, and Doc are gonna fight a war, huh?"

Denny twisted around and grabbed his sleeve with teeth bared. The swollen knot on his jaw looked shiny, the skin stretched taut. "Those motherfuckers are NOT trashin my house like they did Doc's!"

"They only trashed his house because *we* were in it!" JD shoved his hand away. "And have you stopped to think that some of these things might *already* be at the community center?"

That one stumped Denny. He repositioned himself in the seat, shook his head angrily, and then glared up at the ceiling.

"All right, you convinced me," Doc said. "Community center it is." He pressed the pedal and made the hybrid's engine hum even louder.

TWELVE

As Joy Carson exited the building behind Arthur McIntyre and Mitch Flynn, she honestly couldn't decide if the thudding in her chest was caused by terror...or relief. Yes, the attack by the bat creatures had been awful; she would never forget the nightmarish feeling of one of them biting into her scalp like a ripe apple, and her hand still felt tacky with its blood. She certainly wasn't eager to go back outside and offer herself up again. But the dread didn't come close to the terrible, stomach-churning fear that gripped her even before they appeared.

Fear of the moment when she would have to go home and face her husband.

She still couldn't figure out why she'd stood up to him. On the surface, she wanted to believe it was because she truly thought staying had been the right thing to do, but deep down, she figured it more likely that she'd developed a teensy tiny crush on Mr. Flynn over the last month, as he investigated Denny's feud with Lena Henning. Not enough to make her think they would ever be together (she was far too old to entertain delusions of starting over with Prince Charming), but enough to cause a single moment of complete stupidity where she opened her mouth to support him over her domineering husband.

Frankly, if given a choice between facing Denny or going back outside to save people from some messed-up flying monsters, she would take Arthur's 'dino-bats' every time.

But that sure didn't make her suicidal. She was thankful when Mitch set a hesitant pace, easing out into the parking lot as cautiously as a minefield. They could hear the muffled shouts of the people closed up in their cars as soon as they opened the door, Madeline loudest of all. Joy, Mitch, and Arthur ignored them for the moment. They kept their heads up and eyes on the sky, but the creatures really had disappeared. Once they were sure another aerial assault wasn't coming, they started moving toward the closest body on the ground.

Arthur gave a strangled gasp deep in his throat when they reached it. "God in heaven, that's Evelyn Doyle. She bakes cookies for every house on the fourth of July. I didn't even realize she was here tonight. She usually spends winters with her daughter in Tampa."

Joy, whose patriotic cookies were always eaten by her husband and his friends during a drunken stupor before she could have any, remembered the sweet old lady who delivered them, but the torn, bleeding form lying on its side bore little resemblance to her. One eye stared at nothing, above a throat so ripped apart that the spinal column was visible in the ruins. The blood from the wound had already soaked into the tamped down grass beneath her, still so warm that it steamed in the frigid air. Joy's stomach performed a greasy flip-flop at the sight.

"They didn't even feed on them," Arthur continued. "Just

mauled as many as they could and then absconded. That's not animal nature, to attack something so maliciously."

He had a point. The amount of carnage visited on these poor people seemed almost gleeful.

"Hey!" a voice yelled. Joy dragged herself from the inspection of the body. Claude cracked his driver's window a mere half inch and pressed his lips against the gap so he could shout through it. "Hey, what's goin on out there? Is it safe to come out or what?"

"I think so," Mitch answered. Then, to Arthur, he whispered, "See if anybody's alive and do it *fast*. We have to get everyone else inside right now, just in case."

"Will do, lad."

"But what about the ones that...aren't?" Joy asked. "We can't just leave them out here."

Mitch shook his head before she'd even finished. "That's the least of our worries. My one concern at this point is keeping the rest of these people safe 'til we can get some help."

As Arthur moved away to begin checking bodies, Mitch raised his hands and made a come-on gesture to the people still cowering in their cars. "It's okay, they're gone! Hurry and get in the building!"

Doors reluctantly began to open. While the people within—a few of them likely old enough to have seen the start of World War I—made their laborious way toward the community center, Mitch took a few steps in the opposite direction, past the savaged bodies of Tony and his wife, to the still-open hood of the man's Jeep. Joy stood beside him and peeked inside, ready to run if more of the things should come streaming out.

You didn't have to be a mechanic to spot the problem. The vehicle's engine was trashed, parts crushed, wires ripped and chewed.

"Could you...could you fix that?" she asked.

"Not even with a fully stocked garage. The only way this thing would ever run again is with a new engine." He glanced at the owners. "And I don't think they're gonna be buying one any time soon."

"I heard what you and Arthur said inside. Do you really think all the cars are dead?"

"That's what we need to find out."

They turned around. Madeline had emerged from the back of the Jeep at some point and stood in front of them, blocking their path. Joy never liked the gossip queen of 407, and knew the feeling was mutual: several months after she and Denny moved in, the other woman—who looked like she'd walked straight out of a Sears catalog circa 1955—called her 'redneck trash' under her breath in the checkout line of the local grocery store. Madeline glared at Mitch for several seconds, arms rigid at her sides, before one hand flashed out and backhanded across his cheek.

"This is your fault," she snarled. Before either of them could respond, she made a crisp turn and marched toward the community center with her ugly, retro beehive held high.

"That's bullshit," Joy said. "How is *any* of this your fault?"

Mitch touched the red imprint of her hand on his cheek, then turned briskly and continued deeper into the parking lot without a word.

But not before she saw the guilt in his eyes.

A few of the people from the cars stopped to grieve over the creatures' victims. Joy wasn't acquainted with anyone here well enough to know whether these were loved ones or merely friends—being married to Denny had been an isolating experience, to say the least—but she and Mitch urged them to leave the corpses behind and run for the building.

When they reached Mitch's Sierra, he pulled open the door, leaned inside, and twisted the key. Something beneath the hood made a pathetic, rusty garbling. He raised an eyebrow at Joy and kept moving.

Claude climbed down from the high cab of his truck with a Remington hunting rifle in hand. He ducked when he hit the ground and aimed the rifle up at the sky. "Where'd they go?" he demanded. "I ain't gettin more'n a yard from my ride till I know those things're gone!"

"Fine, stay here," Joy told him. He shot her a nasty look, but she saw some surprise in it as well. She'd never been brave enough to smart off to one of Denny's buddies, even when Ned Thompson leered at her ass every time she walked through a room.

"Did you try to start your truck?" Mitch asked.

"Hell yeah I did, I was gonna get the fuck right on outta here when those things came outta Tony's engine!" The man proclaimed this without an ounce of self-consciousness for the cowardice it implied. Probably why his love life consisted entirely of truck-stop-quality prostitutes. "Damn thing wouldn't turn over! I just got it inspected at that shop in town last week, but whatta ya expect? That place is run by a buncha fuckin wetbacks. Prob'ly rigged it to do this just so I'd have to bring it back!"

Before the rant could continue, Mitch said, "Pop your hood and let me have a look."

"What? Fuck you Flynn, I don't want you anywhere near—"

"Jesus Christ, just do it, Claude. What, you think having another man in your engine makes you gay?"

Joy slapped a hand over her mouth to stop an absolutely jubilant peal of laughter from escaping.

Claude looked from her to Mitch with his nostrils flared and upper lip curled, but did as asked. Mitch raised the hood as the other man came back around to join them.

"*Fuck!*" Claude smashed a fist against the side panel when he saw the ruined interior. "Did those things do that?"

"I'd say the chances are good." Mitch looked at Joy. "We can ask everyone else when we get back inside, but yeah, they probably did it to the others, too. Which brings up a whole other set of concerns."

"Like what?" She didn't know if she wanted the answer.

"Like were they just following some kind of instinct...or did they do it *on purpose*, to keep us from leaving?"

"What the hell're you talkin about?" Claude stared at Mitch like he would an algebra problem. "They were just some kinda animal..."

Mitch winced and rubbed at one temple close to the shallow cut across his forehead, then gestured toward the parking lot. "Let's make sure we're not forgetting anyone and then get back inside."

They left Claude standing over the ruins of his engine and hurried on through the lot. Everyone else had either made it inside or were nearly there. Mitch stopped to help Arthur pull a body out from under an SUV while Joy stood nearby, examining the night. Her nose and fingertips burned from the cold, and her bare forearms developed a rash of goosebumps. A few seconds later, she heard a soft whimper from one of the cars to her left.

A green, mud-splattered Toyota Camry sat at the very edge of the lot, with an unmoving body curled into a fetal ball by the rear tire. Joy took a few hesitant steps toward it. She heard the noise again, but this time she realized it came from somewhere in the dark interior. Being careful not to get too close to the corpse, she leaned forward to peer through the glass and made out a human shape in the floorboard of the back seat.

When she opened the rear door, the person inside squealed and shoved back against the opposite side. Joy saw it was a rail thin, gray-haired woman with a shawl wrapped tight around her shoulders.

"It's okay," she told her. "They're gone."

"My husband," the woman sobbed. "I...I think t-they..."

Joy looked over at the body on the ground. "I'm so sorry. But you have to come with me. It might not be safe to stay in here." She held out a hand.

The woman debated for a moment before accepting. Her skin was rough but loose on her bones. Joy helped her slowly out of the car and onto her feet. She caught sight of her husband's body and began to wail.

"Don't look." Joy put an arm around the woman's shoulders and pulled her close, then urged her toward the building. "What's your name, sweetheart?"

"H-Helen," she cried. She allowed herself to be led through the tightly packed vehicles, shivering against Joy's shoulder all the way.

They reached the door just behind Claude, but before they stepped through, a distant humming noise caught Joy's attention. She urged Helen to sit down inside and stood listening with Mitch and Arthur.

The humming grew into the sound of an electric engine. A tiny hybrid vehicle came shooting down 407 and hooked into the parking lot, braking hard just in front of them. When the headlights shut off, Joy could see Doc behind the wheel, with Denny crammed into the passenger seat beside him.

A cold fist hit her in the gut.

It was only at this moment that Joy realized how much she'd truly hoped she would never see her husband alive again.

THIRTEEN

The doors of Doc's tiny car flew open. The cramped occupants sprang from the interior like the contents of a pressurized can. Mitch could sympathize; the only time he'd ridden in the vehicle his knees had been under his chin. Doc—who appeared to be wearing a bathrobe and boxer shorts—paused with one slippered foot on the ground and gazed around at the remains of the parking lot massacre. "Good god almighty, we're too late," he whispered. And then, much louder, "You all right, Mitch?"

"We're fine, but man, am I glad to see you." Mitch walked to meet the veterinarian as he came around the car. "We've got a situation here that's getting worse by the second. We were just attacked by some kind of...weird animals."

"Yeah? Well, join the fuckin club." Denny emerged from the passenger door and then turned to sweep the lot with a shotgun over the roof of the car, like a war movie commando. He looked far worse than when Mitch sent him on this errand an hour ago, clothes torn and stained and a long, swollen bruise down the left side of his jaw. "Where are they, where'd they go?"

"They flew away," Arthur told him.

"*Flew?* What the hell do you mean, *flew?*"

Then JD shoved him out of the way as he wriggled free of the tight backseat.

"Where's Berta? She okay?"

Before Mitch could answer, a hefty blur streaked out of the building past him. JD barely had time to stand before his wife threw her arms around him and all but lifted him into the air. "Don't you *dare* leave me like that again, John Delbert." He hugged her back and planted a kiss on top of her head.

A hard knot rose in Mitch's throat. A severely moot question, but he couldn't help wondering if it would make him feel better or worse to have Allie in this situation with him. He glanced at Joy, waiting to see if she would greet her banged up husband with the same enthusiasm. But she didn't move from her spot beside the door, couldn't even look at him. Denny took the initiative, striding over to throw an arm around her shoulders. "Hey babe, you all right?" The question was perfunctory, asked while he continued to scan the parking lot. She nodded and leaned against him woodenly. They looked like two people in a poorly-acted B movie rather than a real, married couple, just going through the motions that the world expected of them.

It suddenly occurred to Mitch that Doc's car was empty. "Wait, where's Bill?"

The look on JD's face provided all the answer he needed.

"Oh Christ. What happened?"

"We can get into that later," Doc said. "Right now, it's extremely important that we evacuate this building. And anyone else still on 407, if we can find some way to contact them. We can caravan into town and sort this all out there."

"You can run with your tails between your legs if you want, but we ain't gonna be chased off our property," Denny declared, giving his wife another squeeze. From the safety of the building, Claude, Bo and Ned shouted a chorus of agreements.

Mitch ignored them and said to Doc, "I agree, but there's a pretty big problem with that plan. Like the fact that you now appear to have the only working vehicle."

"What? No way, my truck's fine!" JD craned his head around to look at his vehicle, still parked on the first row.

"Try it if you want—in fact, it's probably best if we try them all—but I'm ninety-nine percent sure any car in this lot when we got attacked now has a paperweight for an engine."

Denny nodded. "That don't surprise me. They fucked my ride up, too. Just before they flipped it over like a goddamned flapjack."

"This...this is insane." Doc shivered inside his robe. "Mitch, I have not a single solitary clue about anything that's happened since these two came crashing through my front door tonight, and they sure don't have any answers. The things I saw tonight...just tell me, does it all have something to do with this man JD found?"

"Morgan." In the chaos, Mitch forgot all about their patient. "I honestly don't know, but, at this point, it doesn't matter. We just need to figure out what we're gonna do."

"Then perhaps we should do it inside," Arthur urged. "I'll feel much better with a roof over our heads."

"I agree," Mitch said. "Doc, pull your car up under the awning, as close to the door as you can. We'll need to keep an eye on it while we talk."

Five minutes later, Mitch found himself once again standing in front of his fellow homeowners, except this time, the audience had visibly shrunk. Doc suggested they dim the lights to keep from attracting the attention of anything outside, so they only had every third fluorescent to see by, creating gulfs of deep shadows between them. Stories were exchanged quickly and quietly, without embellishments or questions. Mitch recounted the dino-bats' attack and let everyone who made it to their vehicles in the parking lot confirm that they wouldn't start. Then JD and Denny took their turn. The details of Bill's death were bad, but the news that Sergeant had also been killed made Mitch feel like someone just stomped on his chest while wearing cleats.

"What about Porter or Lena?" he asked when they finished, struggling to keep sudden huskiness from his voice. "You didn't see them out on the road?"

JD shook his head. "I think Lena's door was open. Maybe they made it there."

"Then we need a way to warn them. And anybody else still on 407. You didn't see the bats that attacked us, either?"

"No, nothin like that. We just saw, uh, chickens and a giant centipede."

"Don't forget about the thing that came at me." Denny sat with his posse again, Joy waiting demurely at his side and the shotgun slung across his lap in a casual way that made Mitch a little antsy. Madeline—deprived of her fellow gabbers—had also drifted in with this group, taking a seat just behind him. "Looked like some kinda dog, but with a lotta extra legs."

Mitch crossed his arms and nodded, setting off a chain reaction of painful lurches inside his skull. God, he did *not* have time for a migraine right now. "Whatever they are, there has to be a connection."

"But what *are* they?" a woman at the end of the first row of chairs whispered, while turning to glance at the door. "Where did they come from?"

Mitch opened his mouth to respond, but found himself shouted over by Samuel Whitaker, who stood up from his seat in the far back corner where he and his wife had secluded themselves. "We told you what they are!" His full-volume voice made everyone wince. Deborah looked on defiantly with her chin held high and her nostrils flared as Samuel swung his finger back and forth across the assemblage, like a maestro's baton. "We tried to warn you of the danger to your souls that you face!"

Arthur twisted around in his seat to growl, "Oh, save the holy claptrap for Sunday! You're not converting anyone here, my friend!"

Samuel looked ready to argue until several others echoed the sentiment. He sat down heavily in his seat and huddled in sulky murmurs with Deborah.

When he held attention again, Mitch said, "Doc, you got any idea about these things at all?"

"I really wish people would stop asking me that." The veterinarian had brought in a hefty leather satchel from his car and used the contents to treat several minor injuries, including Joy's bite and the slice across Mitch's forehead. Now he knelt on the stage over Morgan, examining the unconscious man's burns. He looked up with his Hawaiian robe puddled around his knobby knees. "Here's an idea, Mitch: we're all suffering from the most vivid mass hallucination on record."

Some nervous laughter from the audience, capped off by Claude inquiring in a sheepish, embarrassed tone, "Couldn't they be, like, you know...mutations? Just regular animals that crawled through some...some nuclear waste or somethin?"

"Like the Ninja Turtles?" Roberta asked.

"No, not like the fuckin Ninja Turtles, you fat bitch!"

"*Hey!*" JD barked. "You talk to my wife like that again, Claude, and you're gonna be swallowin teeth!"

Claude hefted his hunting rifle, the barrel pointed at the ceiling. "Like to see you try, fuckwit."

"Keep your voices *down*," Mitch told them.

"They could be aliens!" someone else offered from the darkness.

"Or maybe Muslim terrorists!"

"*Muslims?*" Denny groaned. "For fuck's sake, were any of 'em wearin turbans? That is so fuckin stupid."

"This is pointless," Mitch cut in. "The only things we know for sure is that they're dangerous, and there are a lot of them out there. As for where they came from…JD, tell us again what you and Bill saw."

JD was still engaged in a staring contest with Claude, but he finally broke contact and turned back to face Mitch. He'd glossed over this part of his story pretty fast before, taking more time in describing the huge creature that impaled Sergeant. But this time he gave them every detail he could recall about the iridescent fog.

"That's what I saw, too!" Roberta said excitedly. "Those bat-monsters flew into something just like that, floating right over the road!"

"Sounds like husband and wife've been smokin the same shit," one of Denny's other pals muttered.

Mitch might've been inclined to agree…except he couldn't help thinking about Morgan's frantic, nonsensical cries about quarantines and doors. And about that faint glow he and Joy saw in the field behind the building, and the one that poured out of Tony's engine when he popped the hood. "Okay, it's not much, but at least it's something to look for. Maybe those things are gone, but we can't count on that. Since it doesn't look like help is coming and all the car engines are wrecked, we're stuck here for the moment, so—"

"Because of *you*," Madeline said through clenched teeth. Her face looked gaunt and haggard. "If you hadn't made us stay, we'd all be home right now."

"And what makes you think you'd be any better off there?" Arthur asked her.

"He sent my husband out to die!" she snarled, as if this answered the question.

"No ma'am, he sent your husband *home*, which is exactly where you just said you wanted to be."

"Maybe we should just hunker down and wait till morning," another man suggested.

"Did you hear a fuckin word I said?" Denny demanded. "These things bashed their heads against Doc's wall until they busted right through! You think this place is gonna keep them out if they start migratin down from the end of the road? And you just wanna sit on your thumb and *pray*?"

"I have to agree with Denny," Doc added. "We can cower in here and hope they don't find us, but if they do, the community center won't protect us."

"Then what do you suggest?" Mitch asked. "Try to make it out on foot?"

"*Hell* no." Denny lifted the shotgun off his lap and held it aloft like a primitive villager with a pagan idol. "We get armed. At my place. I got enough guns and ammo for everyone in this room. Then we could stand a chance at holdin 'em off."

"And how are we supposed to even get there, if not by walking? All the cars are kaput, remember?"

"'Cept they ain't." Denny grinned and jerked his head back, toward the door. "We got Doc's car right outside."

A tension settled on the room as they waited to hear Mitch's answer. *Tread lightly*, he told himself.

"I thought we might send someone into town to get help, and take along the most injured." Many heads in the room nodded.

"Fine. Send whoever you want. But before you do, let me and Claude make a run down to my place and load up."

"Denny." Mitch strove to keep his voice friendly. "That car is one of our few assets. We can't afford to send it off somewhere in case it doesn't come back."

"You callin me a thief? Or just a coward?"

"Neither. I'm saying we have to get some help out here as soon as possible. There's no time for side trips."

"Okay then, who gets to lead this expedition into town? You?"

"No, absolutely not. We can vote if it makes you feel better."

"Oh, you're such a pussy." Denny held out a hand and curled the fingers into a tight fist. "You wanna be the big shit around here, then squat and dump. At least that'll get you respect. I mean, why don't you just make a goddamn decision?"

"Because I'm not an inbred gun-fucking hick that gets my way by steamrolling over everyone else!"

Mitch regretted the outburst immediately, but, god, did it feel good. Denny stared at him without speaking, his eyes glittering pits in the dim lights. The rest of his posse—the rest of the *room*—remained dead silent as they waited for his response. Beside him, Joy sat bolt upright in her seat like electricity had just been conducted through her body, her lips parted and eyes locked on Mitch.

But it was Doc that finally broke the tense silence in the room.

"There's not gonna be any vote. Unless we all suddenly went communist, it's still *my* car, and I'll be the one that says where it goes. Mitch, if we can take a short recess, I'd like to talk to you for a minute."

Mitch looked across the room. "Everyone, just sit tight. We'll decide who goes as soon as I get back."

Doc waddled off the stage and headed toward the swinging door in the north wall that opened onto the center's kitchen. Mitch followed him, glad to be out from in front of the crowd, but something made him glance back as he pushed through the door. The room broke into hushed whispers and quiet sobbing, but Denny still watched him with narrowed eyes.

Then, from the second row, Madeline leaned forward and whispered in the man's ear. As she did, the anger melted off his face, replaced by a blank, baffled stare. His eyes went from Mitch to his wife.

Just before the door swung closed, Mitch saw Madeline sit back in her seat and shoot him a smug grin.

Then Doc pulled his attention away by asking, "No one knows who this Morgan fella is, or where he might've come from?"

The kitchen was dark enough to leave Mitch blind. He propped open the door of the refrigerator so they would at least have enough light to see one another as they spoke. "Everyone at the meeting claimed they'd never seen him before. Why, what's wrong?"

Doc's pudgy fingers drummed the kitchen counter. The whole room was a narrow, rectangular space lined with Formica, barely enough space in the middle for the overweight vet to walk through. "I can't be a hundred percent sure since I've only seen pictures, but...I think those might be radiation burns on him."

"Radiation?"

Doc nodded. "The shape...the way the tissue is damaged evenly all the way through... But it would have to be massive to flash cook him like that. We're talking Hiroshima levels."

"But how would he have ended up way out here like that? Jesus, you can't tell me he got very far in that condition. And last I checked, we don't have any nuclear reactors on 407."

"You positive about that?" After Mitch squinted at him, the vet added, "Well, who knows what the government is doing out there on the Corp land? That's why I asked if anybody recognized him, saw him around town, maybe." The man paused and wet his froggy lips. "And if he's been exposed to something radioactive around here, then...what's to say this whole area isn't irradiated? Maybe that's what's messing up our phones, some kind of EMP effect."

"Goddamn it. Shit." Mitch leaned over the sink and stared out the tiny window above it. From here he could see a slice of the parking lot, then nothing but dark fields and the distant silhouette of trees. The throb in his head was growing, jabbing at his eyeballs every few seconds, but he had no time to stare into space until it subsided. "He was conscious for just a few seconds when we brought him in. Babbled something about a quarantine and doors and someone named Cybil."

"*Doors?* You think he could've meant this shimmer that JD keeps blabbing about?"

"Maybe so. He said 'anything could come through,' and I guess anything did. But that's not all. I saw a deer earlier tonight. It...it looked like it'd been burned, too."

Doc grimaced. "Even the man himself might be a danger to us. Depending on how many rads he's giving off, we could all get radiation poisoning just from being around him."

Mitch looked down, at the faint outline of the man's

vomit on his shirt. "We need answers before we all start glowing in the dark. Is he in a coma or what?"

"Just unconscious, I think. The body tends to shut down after that much trauma."

"Can we wake him up?"

Doc hesitated. "If you want, I could try giving him some adrenaline. But the shock could very well kill him."

"I think it's a risk we need to take."

Shouting came from the lobby, followed by the muffled purr of an engine revving beyond the wall of the center. Mitch and Doc moved toward the kitchen door, but it opened before they got there. JD rushed through.

"Claude's takin Doc's car!"

"What? *How?*"

"Oh god," Doc moaned. "I left the keys in it! In case we needed to leave in a hurry!"

Mitch shoved past JD and sprinted across the auditorium to the front door, where everyone else stood looking out. He elbowed his way through the crowd to the glass door just in time to see Doc's hybrid spin around in front of the center while spraying dirt from its wheels—a maneuver it was *not* made for—and then it zoomed onto the road and made a squealing right turn.

He pounded a fist against the door. "What the fuck is he doing?"

"Goin to get some guns."

The gruff voice came from directly behind Mitch. He turned to find Denny standing there, shotgun still in hand. They stared at one another, the tension like heat waves on a sunbaked road. The crowd began to withdraw around them, leaving an empty ring with only the two of them in it.

Knowing what the answer would be, Mitch asked, "And

who told him to do that?"

"I did. You got a problem with that?"

"Yeah. Considering he just stole Doc's car and put us all in danger, I fucking well do."

Denny blew air from one corner of his mouth and shook his head sadly. "That's funny, comin from a man who did some stealin of his own tonight."

"What the hell does *that* mean?"

Instead of answering, Denny turned and handed his shotgun off to Ned. Mitch breathed an inward sigh of relief, until the other man faced him once more and began popping the knuckles of both hands.

"Let's do this, *Your Honor.*" His fists rose as he closed in on Mitch.

Then the back door of the community center crashed open, and a feminine scream full of rage echoed through the building.

FOURTEEN

When Mitch and Doc withdrew into the kitchen, the rest of the group broke into frantic conversations. Joy sat in uncomfortable silence beside Denny for a handful of seconds before he abruptly jumped to his feet and stomped away, leaving her behind in her chair like a wad of used chewing gum. She was used to such treatment (on one of their camping trips, she'd been left at a McDonald's for an hour before he realized she wasn't in the car, an oversight which was entirely her fault, of course), but her nerves had been wound as tight as steel cable since Denny came back from Doc's place battered and bruised. She watched as he stood in the corner on the opposite side of the room, talking in animated whispers to his flunkies. Every few seconds, one of them would gesture furtively at the front door of the community center.

And then, from out of nowhere, Denny shot her a fiery glare that made her wither in her seat.

"I think your new boyfriend's in a *lot* of trouble," Madeline said smugly from behind her.

Joy spun to look at her. She'd seen Madeline lean forward

to whisper in her husband's ear, but couldn't hear what she said. "What are you talking about? What did you tell him?"

Madeline didn't respond, just readjusted her thick glasses, fluffed her beehive with one manicured hand, and gave a grin full of gums that looked a little ghoulish on her exhausted face.

Screw this. She might not be able to avoid Denny's wrath forever, but she sure didn't have to put up with this bitch. Joy stood and moved away through the gloomy auditorium, into the main aisle and toward the back rows, where the Whitakers sat. Deborah shot a scowl at her; she obviously hadn't forgotten that hair-pulling business earlier. Off to the left, Arthur sat with JD and his wife, huddled in their own conversation around the burning glow from a cell phone. The big man spotted her and waved her over, a kind gesture that made her feel warm and welcome, until she saw the repulsed look that came over Roberta's face. It hurt, especially since Joy always liked the woman, but it didn't surprise her. Officially, Joy stood as part of the enemy camp; married to its ringleader, in fact. She declined the offer with a shake of her head and kept moving.

Helen sat by herself now, quietly crying with her bony hands gripped tightly in her lap. Joy slid in next to her and put a light hand on her arm.

"How are you?" she asked.

"I j-just can't believe this is happening!" the woman sobbed. "This m-morning Werner and I were talking about the grandkids coming to v-visit next month for Thanksgiving, and now he's...he's..."

"I know," Joy told her. "But you can't think about that right now. There'll be time to grieve when we get out of this."

The old woman's jaw clenched. She shook her head defiantly. "I don't *want* to get out! I want those things to come back and...and kill me too!"

"Please don't say that," Joy pleaded. Sudden envy pricked her. What did it feel like to love someone so much your life held no meaning without them? She sure couldn't imagine Denny's life changing much if one of the bodies lying outside had been her. He'd be out on an ATV or up in a deer blind an hour after her funeral ended.

For Christ's sake, what had she *done* with her life?

Helen's tears tapered for just a moment as she looked over at Joy. "I just don't know if I can go on without him."

"Then don't do it for him. Or you. Do it for those grandkids. They already lost their grandpa tonight; how would they feel if they lost both of you?"

Another pang of sadness made the old woman wince, but then she nodded. Joy opened her mouth to say more when a cry of, "Hey! *Hey!*" drew her attention.

JD flew past her, up the aisle, with Arthur on his heels. She turned to follow them, as did everyone else. They were stopped at the end of the aisle by Bo and Ned, who blocked their path with arms crossed. Behind them, Denny held the community center door open for Claude to go through. A second later, a car door slammed outside.

"What is that idiot doing?" Arthur demanded. Though he loomed over Denny's goons, neither looked intimidated, just smiled and stood their ground.

JD spun and ran down the closest row of folding seats toward the kitchen.

"That's right boy, go tattle to yer daddy!" Bo shouted after him.

By that point, everyone began crowding toward the door. Joy and Helen joined them, standing at the back of the mob to watch as Doc's car was stolen and then Denny attempted to pick a fight with Mitch. And, as her husband accused the other man of doing 'some stealing of his own,' a heavy, sinking sensation filled Joy's stomach, as though she'd just chugged several gallons of sloshing water. She suddenly had a horrible suspicion what Madeline had murmured in Denny's ear.

But all her worries were forgotten as the back door of the center banged open, and a banshee's wail stopped the fight before the first punch could be thrown.

The people around the door—still close to forty individuals, she figured—turned as one, expecting more monsters perhaps. Joy found her position at the back of group gave her a front row seat to the figure standing on the stoop where she and Mitch sat just an hour ago.

It took a few seconds for her to recognize Lena Henning. The wan light just inside the doorway washed across her neighbor's face, revealing rust colored stains smeared across her rough features, but that was far from the strangest thing about her appearance. The woman had always been on the butch side, but now she was dressed like a Rambo cosplayer, with gray and green army fatigues above her combat boots, a midnight black t-shirt, and, silliest of all, a camouflage bandana wrapped around the choppy bowl of her hair. Both of her hands were occupied as well, the contents adding to the soldier-of-fortune Halloween costume.

In one, she held a pump action shotgun that looked big enough to take down a moose.

In the other appeared to be a bottle of vodka with a flaming twist of paper jutting from the neck. The tiny fire backwashed her flat chest with a fierce red glow.

She swept the room with the weapon as she stomped through the door, the motion efficient and somehow professional, like a S.W.A.T. team member checking corners. Her cold gaze lingered on the upraised stage beside the rear door—and the unconscious man who'd kicked off tonight's weirdness, still stretched out in front of the board's podium—but then she continued past, focusing on the tightly packed crowd in front of the entrance.

Joy would remember thinking later, if her brain worked just a little faster, if her reflexes were a little better, she might've done something to stop what came next. But the sight struck her as so bizarre, she could only stare. The rest of the room remained just as hypnotized by the bony lesbian barreling up the aisle toward them, even as she lifted the Molotov cocktail over her head.

"*YOU WILL PAY FOR WHAT YOU DID TO HER!*" Lena roared in her croaking smoker's voice. She launched the glass bottle into the air like a quarterback.

It tumbled in slow motion, arcing high over Joy's head. She followed its path. Watched as it collided with the wall of the community center on the other side of the crowd, beside the door and high up, near the ceiling. The contents blossomed into a beautiful orange and yellow flower bright enough to temporarily blind her, one whose pedals sprayed outward in all directions. Someone screamed, but she couldn't tell who.

And then, in the span of a single heartbeat, the crowd of her neighbors became a panicked herd of stampeding cattle.

FIFTEEN

Mitch understood as soon as he caught a glimpse of Lena Henning's gore-streaked face; the spark of her firebomb's wick revealed a gleam of wild insanity in her eyes that chilled him to the bone. Gladys' words sprang to mind, her warning about how this woman wouldn't bother with lawsuits when pushed too far.

Apparently that push had happened.

But the realization didn't keep him from standing just as frozen as the rest of the crowd while the bottle shattered against the wall to the right of where he and Denny held their fighting stances. The resulting explosion doused a five foot radius with liquid fire.

Burning droplets seared Mitch's face, singed his hair, caught his sleeve on fire. He jerked away and used his hands to beat out the burning spots on his body. In the shifting red glow, he could see Denny and Bo doing the same to themselves. But Ned, still holding Denny's shotgun, had been standing too close to the impact. The man went up in flames shockingly fast. He screamed, dropped the weapon—whose wooden stock and pump were also burning—and ran his hands over his body, as though he could somehow rub the blazing pain away. Then he ran in a confused, jerking circle, spreading the fire that now licked the wall and chewed at the cheap plaster ceiling tiles. Even if Mitch could find something to put the poor bastard out with, he didn't know if he could get close enough to do so.

The crowd broke into hysterical flight. People ran screaming in all directions, pushing and shoving one another in their haste to get away from the growing inferno.

But the only direction they could go was directly toward the woman who started it. Which was probably her intent all along. Through the throng of scattering bodies, Mitch saw Lena bring the shotgun up and open fire into the crowd as they pelted toward her. The shot peppered several people, knocking them down like bowling pins. The rest of the mob trampled right over the fallen. Lena marched forward to meet them with grim determination; if she'd held a saber instead of a shotgun, she would've looked like the ghost of some Civil War general. The old man who lost his wife during the aerial attack outside took a round in the stomach that damn near gutted him. He crumpled, falling hard against one of the folding chairs, which collapsed beneath him.

"*Get down!*" Mitch heard someone bellow. Arthur, he thought, but in the chaos, he couldn't tell where it came from. It felt like hours since this attack began, even though no more than thirty seconds could've elapsed since Lena entered the building. "*Everyone, take cover!*"

In the auditorium, there wasn't much cover *to* take, other than the cheap folding chairs. Those quick-witted enough to grasp the danger threw themselves to the floor and crawled away from the main aisle. Others just continued to run through Lena's field of fire, where she gunned them down like clay pigeons on a skeet range.

Mitch's legs wouldn't work. Panic stole his breath, mired him in indecision. He scanned the room for JD, but spotted Doc instead, blundering back into the kitchen with two other people. Then, all at once, Mitch's paralysis broke. He ducked behind the back row of seats beside Denny.

The shotgun roared again. Mitch risked a peek over the top of the chair. Bodies lay scattered everywhere. A haze of oily black smoke spread across the upper half of the room, but he could still see Lena as she worked her way down the aisle, pausing at every row to execute people where they cowered and then rack shell after shell into the chamber. Her mouth split into a gleeful snarl as someone pleaded for their life.

"*Jesus Christ, this crazy bitch is gonna kill all of us!*" Denny proclaimed.

Even though he knelt right next to Mitch, his words were barely audible over the crackle of the fire at their backs. The heat had gotten so intense, they wouldn't be able to stay longer than a few seconds. They could probably make it to the door, but not without Lena seeing them. Besides, Mitch couldn't save himself while the rest of these people remained trapped.

"*We have to lead her away from the door, give people a chance to get out!*" he told Denny.

"*Yeah, good luck with that! I'm gettin the fuck outta here myself the next time her back is turned!*"

Mitch didn't bother to argue. But he did stand up, grab the chair that Denny hid behind, and fling it across the room with all of his might.

It was an awkward object to launch, but it got the job done. The rear legs struck Lena across the lower back as she pointed her weapon at someone crawling through the chair rows. She stumbled, discharging the shotgun into the floor, then spun around. When she saw Mitch and Denny, her face twisted into a mask of bottomless hatred.

"*I WILL KILL YOUUUUU!*" she howled.

Mitch sprinted across the flaming front of the room with Denny right behind him, cursing his name. Lena spun, tracking them with the shotgun. They reached the corner of the room and dove to the floor again just as the weapon boomed. The folding chair next to Mitch flew away and crashed against the wall, its back a hunk of punctured metal. With his head against the tile, Mitch could see through the forest of chair legs that he'd accomplished his goal: the rest of her victims were forgotten as Lena zeroed in on them. She tossed seats out of her way to clear a path, roaring in fury.

"*Crawl!*" Mitch yelled to Denny, and began moving down the far side of the room.

SIXTEEN

When the crowd broke, Joy moved with them. It was either that, or be plowed under. She grabbed Helen's hand to keep them together, but the mob pulled the older woman away. Then a panicked elbow hit her under the ribcage, shoving her aside. Her feet tangled and, as her balance slipped away, she threw herself into the closest row of seats so she didn't get trampled.

The hollow boom of a gunshot came immediately, followed by several more. The screams of fear turned to pain. *That lunatic just shot at us*, she thought, the idea still too amazing for her to fully comprehend. Another person hit the floor where she'd been standing, a man dressed in a long sleeve polo with a chunk of his head blown off. Joy choked back a scream of her own as blood ran down the man's face and puddled under her foot.

She got to her knees and peered over a chair. To her left, the fire blazed unchecked at the front of the building, casting the whole room in a hazy orange glow. To the right, Lena stood in the aisle just yards away, gunning people down at random as they fled the growing heat. While Joy watched, Roberta Miller's left shoulder caught the edge of a blast that caved in the chest of the man running beside her. The hefty woman spun halfway around and landed on her side in the aisle, where people stepped on her in their haste to escape Lena's wrath.

Joy scurried through the seats on hands and knees, pushing chairs out of her way, until she reached the other woman. Roberta lay on her side, moaning. Joy grabbed the woman's upper arm and pulled.

"*C'mon, we have to go!*" she hissed. Lena marched up the aisle toward them, playing Whack-a-Mole with anyone that popped their head up from the sea of chairs. She even checked each row as she made her way to the front. The methodical approach to the slaughter sent a cold spike through Joy's heart. "*Hurry!*"

Roberta rolled over onto her stomach and got to her hands and knees, grimacing. Blood dribbled down her arm in thin trails. But when she saw Lena approaching, she nodded fearfully.

Joy moved aside to let her into the row, then crawled along close behind her, keeping her head up against the other woman's wide ass. From elsewhere in the room, someone shrieked, a long, ragged note that made Joy's stomach clench. She hoped Helen was all right, but she doubted *any* of them would be at this point. The crackle of flames got louder every second, and the smoke made her eyes burn.

They were midway across the row when Joy looked back over her shoulder.

Lena Henning reached their aisle. Her eyes locked with Joy's. She bared her teeth in a homicidal grin as she raised the shotgun to her shoulder.

Joy stared down the barrel and prayed it wouldn't hurt.

A chair flew out of the smoky gloom to strike Lena in the back. She stumbled, the round meant to end Joy's life instead obliterating several of the scuffed floor tiles. The woman regained her balance and wheeled around, Joy completely forgotten. She screamed something unintelligible before striding away. Joy rose cautiously to see who just saved her life and caught a glimpse of Mitch rushing away into the darkness, with Denny trailing behind. Once again, Joy experienced severely mixed emotions about her husband being alive.

Most of the front wall of the community center blazed now, the flames moving in undulating waves across the plaster. The fire worked its way along the ceiling as well; flaming, fist-sized chunks rained down from the center of the inferno, miniature bombs that exploded against the floor. Something up there gave a deep, rattling groan. It wouldn't be long before the entire roof collapsed.

"*Joy!*"

She turned back around. Roberta had gone on without her and reached the end of the row, where Arthur's tall form waited. A group of fifteen or so other people stood clustered around him, including Madeline and both Whitakers. He beckoned to Joy and shouted, "*We have to get out!*"

Joy stood and went to him. As a group, they ran single file along the side of the room, around the last row of chairs, and on to the front door. This path took them toward the heart of the fire, but it was still the closest exit, and trying to reach the rear door would send them right back in Lena's direction. Several other people joined the caravan along the way including Helen, who lurched out of the smoke, hacking and coughing. Joy could barely breathe herself, and the air got worse as they hustled down the narrow space between the fire and the last row of chairs.

The glass door remained intact, a clear pane surrounded by an ocean of flames. Arthur avoided the metal handle, opening it instead with his foot. "*Go, run!*"

"*JD!*" Roberta shouted, as the others hurried through. She kept one hand against her shoulder, applying pressure to the gunshot wound. "*Where's JD? I can't leave without him!*"

Joy looked across the room, pulling her shirt up over mouth and nose. The smoke was too thick for the firelight to penetrate; beyond a few yards, roiling darkness shrouded everything. Then came the flash of another gunshot off to their left, like lightning in the heart of a storm cloud.

From the other direction, a car-sized chunk of burning wood and plaster crashed to the floor, crushing the chairs beneath it. Joy's ears rang so much from the shotgun blasts, the noise barely registered over the roar of the fire.

"*We can't stay!*" she said. "*The whole place is coming down!*"

"*Ladies, let's go!*" Arthur shouted.

He held the door for them and then jumped through himself. Outside, Joy sucked greedily at the crisp night air, which tasted as sweet as cotton candy. She wanted nothing more than to lie down and breathe it, but they weren't out of danger yet. Fire crawled across the exterior of the building as well, the heat blistering her skin, and the surrounding grass had begun to catch. Already the flames worked their way across to the first of the vehicles parked in the meadow, creating a line of demarcation that forced the survivors away from the building and toward the scrubby shoulder of 407.

"We should get back further, in case she comes out," Arthur told the people gathered beside the road, as he wiped burning ash from his shirt.

“I don’t think anyone’s coming outta there.” Madeline pointed at the glass door they’d just come through.

A pile of burning debris clogged the exit. The flames on the outside of the community center climbed twenty feet in the air, releasing a pillar of greasy smoke that disappeared into the night sky. During the day, that billowing column would’ve been a signal for miles around, but against the night sky, they could barely see it themselves from across the road.

C’mon Mitch, Joy thought. *Get out.*

“That stupid, insane *bitch*,” Roberta sobbed angrily. Tears ran freely down both of her pudgy cheeks, washing clean streaks through the soot. One hand fisted at her waist, the other still squeezed up tight against her bloody shoulder. “All this because we told her she couldn’t have up some goddamn lights?”

Joy shook her head. “I don’t know if that was it. She said something before she threw the bottle. Something about us ‘paying for what we did to her.’”

“The devil speaks through her,” Deborah Whitaker declared.

“Gibberish,” Arthur added, and Joy wondered if he meant Lena or Deborah.

The fuel tank of one of the cars on the edge of the parking lot exploded with a surprisingly subdued *whoomp!* The resulting fireball spread the flames to the surrounding vehicles, a deadly domino effect. The corpses that lay scattered between them began to burn as well. The survivors of the community center massacre backed up further, crossing the road and standing in the underbrush on the far side. Still no sign of life from inside the building, and, as the seconds ticked on and the brick façade began to buckle, it looked like there never would be. The inferno spread into the trees on the opposite end of the structure, cutting them off completely from the south side of the road. Joy wondered if it was dry enough at this time of year for a wildfire to grow out of control.

"We have to go back," she said aloud, to no one in particular. Drops of sweat cascaded down her cheeks and forehead; she wiped them away. "See if we can help anyone else."

Arthur turned to her and gently grasped her upper arms with his large hands. "I know Denny's still in there, but—"

"*Fuck Denny!*" She shook his hands off. "This isn't about Denny, it's about..."

The words died as she looked around at the haggard, vacant faces of the others. They were all in shock, none of them in any condition to attempt a rescue into that hell, even if they could find a way inside.

"There's nothing we can do for *any* of them," Arthur told her. "Their only chance at this point is to make it out through the back. Even if they do, we have no way to reach them as long as the fire keeps spreading."

"Then w-what do we do now?" someone at the far end of the line asked.

"The problem is the same. We need shelter and a way to get help."

Samuel stepped forward eagerly. "Our house is closest."

"No, it isn't," Madeline argued. "*Mine* is."

"Only if you follow the road." He pointed into the mess of underbrush and trees behind them. "But if we cut across the hillside and rejoin 407 where it doubles back, we could get to our house in half the time."

"We can even try calling the police from our phone," Deborah added quickly.

Helen stared into the tree line and shook her head. "No. I don't want to go through that."

"I don't either," Arthur said. "But I'm afraid we don't have much choice. We're in more danger if we just stand here."

A shrieking howl punctuated his claim, drifting to them from somewhere further up the road, a high-pitched caterwaul like that of a mountain cat.

Except this held a buzzing, alien undertone that set Joy's hair on end.

What in hell was going on here?

She took the old woman's hand. "Let's just do this as fast as possible."

Arthur lead the way into the dark woodland, and the rest of their shrinking group reluctantly followed. Joy took one more look back at the burning building before going with them.

SEVENTEEN

Mitch army-crawled across the tile, down the side of the room and away from the fire, which had turned the entire front half of the community center into a vision of hell. Denny followed his lead. From somewhere to their right, over the grinding rumble of the inferno, he could hear Lena tossing chairs aside as she searched for them, coughing harder with every step. The air quality in here had become uncomfortably hot and thick with smoke, the equivalent of trying to breathe in a cloud of fine-grained sand, but near the floor Mitch could take shallow sips into his lungs, just enough to let him keep his wits.

The swinging door to the kitchen appeared on his left. Mitch considered ducking inside, but knew it wouldn't get them out of the building; not even the window over the sink was big enough to squeeze through. He would just be trapped in a shooting gallery, along with Doc and whoever else had taken shelter within. Better to keep leading Lena away from the others until he could lose her. Preferably before they all burned to death.

He slid past the entrance on his belly, then looked back in time to see Denny push open the door anyway and roll through. Mitch clenched his teeth in frustration.

Out in the smoke, Lena screeched triumphantly, drawn by the movement of the door. Her silhouette appeared against the red-hued backdrop of the fire as she ran toward the kitchen. She hurdled over the chairs in her way with the precision of a military cadet, rather than a sixty-something string bean.

Still on the ground and hidden in the smoke, Mitch stuck out his foot.

She was still flat-out sprinting when she tripped, ankles swept neatly out from under her. Lena flew forward and smashed face first into the wall beside the door with a bone-shattering crunch. Mitch thought for sure she must be unconscious or even dead, but she lurched back up, shotgun dangling from one hand. Blood cascaded down her lips and chin from the ruins of her nose as she turned drunkenly toward him.

Knowing it was useless, Mitch scrambled to his feet and fled into the smoke.

The shotgun blast came a scant few seconds later. A sharp pain tore at his backside, like a hundred wasps stinging him at once. The force of it pitched him forward onto the tile again. *My ass, she shot me in my ass*, he thought in amazement. The agony was bright and constant, a fire in his brain, but he ignored it and forced himself to crawl before she caught him.

Scattered chairs loomed ahead, strange islands in the darkness. He quickly became lost in the room, the smoke too thick to see more than a few yards ahead. Panic leeched into his brain as he struggled to catch a clear breath. Mitch pulled himself into a group of chairs, hunkered down in the narrow space between their legs, and concentrated on inhaling. Sweat poured down his neck, the air far hotter than any sauna now. The seat of his jeans felt wet also, but he was too terrified to put his hand back there to feel how big a hole she'd put in him.

Mitch could see Lena's ghostly form lurching through the haze. She didn't seem to know where he'd gone. Maybe if he just stayed still, she would pass him by.

Another shadow blundered into his field of vision from the left, one hand held to its mouth as it gagged. Mitch recognized JD's squat silhouette even before he shouted his wife's name.

Lena's shotgun swung in his best friend's direction.

"*JD, look out!*" Mitch jumped up and ran, the pain of his wound pushed aside. He barreled into Lena's flat chest with both hands, driving her backward before she could fire. She snarled in his face, teeth coated in blood, eyes crazed and bulging, but couldn't get her feet planted to stop his momentum.

The wall of the center appeared behind her. Mitch slammed the skinny woman into it for the second time, bouncing her off the plaster just beside the door of the coat closet. Again he thought this would take the wind out of her, and again she surprised him by ramming the butt of the shotgun into his stomach. He stumbled back, lungs struggling even more, and ran into JD.

"*You killed her, you hateful bastards!*" Lena screamed. She stepped away from the wall and stalked toward them, bringing the shotgun to bear on both men from just feet away. "*You killed my Cynthia!*"

The door of the coat closet burst open behind her. Gladys emerged, carrying a golf club in her good arm, which she swung in a whistling arc without a moment's hesitation. The heavy head of the five wood made a low *clonk!* as it connected with the back of Lena's skull. This time she collapsed to the floor for good.

Gladys pushed her coke-bottle glasses up on her nose and asked, "*Jesus, Mitchy, what'd you do to the place?*" before she launched into a coughing fit.

Mitch ran forward and wrenched the shotgun out of Lena's slack grip. His ass still throbbed, but there would be time for that later. He pointed to Gladys. "*Get her out the back door!*" he ordered JD.

"*But Roberta—!*"

"*We don't have time, JD! Just do it!*" Without waiting to see if he listened, Mitch pulled his shirt up over his face, then followed the wall down to the kitchen door and pushed it open. A cooking pan flew out of the smoky darkness within and struck the wall a half foot from his head. "*It's me, it's Mitch!*" he shouted before entering.

Doc and Denny huddled halfway across the room, along with Bo and another man and a woman that Mitch didn't know. "*Where is she?*" Doc managed to get out between coughs.

"*She's out cold! Now get outside, the fire's almost here!*"

The five of them hurried out. Mitch led the way to the back door as blazing embers rained down around them. By the time they reached her, Lena was stirring.

"*Get up!*" Mitch told her.

"*Fuck her, that bitch can burn!*" Denny yelled.

Mitch ignored him and nudged the woman with the barrel of the shotgun. "*Get up and walk! If you try anything else, I swear to Christ, I will shoot you without a second thought!*"

Lena looked unaware of her surroundings as she rose to her feet and stumbled out ahead of them. A moonlit rectangle marked the door through the smoke ahead. The rest of them ran outside, where JD and Gladys waited, but as

Mitch started through, the edge of the stage caught his eye. Morgan's feet were barely visible where he lay.

"*Poor man's been burned enough for one day!*" Doc shouted.

Mitch pressed the shotgun into the vet's bloated hands, then signaled JD to help him. Together, they went back into the smoke, picked Morgan up by the arms, and dragged him through the door just as the middle of the roof crashed down. A concussive wave slammed into them from behind, a giant hand that shoved Mitch forward. Plumes of soot billowed out around them, coating all three men in a uniform gray.

The shaggy grass outside burned on both sides of the building, a sea of waist high flames spreading in all directions. Mitch and JD dragged the unconscious man away from the building, toward the woods, where the other seven people waited far back from the community center. They put him down in the grass near Lena, who sat cross-legged, staring at the fire with the blank fascination of a newborn. Her nose crooked over to the right at a drastic angle, and a visible knot grew on the back of her head where Gladys used her skull as a golf tee. With her fury abated, she looked smaller somehow, shrunken in on herself. Doc stood guard over her with the shotgun.

"Have you seen anyone else?" Mitch asked, then paused to spit out a mouthful of ash. "I thought some people went out the front."

"Cain't tell," Bo answered, his drawling accent turning the first word into two syllables. "Fire's got us cut off for fifty or sixty yards in either direction, and still spreadin. Few of the cars in the parkin lot even went up."

He was right. The flames ate up the dry October grass in an expanding circle that would reach them in moments. They wouldn't be able to get to the road unless they could outpace it by going around. Mitch didn't know if he could take another step.

"*You fuckin cunt!*" JD suddenly bellowed. He charged at Lena before any of them could grab him, reared back, and brought the back of one hand cracking across her bloody cheek, far harder than Madeline had struck Mitch, the sound as sharp as a gunshot. She took it without acknowledgment, face flying to the side and then returning to gaze at the fire. JD lifted his arm to hit her again, but by then Mitch grabbed his wrist and pulled him away.

"She's not worth it," Mitch told him.

"R-Roberta," JD stammered, his face screwing up in anguish. "She k-killed my *wife*, Mitch."

"We don't know that. She might've made it out. Once the fire dies down, we can start looking."

Denny watched all of this in silence, without a single quip. Then he turned and started away from them, heading northeast toward the tree line.

"Where are you going?" Mitch asked.

"Home, like I shoulda done in the first place," he said over his shoulder without stopping. "I sure as hell ain't gonna stand here with my dick in my hand, waitin for one of those goddamn monsters to eat me. I suppose the rest of you can come, long as that crazy lesbo ain't with you."

Bo joined him first, hurrying after Denny like a faithful dog. The couple Mitch didn't know went next. Doc, JD, and Gladys all looked over at Mitch, but no one spoke until the secretary asked, "*Monsters?*"

"We'll explain on the way," Mitch told her. He looked at Doc. "Just keep that shotgun handy. I have a feeling we're gonna need it."

EIGHTEEN

The nineteen survivors of the community center massacre trudged through the dark woods with the listlessness of sleepwalkers, their path lit only by weak cell phone flashlights that cast a dim haze of illumination. For a while, they were helped by the orange glow of the fire washing across the horizon at their backs, but it quickly grew dimmer as the tree canopy closed in around them.

Samuel Whitaker led the pack. He set a brisk pace just short of a jog that none of the weary 407ers even tried to match, then halted every twenty or thirty yards to wait impatiently for them to catch up. Thin runners of sweat carved through the grime smeared across his bald head and harsh, angular face, despite the fact that the temperature continued to drop as midnight approached. Even though few folks wore jackets, the cold didn't bother anyone after the unbearable heat inside the community center.

Joy walked with Helen to her left, helping the old woman along, and Arthur and Roberta off to her right. The rest of the group spread out in a straggling line as they wove between trees and struggled through heavy brush. Most of them still coughed from smoke inhalation, and Joy could hear a few people quietly sobbing, but no one spoke, either from exhaustion, shock, or fear of what might hear them.

Except Deborah and Madeline. Those two engaged in hushed conversation non-stop as they followed right behind the former's husband. They didn't seem like people who would normally associate with one another to Joy, but then again, maybe bitches of a feather flocked together. Every few minutes, when they caught up with him, Samuel would turn his head and murmur something to the women over his shoulder before bounding forward again like Tarzan of the Jungle.

Joy couldn't care less what they said to one another. At first, she'd been too terrified, waiting for more of those flying horrors to swoop out of the trees as she picked her way through brambles and held branches aside for Helen to pass. When the monotony of walking finally caused that fear to fade into mental background noise, her thoughts turned to Denny and Mitch.

Both men were most likely dead. Though she'd wished that on Denny a few times over the last decade, they had history together and even some good times, so she would never be able to celebrate the idea of him dying.

And Mitch… Christ, after everything that man had gone through, she considered his demise an absolute tragedy, an epic prank pulled by a cold and indifferent universe.

Yet she could feel nothing for either of them. Grief took energy, and she had none to spare. As she'd told Helen, there would be time for that later, when they escaped this nightmare.

Roberta brought her out of these thoughts when she drifted closer and murmured, "You saved my life."

Joy frowned as she moved her flashlight close enough for the glare to illuminate the other woman. "I didn't do anything."

"You did," Roberta insisted. Joy might've argued further, but the other woman was having trouble speaking. And breathing. Her chest heaved in and out, that prodigious bosom riding the crest of each inhalation until it touched her chin. One maroon hand stayed pressed against the wound in her meaty shoulder. "If you hadn't gotten me up, I'da laid there on the floor until Lena finished the job. So...thank you."

"Uh, well...glad I could help," Joy said sheepishly, then turned to help Helen over a depression in the ground so she wouldn't have to meet the other woman's gaze. She'd never been any good at accepting praise. Probably because she'd gotten so little of it in her life, not from her parents, and certainly not from Denny.

But she also didn't want the conversation to die. This might be her only chance to get someone around here to change their mind about her. She finished helping Helen and then forced herself to look at Roberta just in time to see the woman collapse.

Her legs folded and lowered her gently to the ground amid a thicket of wild raspberry. Joy reached her side a second later, followed by Arthur. The big man knelt next to her in the brush, one hand on the trunk of a gnarly old oak tree to support himself. "What's wrong, my dear?"

"I don't know, I...I just feel dizzy..." The words slurred together. Her hand finally fell away from her shoulder, revealing a shredded patch of flesh through a hole in her blouse. Joy pointed her cell phone's flashlight at the wound and saw a trickle of maroon spreading down her entire side.

"That looks bad," she whispered, and thought, *Jesus, I didn't save her life, I just granted her an extension.*

"For a shotgun, it could be a lot worse," Arthur said. "I'd planned on bandaging it as soon as we reached the Whitakers', but now I'm afraid she won't make it that far."

"It's all right, just gimme a second to catch m'wind," Roberta told them.

"Nonsense." He turned and shouted, "Hey there, Samuel, hold on! We need help!"

The entire group stopped, many of them cringing away from Arthur's raised voice in the otherwise silent woods. Their cell phones created a dim pallor around Roberta as they crept closer. Samuel came tromping back through the trees, flanked by Deborah and Madeline, the latter of which hissed, "Would you keep it down? You want those things to find us?" Joy was delighted to realize a chunk of the woman's beehive hairdo had been singed off, leaving a lopsided pile on top of her head.

Arthur ignored her, but lowered his voice. "Roberta's hurt. I don't know if she can walk much farther."

Samuel shrugged. "Well, she's gonna have to. She's too big for us to carry."

"There's that ol' neighborly Christian spirit," Joy mumbled.

He shot her a nasty glare. His eyes were beady and placed far back in his skull, giving him the angry look of a rat. "Our house is just over the next ridge. If she can't make it, the rest of us can go on ahead and then you can bring back a wheelbarrow for her."

"Yeah, and I'm guessing that's not a mission you'll be assisting with, am I right?"

His spine went rigid. "I'll be tending to the needs of my flock."

Joy choked on bitter laughter. "Is that what we are now? Your 'flock?'"

"You're in my care, aren't you? You'll be under my roof. In the eyes of the Lord, it's my responsibility to see to your needs. Both physical and spiritual."

The way he stressed this last word made Joy slightly uncomfortable, deep in the pit of her stomach. Those recessed eyes looked even more hooded than usual. She realized she didn't even know what religion these two were.

Deborah raised a hand toward Roberta—palm up, as theatrical as a carny inviting the rubes to a show—then spoke in a haughty, authoritative voice while looking down her soot-stained nose. "If her faith in the Good Lord was strong enough, He would raise her up and make her strong."

"Really? Just that easy? Cause I don't see Him sending in a heavenly helicopter to airlift *your* holier-than-thou ass outta this mess, sweetheart."

"What would you like us to do, Roberta?" Arthur asked softly, interrupting the hushed argument.

"I'll be damned if anybody's puttin me in a wheelbarrow like a load of fat bricks," the woman growled. "I got dizzy, but I'm feelin better already. Just help me up."

Joy took one of her offered hands. Arthur took the other. Roberta winced as they hauled her back to her feet, then gave a shaky thumbs up. "See? Right as rain."

Arthur placed a hand on the oak beside him again and leaned against it wearily. He might be a big, strapping galoot-of-a-man, but he suddenly looked all of his sixty-plus years. "Lead on then, Samuel. The sooner we reach your home, the better off we'll b—"

His words cut off as something on the tree snapped closed with the finality of a bear trap, taking three of his fingers with it.

Arthur howled and stumbled backward, bringing his right hand up to his face. Tiny gouts of blood squirted up from the stumps of his pointer, middle, and ring fingers. He examined the injury for only a moment before jamming it into his other armpit and bringing his arm down hard to put pressure on it.

Joy swung her cell phone around and trained the beam on the oak tree. With the shadows thrown long, they could see the thing that clung to the trunk, though its rough, brown flesh helped it blend in with the bark. The body was narrow, flat, and two feet long, but a set of wide, grinning jaws took up most of that length, jutting from one end like an alligator's snout. Not only did this huge maw look disproportional to the rest of its body, it was so swollen with crooked teeth it couldn't even close correctly, the lower mandible skewed to an offset angle. Arthur's fingers were still visible between those yellowed fangs, but, as they watched, the jaws opened and let them spill onto the ground. The rest of its figure was an odd conglomeration of legs with split-toed feet and a long tail that stretched up and out of sight into the canopy.

Her mind recoiled in disgust. Yes, the thing was ugly, but that was only a small part of its hideousness. It was the awkwardness of its form that truly offended, an artless collection of mismatched parts assembled by a bumbling Frankenstein. Nature could never produce something so uneven, so asymmetrical, so utterly wrong.

Before anyone else could react to the wriggling horror, someone at the far end of the line let out a scream. A woman blundered through the trees toward them with her arm held stiffly out in front of her, as though waiting for her hand to be kissed. Another of the monsters clung to it, tail curled around her waist like a belt and jaws locked around her bicep. "*Get it off!*" she cried, as the thing worked to gnaw her appendage off.

The treetops over their heads rattled and shook as more of these creatures dropped down, hanging by their prehensile tails, fearsome maws opening wide and then snapping closed again.

"*Run!*" Arthur bellowed, giving Roberta a shove to get her moving.

"*This way!*" Samuel turned, ducked under one of the beasts as it snapped at his head, and fled into the woods. His wife and Madeline followed without looking back.

Joy grabbed Helen's hand and ran. Shrieks of pain and terror floated through the trees. Shadows flickered in confusing displays as flashlights swung wildly. For the first few seconds of flight, Arthur and Roberta were off to their left, but Joy soon lost track of them. People ran haphazard, disoriented in the dark, tripping over the underbrush, crisscrossing in and out of the trees only to run into one another. And the monsters were *everywhere*, dangling from the trees and snapping at anyone who came close. The clacking of their teeth formed a terrible chorus. Joy dodged around them with Helen in tow, moving purely on instinct. A man grabbed at her as she passed by in the black woods. His face had been torn away, exposing bloody shreds of muscle, one eyeball hanging limp against his bare cheekbone. He knocked her cell phone out of her hand and sent it spinning into the bushes as they fled past him.

After that, she kept her eyes on the glow from Samuel's phone, but it drew farther away with each passing second. Helen weighed on her arm, slowing her pace more with each step. The old woman panted as she tried to keep up. The screams faded around them, replaced by wet chomping sounds as the stubby crocodile creatures tore apart their neighbors. Not to eat, of course; oh no, these things were far more into destruction than digestion. For one shameful moment, Joy considered letting go of the woman's hand and sprinting ahead on her own.

But she was very grateful for the hold up when she glimpsed a quicksilver flash between the trees immediately in front of her.

Joy came to a sudden halt, jerking backward to counter her speed. Just inches in front of her, a shimmering, translucent wall floated in the air. It looked exactly like JD described, a rough oval that stretched through the trees, as ghostly and ephemeral as a spider web adorned with heavy dew. She stood so close that, if she focused her eyes just right, she could see the strange glow came from thousands of tiny, glittering particles suspended in midair. An electric charge tingled across her skin, stiffening the roots of her hair.

Even as Joy processed all this, Helen kept running past her, heedless of the danger.

"Wait, stop!" Joy tightened her grip on the old woman's hand and pulled as hard as she could.

The force yanked Helen off balance and spun her halfway around. Her other hand flew outward to steady her...

...and plunged right into that wall of gossamer radiance.

NINETEEN

The fire chased Mitch's group for ten minutes after they left the community center, even started to consume the short stretch of woods they cut through, but it finally guttered on the moist ground beneath the canopy, leaving a trail of smoldering ruin in their wake. Mitch and JD lugged Morgan's unconscious body between them with his arms slung over their shoulders, while doing their best to explain to Gladys what happened since she zonked out. She gave little comment about the vicious creatures and glowing holes in reality, but finally spoke when he reached the part about Lena's attack.

"I told you she was trouble, Mitchy," she whispered, flapping her good hand at the other woman's backside. Lena marched in front of them with Doc just behind, shotgun held ready. The swollen knot on her scalp gave her whole head an odd, lumpy appearance.

"Yeah," Mitch agreed, grimacing as he stumbled under Morgan's weight. Every step caused dull pain to radiate from his right ass cheek, all along his hip and down his leg. At least he knew this was *real* pain, pain with a root cause, not like the migraines. He had no urge to sit somewhere and shut his brain off to escape it either; if anything, this kept him hyper alert. He still didn't know how much damage the shot did, but he could feel blood trickling down his calf and even squelching in his shoe. Nothing to do for now but keep walking until he dropped. "I'm just glad you figured out what was going on from inside the closet."

"I didn't." Gladys dropped him a weary wink, magnified by her enormous glasses. "I just really wanted to brain that chain-smoking harpy with a golf club."

Ahead, the woods began to lighten in drastic increments. At first, Mitch thought the brilliance was daybreak, though his body clock insisted otherwise. Then he and JD emerged from the tree line—still supporting Morgan's limp form—and spotted Lena's avant-garde cabin atop a gentle incline in front of them, surrounded by those high intensity lamps. Mitch had never actually seen these lights at night (had suspected Denny might be exaggerating a bit about them) but damned if they weren't bright enough to make your eyes water when you looked directly at them.

A few yards away, Lena began to shriek.

She'd remained in her docile, near catatonic state throughout the hike. But when she entered the clearing where her house sat, she tilted her head back and wailed to the heavens. The awful noise continued as she sank to her knees in the grass, then brought her hands to her face and raked furrows down her cheeks.

"Jesus, what's wrong with her?" JD asked.

Doc started toward her, but Mitch held up a hand. "Let me. You just keep the gun on her." He passed Morgan off to JD and then approached Lena cautiously, trying not to limp.

When he felt confident this wasn't some trick, Mitch hunkered in front of her in the glare of the lights. The resulting throb from his rear end made the world wobble for a split second.

"Miss Henning? Lena?" Mitch marveled at how gentle—how *normal*—his voice sounded. Twenty minutes ago, he'd been locked in mortal combat with this woman. He could still recall the feeling of driving her head into the wall, the way she snarled in his face like a rabid animal. "What is it, what's wrong?"

She didn't answer, didn't even acknowledge him, but her screams spiraled down into a croaking moan, interrupted only by shuddering breaths that blasted from her mouth in white plumes. She'd lost her Rambo bandana, and sweat plastered her hair to her scalp. A thick crust of blood covered her mouth and chin from her broken nose, which was no more than a swollen, formless wad of dough stuck to the middle of her face. Her fingers pulled at the fleshy bags of her cheeks, stretching her eyes open so wide they looked ready to fall out of their sockets. They stared right past Mitch, locked on the house over his shoulder.

"Can't you shut that bitch up?" Denny appeared to his left with Bo. Behind them, Mitch could see the other two survivors—a fifty-something married couple whose names turned out to be Eli and Carla—cowering in each other's arms. "She's gonna bring every last one of those things down on us."

"I don't know what's wrong with her."

"Looks like some sort of PTSD," Doc murmured. "Something sure rattled her cage, anyway."

"Mass murder tends to do that to a person," JD said, in an icy tone Mitch had never heard him use before.

Mitch followed her line of sight to the cabin. All at once, he remembered what she screeched at him inside the community center. "Lena...what happened to Cynthia?"

She still didn't answer, just wrapped her arms around her stomach and rocked back and forth as she let out another anguished moan.

"Oh, for fuck's sake," Denny hissed, giving a quick glance around. "Bad enough we got Mr. Flame Broiled slowin us down, but you had to bring her too, didn't ya?"

Mitch looked up at him. "Did you really want her out of our sight so she could grab another firebomb and come find us again?"

"No. What I want is for Doc to hand over that shotgun so I can put this insane bull dyke outta her misery once and for all."

"Good luck explaining that to the police when this is all over," Doc told him.

Denny reached behind his head, grabbed the tail of his mullet with both hands, and pulled. "Why the hell are you all so gung-ho to protect her? Duh, she just tried to kill us! She *did* kill a fuck of a lot of other people, includin your best friend's wife, Flynn! Oh, and mine too, if that lights a bigger fire under your ass."

Mitch didn't know what the last comment meant and didn't think now was the time to ask. "That's why I wanna make sure she's punished for what she did."

"Then leave her here. Getting eaten by some of those fuckin things sounds like punishment to me."

"I won't do that. There's been enough death already." Mitch reigned in his anger and let a pleading note slip into his tone. "Please Denny...just let us get her to your place and then we can...I don't know, tie her to a chair or something so we don't have to worry about her."

Denny's nostrils flared. The muscles along his bruised jaw stood out in banded cords. Finally he waved a hand and shook his head. "Fine. Whatever gets us goddamn movin again." He walked away without waiting for an answer. Eli came over to help JD with Morgan, and then the rest of the group moved on as well.

Mitch turned back to Lena and put a tentative hand on her bony shoulder. She flinched away from him. "C'mon Lena, we need to go."

She rose, her movements wooden and robotic. Once she began walking again—casting another glance at her house as she followed Denny and the others—Mitch fell in beside Doc.

"Not that she was the most sane gal before all this, but her mind could very well be broken," the vet said softly. "She might never snap out of this."

Mitch considered that, then told him the theory coming together in his head. "Back at the center, she said something about us killing Cynthia. I think some of these creatures must've gotten her, and the grief just drove Lena insane."

"Maybe, but that's no excuse for murdering a few dozen people." He remained quiet a moment before asking, "How bad are you hurt, Mitch?"

"I don't know. Let's just get to Denny's and then I'll take a look."

He left Doc on guard duty as he worked his way forward in the group. They were out of Lena's yard now and about to cross another narrow band of sparse oaks that separated them from Denny's property. The trees cut the glare from the bright lights into jagged pieces, but there was still plenty of illumination to see by. Mitch passed Bo, whose upper lip curled in a sneer, and then came abreast of Denny to ask, "So what're you thinking once we get to your place?"

Denny's answer came with such military precision, it gave Mitch some comfort to know that he'd thought about it so much. At least *someone* had a plan. "We rendezvous with Claude and distribute whatever firearms he's got prepped. Then most of us set about fortifyin the house and perimeter while someone calls for help and someone else sets off a few flares, so anyone else still alive from the community center can make their way to us. Then, dependin on what the sheriff says, those that wanna leave can pile in Doc's car and head for Bear Creek."

"'Those that wanna leave?'" Mitch repeated. "That mean you're staying?"

"They ain't gettin my house." Denny's footsteps faltered as he lowered his head and murmured into his chest, "It's all I got left."

Mitch thought about reminding him that those creatures would probably only want his house if he was in it, but the man looked so dejected, he let it go.

A minute later, they reached Denny's fence, a chest-high chain link topped with taut lines of razor wire. A square, five-acre field waited on the other side, tamed from the surrounding wilderness but still in need of a good mow. The one-story, camouflaged dwelling sat directly in the middle, squat and somehow muscular. His rectangular metal shed waited in the far northeast corner, a good fifty yards from the house. Denny stood looking across the sea of overgrown grass for a moment before muttering, "Son of a bitch. He ain't here."

It took Mitch a moment to understand what he meant. Denny's home and the property around it were quiet and empty. Doc's stolen car was nowhere in sight. The only vehicle on the property was the huge ATV parked beneath the carport.

Claude wasn't here.

"Where the fuck'd he go?" Bo drawled. "It's a half mile from the community center ta here. Not like the stupid shit could get lost."

"He must've finished loadin up the guns already and headed back," Denny said. "Goddamn it, I was hopin to catch 'im before he left."

Mitch frowned. "Don't you think we would've heard him pass by on the road?"

"That hybrid's engine ain't any louder'n a fart. Naw, he went right by us while we traipsed through the woods."

"So I guess the question now is, what will he do when he sees the place is burned down and we're not there?"

"He'll get the fuck outta Dodge." Denny sighed and shook his head. "But at least he'll send help when he gets there. C'mon, let's see what he left us."

TWENTY

Joy saw it all, each image burned into her brain, although it took no longer than a single heartbeat.

As Helen's fingertips touched that twinkling surface, the curtain instantly cleared, like a static-filled television being switched off. The shimmer was replaced by a darkness so deep and black and endless it actually brightened the night around it by comparison. The effect was like looking through a window into the heart of outer space, except there were no stars, no galaxies, nothing at all to alter that smooth, lightless eternity. Staring into such an abyss made the moorings of Joy's sanity quake.

Helen's hand swung deeper into the hole, all the way up to her forearm, vanishing as it crossed the threshold. For the moment that they were connected—Joy to Helen and Helen to the portal—that sensation of a mild electrical discharge increased, until the fillings in Joy's teeth began to ache. The old woman opened her mouth and wailed, screaming so high and loud that her voice blew out, reduced to a tattered wheeze.

Then Joy yanked her back out. The void disappeared behind the wall of static as they both tumbled backward into the brush.

Joy scrambled up again and leaned over Helen. In the shifting glow, she could just make out the other woman's arm, held tight against her chest, although it looked like the appendage had been replaced by a blackened hunk of wood.

Helen's mouth stretched in a grimace, her teeth gritted. A thin moan escaped her.

"C'mon, we have to go," Joy whispered desperately. She stood and pulled at Helen's good hand. The old woman whimpered, but climbed to her feet. Joy put an arm around her to support her small frame. They gave the glowing hole a wide berth and continued on, but at a much more cautious pace.

A half minute later they left the trees. A short, overgrown meadow separated them from a stoic ranch house just ahead, with a warm porch light above the front door. Samuel stood beside the entrance, beckoning frantically. The two of them reached the house and clambered onto the porch.

"Did you see anyone else?" he demanded, as they limped through.

"I don't think so," Joy told him. Her arms and back ached from supporting Helen. "I think we were the last ones who...who made it."

He closed the heavy wooden door, then flipped a switch beside it. The light on the front porch winked out. Samuel stood with his face pressed against the vertical window beside the door, glaring out at the night, then spun and sprinted down a hallway that ran along the front of the house without another word.

Joy turned to examine the rest of the place. They stood in a luxurious living room with cherrywood floors and an empty stone fireplace to their right, lit by somber recessed tract lighting along the periphery. Not the kind of place she imagined the uber-religious couple living, except for the ornate steelwork crosses that hung on every inch of free wall space. Actually, it was more like what she'd envisioned when Denny told her he wanted to build a cabin in the country, instead of the Manly Man Hunting Lodge in which they'd ended up. Arthur sat on a huge, puffy leather couch with Roberta beside him. She held a wadded up towel against the ruins of his right hand while he squeezed his eyes shut and hissed in pain through clenched teeth. Madeline watched from the shadows across the room, standing next to a bar top that opened onto a dim, spacious kitchen beyond. Three other people from their dwindling group that Joy didn't know huddled on the fireplace hearth, two men and a woman.

The door into that fancy kitchen opened and Deborah emerged with a first aid kit. "I'm afraid this is all we have," she said, handing the box to Roberta. Joy noticed her skin was freshly scrubbed and free of ash; the woman actually took the time to clean herself up before bringing medical supplies to badly injured people. "Try not to get any blood on my couch, please."

"Is this it?" Joy asked. "No one else…?"

"We're it," Madeline confirmed. A bit smugly, Joy thought. "Read it and weep."

Nine people. They'd lost nine more people in the woods, human beings who'd been torn apart by those mutant tree crocodiles. It sounded like a concept that belonged in a late-night sci-fi horror movie from the seventies, yet it was real, it was happening, and the rest of them were trapped in it. A frustrated scream rattled in the back of Joy's throat, but she swallowed it back down.

As Roberta bandaged his hand with gauze and padding, Arthur opened his pain-clouded eyes and caught sight of Helen. "Good Lord, did those things do that?"

"No. We had a run-in with one of JD's magic holes." Joy saw Roberta wince at the mention of her husband. She struggled to move forward, but her back threatened to give out from Helen's weight. The old woman had slipped into unconsciousness.

"That's good enough, my dear," Arthur told Roberta, taking the roll of gauze from her. With only the thumb and pinky remaining on his injured hand, he was stuck in a permanent surfer 'hang ten' gesture. "See if you can bandage yourself and I'll help them."

Helen couldn't weigh more than ninety pounds, but with Arthur's injuries, they still struggled to get her to a nearby recliner and lower her into the seat. Her eyes were closed but moving rapidly beneath the lids. A thin, brown fluid dribbled from the corner of her mouth.

"Oh my god, her hand," Roberta whispered.

Joy examined the appendage again in the light. The flesh that went through the hole was utterly scorched. Helen's hand curled into a withered black claw, the charbroiled skin sloughing off, gleaming white bone visible at the fingertips. Near the forearm, the burns became less severe, the tissue red and covered with angry boils, but all of it ended in a neat line just below her elbow.

"We should probably wrap it in cool towels, like Gladys said." Joy looked at Deborah. "Do you have any painkillers?"

"Absolutely not. We allow no mood-altering pharmaceuticals in this house."

So much for tending to the needs of your flock, Joy thought.

Arthur examined Helen's arm for a long moment, then

said, "Tell me exactly what happened."

Joy sank down on the edge of the heavy wooden coffee table in the middle of the room, next to a framed picture of Christ with his hand held skyward. She rubbed at her eyes as she recounted what she'd seen, the half-glimpsed shimmer, Helen's hand swinging into it, the impossibly black gulf that appeared.

When she finished, Arthur asked, "And you say her hand stayed in this...this portal...for only a few *seconds?*"

"Probably less than that. It went in, and I pulled her right back out."

"How?" Roberta asked. She'd used nearly a whole bottle of alcohol cleaning her shoulder, and padded it with flat strips of gauze. The bleeding had slowed considerably. "How could something cook her like that so fast?"

Arthur raised his bandaged hand to rub at his chin but stopped himself before making contact. "I have no idea, but I think we *do* know what happened to the man you and JD found on the road. Unfortunately, given the circumstances, I fear we may never know just how he came into contact with one of them."

"Poor bastard," Joy said. "Guy survives getting burned to a cinder, just to have another fire finish the job."

"I would appreciate you not cursing in my home," Deborah snapped.

Roberta clapped a hand to her mouth and loosed a sudden harsh sob.

"I'm...I'm sorry, Roberta," Joy said. Once again, she'd put her foot right in her mouth tonight. "I didn't mean to be so—"

"It's fine." She waved the words away and looked to the lady of the house. "May I use your restroom?" After receiving directions down another hallway, Roberta left, tugging her blouse back into place.

"We need to move quickly," Arthur told the rest of them. "First though, we must make sure some sort of help is on the way. Not just for us, but for anyone else that might still be alive out there. Deborah, have you tried your landline?"

The woman frowned slowly and shook her head. "No, not yet."

"Then take us to it. Once we speak to the authorities, maybe they can help us plan our next step."

She hesitated, looking flustered for the first time tonight. But before she could answer, Samuel returned. He'd also cleaned the grime from his face and hands, and carried a large hunting rifle with a mounted scope. A revolver dangled from one side of his belt by a holster, the black rubber grip protruding off his hip. The sight of him suddenly decked out in weapons like he was ready to safari into the jungles of Africa made Joy's skin turn to ice.

"No, first we need to board this place up," he argued. "Every window, every door."

Arthur shook his head. "I thought we'd established that digging in is a mistake. We need help, either to bring it here, or get to it. Tell me, what's your vehicle situation?"

Samuel answered after a brief hesitation, but Joy saw his jaw clench in annoyance first. "My car was at the community center. Deborah's Beemer is in the garage, but...but it would only hold five or six."

"I'm sure we can stretch that. I, for one, would be willing to ride in the trunk if it meant us all leaving. But, first things first, let's try calling town."

Samuel said nothing. His eyes flicked to Deborah. A look passed between husband and wife that Joy could not decipher.

"*For God's sake, what's wrong with you?*" Arthur thundered. "*Give us the damn phone!*"

An angry muscle twitched in Samuel's cheek. "It's in the kitchen."

"Thank you." Arthur turned to Joy. "Why don't you try to contact the sheriff? Or anyone else, for that matter. Hell, I don't care if you call Washington D.C. or Bumpkin, Iowa, so long as someone else knows what's happening here. I'll go with Samuel to look at his car. Maybe we can fit a few more if we tear out a seat."

Joy nodded. Samuel looked at his wife—Joy saw that same look pass between them again, part knowing, part resolute—and then led Arthur down the same hall that Roberta disappeared into.

"This way," Deborah said stiffly. She pushed back through the swinging door into the kitchen. Joy walked past Madeline, who shot her another of those acidic smiles, and then into the kitchen.

Much darker in here than the living room, even with the light coming through the open bar. Shadows painted every surface. Three more huge iron crosses hung on the blank space at the back of the kitchen, a quaint modern day Golgotha. They were several inches thick and big enough to use in an actual crucifixion, their interiors filled with ornate loops and swirls of metal. Deborah didn't move to turn on any lights, just motioned to a wall-mounted phone on the other side of the island stove.

Joy made her away around the room and picked up the handset. A dial tone greeted her instantly. "Thank god." She extended a finger to dial 911, but before she could punch the first numeral, the tone cut off.

"What? Wait, no. No way!" She hit the hang-up button several times, got nothing but silence. "Hey, your phone—"

She turned around, gasped, and dropped the handset.

The coiled cord caught the hunk of plastic before it could hit the ground and caused it to clatter against the wall.

Deborah had crept across the room and stood just behind her with the handle of a large carving knife held tight against her stomach, the blade pointed at a spot between Joy's breasts. The darkness of the kitchen turned her face into an impassive mask. Joy could see that the cord from the phone into the wall jack beside her had been neatly severed.

"Don't you thank *my* God," the other woman growled.

"Deborah...what are you doing?"

"Saving our souls."

"Listen...if this is about before...when I pulled your hair—"

"Shut up." Deborah's eyes narrowed as she flicked the tip of the knife toward the door. "Get back out there. And if you try to run, I will not hesitate to slit your whoring little throat."

Joy turned and moved toward the door. In the living room, Roberta had returned, but confusion clouded her face when she spotted the knife in Deborah's hand. Everyone else in the room mirrored the look.

Except Madeline, who just looked at her with that devious grin.

A heavy gunshot boomed from the hallway where Arthur and Samuel had disappeared. Joy jumped so much, the tip of Deborah's knife pressed painfully against her spine. A second later, the two men came marching up the corridor, Arthur with his hands hoisted in the air and Samuel prodding him with the rifle barrel.

"Get up, all of you!" Samuel ordered. The people on the fireplace slowly stood as he came around Arthur and went to another door in the corner, just down the wall from the kitchen. He shoved this open, revealing a short landing and a narrow staircase that descended into darkness. "Come on, everyone inside! Now! And bring the old woman with you!"

Arthur slowly lowered his arms. "What is this?"

Samuel brought the rifle butt to his shoulder and aimed the weapon at his head. "Stop talking and *get down there!*"

One by one they complied, falling into line and shuffling through the door. At direction from Samuel, the two other men hefted Helen and carried her by the arms and waist. Joy fell in behind them, with Arthur bringing up the rear. Only Madeline and Deborah were left behind. At the head of the stairs, Joy saw the walls on either side became bare earth below floor level. The steps squeaked as the others descended ahead of her, but she couldn't see more than a yard or so. She caught a whiff of stale, musty dirt as she stepped through and realized they were being forced into a basement.

Behind her, Arthur spun around on the landing and stuck his foot in the door as Samuel tried to close it. Joy halted on the first stair and watched him shout through the gap.

"*You can't do this, you lunatic!*" he yelled as he braced the door with his shoulder. "*Don't you understand what's going on out there?*"

"Yes, I do. Too bad you don't." Samuel stopped trying to close the door long enough to slide the barrel of the rifle into the gap in front of Arthur's stomach. "Now get down there!"

"I'm not going anywhere!" Arthur stopped pushing, but left his foot in the door. "Just tell me, what in blazes do you want from us?"

"We want to help you," Samuel answered coldly.

The rifle blasted. Joy winced and closed her eyes as something warm splattered her cheek. When she opened them,

Arthur stumbled back into her. His weight hit her hard, shoving her backward. She threw herself against the splintery wall and managed to catch her footing, but could do nothing to stop Arthur's huge frame from crashing down the staircase.

Then Samuel slammed the door, sealing them up in darkness.

TWENTY ONE

Casa Carson had an overwhelming motif of camouflage and hunting. Mounted animal heads and fishing catches lined every wall, including a huge ten-point buck over a massive entertainment center in the den. One room just off the entrance smelled of gun oil and contained shelves upon shelves of tools, bins of bullets, and a table full of disassembled weapons, including an AR-15 with some modifications that didn't look entirely legal to Mitch. Even the kitchen was spartan, a cramped little corner with all steel fixtures and a fish gutting station built into the counter beside the sink.

Nothing in this house indicated a woman lived here.

Mitch remembered his and Allie's home, the way she left her decorating fingerprint on each room, making the place feel warm and vibrant. The artwork of world landmarks in their bedroom. Her cutesy knob covers for the kitchen cabinets.

The room upstairs for the life growing inside her, with the balloons she'd hand-painted on the walls.

And when she died, he couldn't bear to look at any of it. He'd put the goddamned place on the market three days after the funeral and sold it exactly as she'd left it.

Right between his temples, that familiar throbbing woke up and stretched its fingers across his brain.

Denny buzzed through his house ahead of everyone else, turning on lights. Mitch thought about telling him to keep them off, but didn't feel like sitting in the dark either. Once they were all gathered in his living room, Denny began barking orders. "Bo, hit the shed and see if Claude left anything useful. JD, you and Eli can put the human torch on my couch, but lay down some towels or a blanket first, for God's sake. There's a first aid kit under the kitchen sink if you need it, Doc. Carla, sweetheart, can you rustle us some grub? Whatever you can find in the fridge is fine. And I want the psycho tied to that, like yesterday." He pointed to a sturdy wooden rocking chair in the corner of the dining nook, then glanced at Mitch. "There's some bungee cord in the drawer over there you can use. Make sure it's tight, too. I'm gonna call the sheriff." Denny strode through the door of that cluttered room at the front of the house.

By the time Mitch found the cords, Doc had gotten Lena in the chair. She sat bolt upright and didn't move as Mitch wrapped the cords around her arms, ankles and waist, tight enough that he couldn't fit even a finger under them. When he finished, Doc gave a huge sigh of relief and put the shotgun down on the scuffed dining table like it had turned into a poisonous snake.

"Lord, I never exactly loved guns before, but now I know I hate pointing them at another human being. If you can even call her that." He pulled the soot-stained flaps of his robe closed over his rotund belly and shoved his hands in the pockets. "Now, let's have a look at that cheek, Mitch."

They retrieved the first aid kit and found a secluded corner of the living room behind a leather recliner with a built-in mini fridge. Doc knelt behind him while Mitch undid his jeans. Dried blood had glued the fabric to his skin; he bit down on a scream as Doc ripped them away from the wound.

"Well," the vet said, swabbing his ass with alcohol-soaked cotton balls that felt like flaming sandpaper. "She definitely took a chunk out of you, but the shot came in at a steep angle from the side. Didn't get too far past the sub-cutaneous. Could probably use a few stitches, but for now, I should be able to bandage you tight enough to contain the bleeding. Denny's even got some local anesthetic in here that should numb your padding."

It *did* help, taking the pain from a burning ache to an irritating throb. If only something would work so well on his migraine. Mitch pulled his pants up, helped Doc to his feet, then nodded at Morgan, now stretched out on Denny's couch and being fretted over by Gladys even though she could only use one arm. "Can you still try to wake him up?"

"Left my bag at the center." Doc shrugged helplessly. "If Denny has some other medication, I might be able to cook something up."

"I'll check. See if you can do something about Gladys' arm."

Mitch walked into the room where Denny went. He found the man amid his ammo stockpile with an electronic device that looked like a huge walkie-talkie, punching buttons on its face in frustration.

"What is that?" Mitch asked.

"Sat phone. But it ain't workin."

"Well, where's your landline?"

"Don't have one."

"*What?*"

"Sat phones're better'n landlines or cells. If the apocalypse happens and everything else goes down, this can still place a call directly through a satellite."

"I know what a sat phone is. So why isn't it working?"

"Whatever's knockin out the cells must be jammin this up, too."

"Yeah, so much for the apocalypse." Mitch squeezed his temples until he thought his skull might crack. "You don't have any other way to contact the outside world? What about internet access?"

"Just Wi-Fi. Tried to get my phone to connect as we came inside. Nuthin." A heavy crease split his brow. "Between this, the cells, and the radios, I'd say it has to be some kinda EMP, but the rest of the electricity obviously works. So what the hell could be affecting *only* wireless comms?"

Mitch leaned against the wall next to a bullet caster and closed his eyes. He briefly considered trying to find that mental dead space, just switch off his mind and drift away into the darkness inside his head and let somebody else deal with it all. "This is an utter disaster. We came here for nothing."

Footsteps pounded in the hallway and then Bo skidded to a stop in the doorway. The orange handle of a flare gun jutted from his waistband. "It's all still there, Den!"

"Huh? What's still there?"

"Yer guns. Far as I can tell, Claude didn't take nuthin."

Mitch threw his hands in the air. "So the son of a bitch never even came here?"

"Or he never *made* it here," Denny countered. "Let me go take a look."

He started out, but Mitch grabbed his arm. "Doc needs any medication you have in the house."

"What for?"

"He's gonna try to wake up this Morgan guy and see what he can tell us."

Denny rolled his eyes, but opened a drawer in a filing cabinet beside the door. Stacks of cellophane wrapped medication, pill bottles, and even syringes stood inside. "Take whatever," he said on the way out.

In the living room, the others were cleaning the ash off their faces. Eli plopped down in the middle of the floor and lay on his back with his eyes closed. Doc set and re-splinted Gladys' arm and then left to peruse Denny's pharmaceuticals. Someone had turned on the TV, but the screen displayed only static. No real surprise there, if Denny's theory was correct. Mitch stood against the wall for a moment, nursing his headache, and accepted half a sandwich and a can of cold Coke when Carla came around to distribute them, then wolfed both in a few swallows.

Lena caught his eye as he finished. She sat perfectly still in her bindings, staring at the far wall with a bland—if somewhat gory—expression. He grabbed another half sandwich and approached her.

"You want something to eat?"

She didn't answer, but her dull eyes flicked to the food in his hand. Mitch put it down on the edge of an end table, went into the kitchen, and wet a paper towel in the sink. He used this to clean her face, wiping away the dark soot and the blood from her lips and cheeks while trying not to touch her puffy nose. The act was just mundane enough to be soothing; the pain in his own skull ebbed a bit. He also wiped at the crusty lump on the back of her skull where Gladys brained her with the golf club, the swelling so bad it split the skin. How she didn't have a concussion, Mitch would never know. It must be nothing more than pure hate that kept her going. Once clean, Lena's severe features still held that vacant sheen, but at least she didn't look quite so ghoulish. He held the sandwich to her mouth while she took a bite and chewed mechanically.

"Denny was right about her." JD stood just a few feet away, glaring at them. Mitch hadn't seen him since they entered the house, but based on his red eyes, Mitch figured he'd been somewhere weeping. "She's not a person, she's just a...a wild animal. We should've left her in the woods."

"And you think pulling a Hansel and Gretel would've solved anything?" Mitch asked, giving her another bite. As he did, he saw her eyes move again, twitching into focus to settle briefly on JD. Dark rage bloomed in them, there and then gone, like a spark of distant light.

Gotta stay careful around her, he thought. *Might be she's not as broken as she wants us to believe.*

His friend trembled with barely concealed rage. "Don't you give me any hogwash about crime and punishment, Mitch. Don't you dare. She's gonna pay for what she did, even if I have to do it myself."

"Okay. Yes, you're right." Having JD around Lena was like storing your dynamite in the oven. Mitch took his best friend by the arm and gently guided him out of the dining room and into the kitchen, close to the back door of the house. "Listen, everyone here has reason to want her dead. Don't forget, she killed Arthur, too. And...and Joy." A surprisingly hard pang hit him as he said this last name. "But what kind of people would we be if we all just ganged up and lynched her?"

"Happy ones." JD's anger shattered like a glass vase hit with a baseball bat, his face fuming one second then screwed up and bawling the next. Mitch pulled him into an unashamed embrace. The other man buried his face in Mitch's shoulder and sobbed. "It's my fault. I shouldn'ta left her alone. I shoulda stayed with her. I looked for her in all the smoke, but..."

Mitch remained quiet, just held him until he finished. It was tempting to say that he knew what the man was going through, but he didn't. Not really. He and Allie had only been granted three years together; three blissful years, three years he was having a hard time letting go of, but still just a blip compared to his best friend's marriage. JD met Roberta just after high school graduation, knocked her up, and got hitched all within a few months. Mitch never thought it would last, but, thankfully, he never said so, because the two of them proved to be made for each other. Losing a spouse after you've been together that long had to be like losing a limb.

JD raised his head and wiped at his bleary eyes. "God, what am I gonna tell Aaron? How'm I gonna look my boy in the face?"

"I had to tell Allie's parents," Mitch said, releasing him. "Dialing their number was the hardest thing I ever did. I thought they'd blame me for it. But they didn't. And, if Roberta is really...then Aaron won't blame you either. But you have to promise me, JD. Promise me you won't do anything to Lena. We get through this, then we hand her over to the sheriff. End of story."

"Okay. I promise."

The back door opened as they finished. Bo stuck his head inside and looked at Mitch. "Denny needs you." Mitch nodded and stepped toward the door. JD started to follow, but Bo held up a hand. "Just you, Flynn."

Mitch frowned. "We don't have any secrets right now."

Bo regarded JD for a moment, then shrugged and turned away.

They stepped back outside. Mitch's arms goose-pimpled as soon as the cold air touched them. Silence ruled the night, no more squawking bird cries or bleating deer. He wondered if the bonfire at the community center had chased away any wildlife left in the area. Or if maybe the whole thing was over, that whatever strange event caused the glowing holes to appear and spill out a host of ungodly monstrosities quietly ended while they were preoccupied with escaping Lena's wrath. He recognized that as dangerously wishful thinking, and kept his guard up as Bo led them along a well-worn dirt path that carved through the overgrown grass, all the way from the house to the huge shed that sat in the corner of the property.

Lena's blazing exterior lights stretched well across the field on the south side of Denny's house, but shadows bathed the north half, where the shed sat. The structure looked like a shipping container, maybe twenty yards long by ten wide, with midnight blue sheet metal for the sides and roof. Denny had filed no application with the HOA to erect the building, but it wouldn't have mattered even if he did. Besides being an eyesore, such construction with no permanent foundation violated 407 bylaws.

But if it kept them alive through the rest of the night, Mitch would retroactively approve the damn thing himself.

Bo pushed open a door in the short side and waved them through.

Mitch blinked at the bright interior. Fluorescents marched down the length of the shed in a single row. Various guns mounted the walls like something out of a spy movie, and several pallets of dry food and supplies were stacked up above his head. Down the aisle stood a workstation with some kind of rounded metal bulbs on it, but Mitch studied them for only a moment before Denny swung around from behind the door and whammed the stock of a semi-automatic rifle into his stomach.

Pain rocketed through his abdomen. Mitch doubled over and then went to his knees, clutching his belly in both arms. The blow—a complete shock—emptied his lungs like two crumpled plastic bags. As he tried to remember how to breathe, he heard JD shout, "*Hey, what the hell are you doin?*"

"Keep 'im back," Denny told Bo. "This is between me and the boy scout."

Air found its way back into Mitch's chest just as his vision started to cloud. He fell over on his side, still gasping, and looked around. Bo kept JD pinned against the wall with one hairy forearm across his throat and the orange flare gun in his other hand. Denny strolled around in front of Mitch, still clutching the rifle, and looked down at him with a smirk made crooked by his swollen jaw.

"We got a lotta work to do, but I figured we should get this outta the way first." For a moment, Mitch thought he might level the weapon and open fire, disintegrate him from the neck up, but instead, Denny set the weapon atop a stack of gallon water jugs, then leaned over until his face hovered above Mitch's. "What? You think I forgot I owed you an ass-kickin?"

"You gotta be kidding me," Mitch wheezed. "Half our neighborhood just got slaughtered, we're being hunted by Lovecraft rejects, and you wanna put everything on hold to beat me to a pulp?"

"We haven't seen any of those fuckers since before we got back to the community center. For all we know, they're long gone." He didn't sound like he believed this any more than Mitch. "So before we all get rescued and life goes on…let's get this thing between us hashed out."

Mitch shook his head to clear it, which turned out to be a mistake. "*What* thing? Christ, what did I do to you, except help you out with Lena?"

"You know what the fuck this is about, and it don't have anything to do with that looney tunes lesbo!" Denny snarled. He came even closer, his nose thrust in Mitch's face. "Just tell me, did you fuck her?"

Mitch blinked, trying to imagine the sequence of events that would ever get him to strip naked and lay on top of Lena Henning. "Huh?"

"*Did* you?" Denny pressed. "Or did I catch this thing before you two got that far?"

"I have no idea what you're talking about."

"Joy." Denny swallowed hard, but his face remained set in stone. "Did you have sex with my wife, Flynn? If so, I just wanna hear you say it. Cause even if she's dead, I still got a right to know."

"W-what?" Even though the accusation was just as insane as the thought of him making love to Lena, Mitch was terrified that a slight trace of misplaced guilt might somehow work its way onto his face. "Absolutely not. I barely know her."

"That's not what Madeline told me. She said you two were cozied up the whole time I was gone. You know, when you sent me off as your errand boy."

"Then Madeline lied."

Denny lifted one shoulder and let it fall. "Maybe. Lord knows it wouldn't be the first time. I even told myself that... but then I remembered Joy standin up for you, back at the meeting. Choosin you over me. And I keep thinkin...why would she do somethin like that if the two of you weren't hoppin in the sack?"

Mitch groaned. "Jesus, would you listen to yourself? *If my wife doesn't agree with everything that comes outta my mouth, it must be because some other guy's dick has her hypnotized.* You can think what you want, but I never touched Joy." The words made him feel degraded just coming out of his mouth...but still, that nugget of guilt burned like a hot coal in the pit of his stomach.

Denny pursed his lips and nodded thoughtfully. "That's good. Keep sayin that. Cause I really wanna see if your story changes after I bust a few of your teeth out." He reared back with one arm, forming a huge fist.

Mitch pistoned one foot into his leg, catching him just inside the knee.

Denny howled, went down, then rolled to the side all in one motion, his reflexes startlingly fast. Mitch lunged at him, not wanting to give the other man a chance to recover. He landed on Denny's back as he scuttled away, then received an elbow in the eye that set off a white flare across his vision.

JD shouted something, but Mitch was too busy hanging on to Denny to hear him. The two of them tumbled across the concrete floor of the shed in a flurry of grunts and punches. Mitch got in a few good hits to his opponent's torso, but, in the end, he couldn't match Denny's strength. They hit the wall beside the door and the other man squirmed out of his grasp, then kneed him in the groin as they separated.

"*Admit it!*" Denny roared, hands held out in frustrated fists as he stood in the doorway. "Admit you tried to steal my woman or I will *cave your skull in!*"

"*Heeeelp!*"

They all froze as the cry drifted through the open door of the shed. When it came again, Denny and Bo scrambled to the exit, fights and grudges forgotten. Mitch's heart hammered as JD helped him up and then they peeked out into the night around the other two men.

The shout came again, just that single word, but full of fear and misery. It issued from somewhere in the sea of high grass between the house and the shed. Denny grabbed a pair of binoculars from a hook beside the door and scanned his property.

"What is it? Whatcha see?" Bo's voice quavered.

"Nuthin, it's too dark. Fire off one of them flares."

Bo leaned through the doorway, pointed the orange pistol at the sky, and pulled the trigger. There was a pop and a sizzle as the phosphorus cartridge arced high into the night, trailing a wispy column of smoke. It bloomed against the black sky, creating a miniature sun that bathed the land in a flickering, reddish glow.

"Holy shit," Denny whispered. "It's Claude." He held the binoculars out. Bo reached for them, but Mitch grabbed them first. He put them to his eyes and studied the magnified image for a few seconds before he spotted the man.

Halfway between here and the house, just off the beaten dirt path, a figure sat in the overgrown field. Only its head and one arm were visible, the latter waving from side-to-side in the air in big sweeps, like a drowning swimmer signaling for help. Grass obscured the lower half of his face, but it was unmistakably Claude, his eyes huge and his mouth open as he shouted again.

And yet...something felt off. Mitch tried to study the man to figure out what bothered him, but Bo snatched the binoculars away.

Denny cupped his hands around his mouth and shouted, "*Claude! What's wrong, man? You hurt?*"

A pause before another plea of "*Heeeelp!*"

"This is freakin me out!" JD exclaimed. "Just close the door!"

Bo put a hand on his shoulder and shoved. "We cain't just leave him out there!"

Oh yes you can, Mitch thought. That repetitive call made the hair on the back of his neck feel as stiff as needles. It sounded more like the call of some lonely wild animal.

JD glared at Bo and pointed outside. "Fine, he's your friend, go see what's wrong with him!"

Bo hesitated and looked around the room like a caged animal, seeking some way out of the challenge without looking scared.

Denny did it for him, by slinging an arm around Mitch's neck and pulling him into a loose headlock.

"Guess what, El Presidente?" he said. "I just figured out how you're gonna pay me back for sleepin with my wife."

TWENTY TWO

The Whitaker's basement stretched only a few yards to either side of the foot of the stairs. Crumbly bare earth formed the walls, the floor was a concrete slab, the ceiling beams low enough to bang your head on. Not five-star accommodations, but at least they weren't stumbling around in the dark; when Samuel closed off the light from upstairs, someone found the dangling chain for a naked bulb in the middle of the room.

Joy raced down as fast as she dared, wiping Arthur's blood from her cheek. She found the man at the base of the steps, stretched out on the concrete with Roberta already kneeling over him. Blood spread down his side, creating a shiny black puddle beside him. He was conscious though, his eyes following her as she hunkered beside him.

"Here, let me see." Joy lifted his shirt, revealing a surprising fit and well-toned torso for a man his age. Hell, considering Denny's expanding paunch, even a man fifteen years younger would be envious. The bullet hit him low in the side, just under the stack of his ribs, creating a hole no bigger than a quarter. It looked much neater and cleaner than the chewed flesh around Roberta's shotgun wound, but the crimson flood pumping out of it alarmed Joy far more. Between that and his amputated fingers, he couldn't have much blood left. "Goddamn it, first Lena and now those assholes! Has everyone in this fucking neighborhood gone insane?"

He took one of her hands and pulled it gently away from his side. "Just leave me," he rasped. "You have to escape this place. God knows what they have planned for the rest of you."

"Arthur, no offense, but shut the fuck up. We're not just gonna let you bleed out and we don't have time to argue about it."

"I know." His mouth spread in a weak grin. "But it had to be said."

Joy gave a half-amused grunt and looked to Roberta. "Keep pressure on it. Stick your finger in there and plug it up like a cork, if you have to. I'll see if there's anything else down here that can help."

She stood and took in the rest of the basement and the people sharing it with her. A side-by-side washer-dryer combo occupied one end of the space, connected to pipes that ran up into the subflooring above their heads, where they could hear quick footsteps every few minutes. The rest of the room's periphery held plastic storage bins, lawn decorations, and worn luggage, the sort of detritus that results from living in one place for too long. Narrow slit windows lined the very top of the wall opposite the stairs. An old wicker chair sat in one corner, and the men that carried Helen down had placed her limp body in it. These two fifty-somethings stood uncertainly beside her, along with the woman that had been with them upstairs.

"I'm Joy," she introduced herself.

One of the men, a gawky-looking fellow with a huge schnoz, pointed to himself and said, "Barry. This is my neighbor Conrad, and his wife Shirley." These two, both curly-haired brunettes that resembled one another closely enough to be siblings rather than spouses, huddled together and gave her a frightened wave.

"All right, I need your help," she told them. "We need to go through this entire basement and every one of these boxes. We're looking for medical supplies or anything we can use to defend ourselves. Just...just in case it comes to that. Can you three do that?"

They nodded eagerly and set to work without a single question. As they began pulling down boxes and dumping them out on the floor, Joy went first to the door at the top of the stairs, confirmed it was locked and too solid to break down, then turned to the windows that lined the upper half of the room.

Dust and cobwebs caked the glass panes. She wiped them clear and saw that they were positioned at ground level, with grass growing just on the other side. They looked out on a short clearing and another stretch of dark woods behind the house. The windows weren't designed to open, but even if she broke them, none of the people trapped here could've squeezed through the frames.

As she stared through one, trying to force her brain to come up with a plan, a sudden blaze of light shot into the sky above the trees in the distance and burst into a flaming red ball. It hovered there for a moment, tingeing the black with dull crimson.

Conrad paused in the act of tearing open a cardboard box. "Are those fireworks?"

"No. It's a flare." A small bubble of hope floated up from her stomach. "Apparently my husband is still alive. Which means other people might be, too." She glanced at Roberta. The woman wore red gloves from holding her hands over Arthur's wound, but a tearful grin touched the corners of her mouth. "Now we just need to survive until they can get help."

They spent the next twenty minutes tearing through the bins that dominated the basement. Most of them contained old clothes, shoes, towels, and kids' toys, although Joy shuddered to think what it would've been like for any Whitaker offspring to grow up under such parents. One of them held a collection of dusty religious pamphlets for The Church of the End Times Redeemer. Joy always expected people with those sort of beliefs to dress in potato sacks and live like the Amish, but she supposed there were cults that catered to more upscale parishioners also. At least this revelation made Samuel and Deborah's behavior a little easier to understand. No less insane, just easier to understand.

Throughout all this, those fast footsteps came and went over their heads. If Joy envisioned the layout of the house correctly, it must be coming from that cavernous kitchen, with its garish collection of life size crucifixes. At one point, she could even swear she heard the buzz of power tools.

They used the towels to create a compress for Arthur. His skin looked pale and waxy in the dark, his breathing labored. Otherwise, with the basement now resembling a garbage dump, Joy lost hope they would find anything useful. She was on the verge of sinking back into the floor when Shirley called her over.

The woman knelt over another open storage bin. Joy looked inside over her shoulder. Various crafting elements sat inside—yarn, construction paper, photographs and scrapbooking components—but among them rested a pair of long-bladed scissors.

The door to the basement squealed open and thudding footsteps started down the stairs. Joy managed to grab the scissors, stuff them under her shirt and down the back of her pants, and kick the box away before Samuel clomped into view.

He held the rifle up, butt against his shoulder, and panned the sights across each person before demanding, "What the fudge did you do to my basement?"

"Language," Deborah chided sharply, as she and Madeline marched down the steps single file behind him. They reached the bottom and Deborah stepped over Arthur with hardly a downward glance. Roberta remained crouched over his wound, but Barry and Conrad shrank away against the far wall.

"Lord forgive me my transgression," Samuel murmured, taking one hand off the rifle barrel and pressing a fist to his chest, just over his heart. Sure, fake cussing he would apologize for, but taking his neighbors prisoner didn't even rate a mention to the Man Upstairs.

"Arthur's losing a lot of blood," Joy said slowly. "We need to get him to a hospital. We'll...we'll tell them the shooting was an accident, won't we?" Everyone in the room nodded so hard Joy was surprised they didn't sprain their necks.

"There are no more hospitals," Deborah said. Her narrow nostrils flared as she made this declaration. "No more sheriffs nor fire stations nor temples. The end has come. You all saw the harbingers for yourselves."

"That is...not true." Joy picked each word carefully, swerving far away from her first choices, such as 'brain dead retarded' and 'ball-achingly crazy'.

"Oh, yes, it is," Deborah replied, as sweetly as June Cleaver. "Those creatures were demons, and they are here to scour the land of the righteous in order to prepare for Satan's reign on earth. Civilization *will* fall; there's no stopping that. Now we can only prepare for what happens next."

Joy gaped at her. The idea seemed to thrill the other woman, as though ushering in the apocalypse should be a point of pride. Or arousal. She suddenly conjured an image of these two in bed, Samuel whispering about how hellish the vistas would be after the collapse of society as Deborah worked toward orgasm. "But upstairs, your phone, it had a dial tone! If we can just get in your car and drive to town, I'm sure you'll see—"

"Doesn't matter," Samuel cut her off with a finality that turned her veins into a river of ice. "Our ears are closed to the lies of sinners like you. Your kind is responsible for all of this." His beady eyes narrowed. "But we can help you."

"Please let us go," Shirley whimpered beside Joy.

Deborah ignored her and said, "Enough talk. Who goes first, Samuel?"

"First for what?" Joy asked.

"Be quiet a minute and let me think, all of you!" Samuel barked. He still held the rifle up and ready, but the barrel drifted to a spot on the wall behind them. To Joy's utter amazement, he squeezed his eyes closed hard enough to wrinkle his brow all the way up his balding pate, tilted his head back, and whispered, "Dear God, please guide my hand and allow me to make the choices that would most honor You..."

He continued to pray with eyes closed, and Joy tensed, moving her hand slowly behind her, toward the handle of the scissors jutting from her waistband. She wouldn't give herself time to doubt or consider the consequences, she would just rush him, grab the weapon with one hand, and plunge the scissors into his neck with the other.

She could do it.

She *had* to do it.

Madeline's eye fell upon her as her fingers caressed the round handles. She still looked drawn and gruesome, with dark circles under her eyes that reached all the way to her cheeks. So far, she'd only watched and listened to the rantings of her new friends, but now she came forward and stood in front of Joy with a sneer playing at the corner of her thin lips. "This little whore needs to be in the first group, don't you think?"

"I agree," Deborah said quickly, with a prim smile that made Joy want to pull her hair all over again. "Delaying her cleansing implies that we condone her sin."

Samuel's eyes opened. Relief smoothed out his long forehead. "Yeah, okay, that's good. We'll take both the girls over there." Shirley let out a bleat of fear.

Conrad stepped forward from the wall across the room with his fists up. "You're not taking my wife anywhere without me!"

"Fine. Then you're coming too." Samuel stepped away from the stairs and waved with the barrel. "C'mon, all three of you, back up. Deborah, take the other gun and go ahead of them."

His wife walked over, pulled the revolver from the holster on his waist, and went primly up the stairs. After another shouted order from Samuel, Conrad and Shirley followed her, holding hands. Joy stood still, seeking an opening, until Madeline grabbed her neck and shoved.

"Get moving, whore!"

As she approached the foot of the stairs, Arthur reached out with his bandaged hand to touch her leg. Joy paused and met his gaze. He gave her a single, solemn nod, then rasped, "Denny...doesn't deserve you."

"Yeah...but I probably deserve him." She continued up the stairs with the barrel of the rifle poking her between the shoulders. Each step took monumental effort. She couldn't remember ever feeling so exhausted and emotionally raw in her entire life.

Deborah, Conrad, and Shirley waited in the living room. Joy expected to be taken into the kitchen, where all that noise came from, but instead, Samuel relocked the basement door, tossed the keys onto the bar top, and ushered them quickly down the hall, past the open garage, to a side door of the house. The window looked out onto another short field like the one she saw through the basement windows. A rolling thicket of trees began just thirty feet from the house, but right in front of the tree line, some sort of structure stood in the yard, a narrow frame that resembled a child's swing set...

"Stand against the wall and don't move!" Samuel commanded. "Madeline, take the gun and watch them until we yell for you to bring them out." He handed her the pistol and slipped through the door with Deborah, out into the night.

Conrad and Shirley stood against the wall, huddled in each other's arms. Joy looked at Madeline, who watched them from beside the door with the revolver held firm and steady. "What are they gonna do to us?"

"You'll find out soon enough."

"Don't tell me they actually got you to believe that garbage."

Madeline snorted and moved her free hand to fluff the pile of hair on top of her head. When she encountered the burned chunks of the beehive, she lowered her arm back to her side. That raccoon mask made her look like she had two black eyes, a condition Joy had seen in the mirror several times over the course of her marriage. "Well, I *am* a Christian woman, but yes, between you and me, those two are quite a few books short of a full Bible." She waggled the gun. "Sure convinced them that I do, though."

"But...*why?*"

"What, you think I'd rather be standing where you are right now? I heard Deborah talking on the way here and made sure I got on the winning team. If any of you had brains, you'd've dropped to your knees and started screaming 'Praise Jesus,' too!"

"Okay, congratulations, you're smarter than us," Joy told her. "But now that you have the gun, you can help us! We have to get away from them!"

"Oh, trust me, I intend to. Those two intend to give all of you first class tickets to paradise and then book themselves on the same flight, but I'm sure as hell not going to drink the Kool-Aid. I'm leaving the first chance I get. But first...I'm gonna enjoy seeing you get what you have coming."

Joy stared at her, dumbfounded. "Why do you hate me so much?"

"I don't hate you. I just think you're trash."

"So I deserve all this?"

"No." Madeline's lips peeled back from her teeth. She came forward until those dark bags under her eyes were just inches away and pressed the snubbed barrel of the revolver into Joy's stomach. "But my husband is dead, and that's because of your man."

"What does Denny have to do with any of this?"

"Not that ignorant redneck!" Madeline snarled, hard

enough for spittle to fly. "Your *man*. Mr. Big Shot HOA President!"

"Mitch is *not* my man," Joy said. The revolver dug into her guts even further, hard enough to make her gasp.

"Don't lie. I saw the way you looked at him all through that meeting, before you two snuck off together. Told Denny about it, too." Though her tone sounded triumphant, a tear appeared at the corner of one eye, behind her glasses. Her whole body looked as tense as a guitar string. "Your boyfriend sent my sweet Jeremiah off to his death. And if I can't watch him suffer for it, *you'll* have to do."

Joy wanted to ask her why the rest of their neighbors needed to suffer for this vendetta, but she was scared to speak, scared to move, scared to *breathe*, lest the other woman shoot her now before the Whitakers could have their way with her. Then again, maybe death by gunshot would be preferable to whatever they had planned.

The door opened and Deborah poked her head through. "We're ready."

"After you." Madeline put a hand on Joy's neck and escorted her roughly to the door, with the gun still pressed into her side.

TWENTY THREE

"It's simple," Denny said, shoving a heavy duty metal flashlight into Mitch's hands. "Just go out there, see what's wrong with the son of a bitch, and then get 'im to the house."

"If it's so simple, then why don't you do it?"

"Cause he's too chickenshit," JD muttered.

Denny took a slow deep breath and then released it through clenched teeth, like a pressure valve letting off tension. "Cause I'm askin you to do it. Then you and I are square."

Mitch closed his eyes as a jagged bolt of lightning lanced behind them. "For the last time...there is nothing you and I need to be square about."

"So you say. But you are goin out there, one way or another." Denny picked up the rifle again, and patted the barrel for emphasis. "If everything's okay, we'll stock up on what we need here, and follow right behind you."

"And if everything's *not* okay?"

Denny started to answer, then cut his eyes to the open door of the shed as another agonized cry drifted in from outside. "Well, we'll jump that mudhole when we come to it."

"You can't just send us out there without some way to defend ourselves!" JD's face reddened, his hands balled into fists at his side. "What if more of those things are out there?"

"I already told you, you ain't gettin a gun," Denny barked. Mitch didn't blame him for that; the first thing he would do if a firearm were placed in his hand right now would be to tell the man to go fuck himself. "Bo and me can cover you from here. 'Sides, I don't know what you're bitchin about anyway, Miller. Nobody's forcin you to go out there."

JD's spine stiffened. "If Mitch goes, I go."

"Yeah, see how far that little life philosophy gets you." Denny turned to the door and scanned the field again with the binoculars, then offered them to Mitch as well. The distance between them and the house stretched out to infinite proportions, with Claude approximately the same distance away from them as Alpha Centauri. "Look, I'm sure it's nuthin. Stupid fuck prob'ly threw his back out again or somethin. Just...keep an eye out. You see anything, give a shout."

Mitch snatched the binoculars from his hand and left the shed before he could suffer the indignity of being forced out. As little as he wanted to do this, they couldn't just sit out here all night. They would have to head back to the house eventually, and they couldn't very well leave Claude out here when they did. After being under the bright fluorescents, the frigid darkness outside attempted to suffocate Mitch until Bo fired another flare into the sky, bathing the land in that eerie reddish glow.

A second later, JD caught up with him, huffing each breath out in a cloud. "Mitch, man, about back there, I'm sorry, I never woulda let Denny go at you like that—"

Mitch held up a hand. "I know. Save the apologies for

later. Take this and make sure nothing sneaks up on us." He handed over the flashlight without stopping.

They followed the meandering dirt path to the house for only a few more yards before Mitch cut away from it, into the overgrown field, on a route that would take them directly to Claude's position. He didn't like the idea of walking through the thigh-high grass, where anything could ambush them, but he also didn't want to be out here any longer than needed. That burning flare in the sky painted each blade of grass a dull crimson, making it look like they were wading through a sea of blood. JD turned the flashlight on and swept the narrow beam back and forth across the field to either side of them, like a searchlight. Mitch watched for movement, or for the strange shimmer he'd seen behind the community center, but the field appeared to be empty.

They'd covered half the distance between Denny's survivalist shed and their destination when Mitch stopped and used the binoculars again. The cold numbed his hands, and he held his breath to keep the plumes from fogging the lenses.

Claude was still there, in the same position. Now that they were closer, Mitch hoped to be able to see what was wrong with the man, but the grass still obscured all but his jowly, piggish face and that one lanky arm moving back and forth in wide arcs above it. His eyes were wide and frightened, his jaw hanging open to reveal his snaggly teeth, and the light from the flare made his pasty skin glow the light orange of a fake tan. Again, something about the scene made Mitch's flesh crawl. As he watched, another of those horrible pleas for help drifted out of the man's open mouth, which only reinforced his discomfort.

Mitch lowered the field glasses and whisper-shouted, "*Claude! What's wrong?*"

Again, they received no reply. The man just continued to stare vacantly in their direction with that one arm waving overhead.

"Christ, has he gone deaf?" JD murmured.

"I don't think that's it."

"He's gotta be hurt. Otherwise, why would he just keep sitting there?"

"Yeah, but if he's hurt so bad he can't walk, how the hell did he get out here in the first place? Where did he come from, and where's Doc's car?"

JD gave no response to that. Mitch's gut still screamed that this was wrong, all wrong. He'd missed something, some nagging detail that might bring everything into focus.

And he couldn't stop thinking about the bat creatures. How crafty they'd been, by sabotaging the vehicles before they attacked. Whether it was actually their intention or not, Mitch thought underestimating any of those monsters would be a mistake.

"Circle around," he told JD. "Let's approach him from both sides. And if you see anything weird, anything at all... just run for the house."

JD nodded and started away from him, swinging out on a wide arc deeper into the field. Mitch shivered in the cold and then looked back at the shed while he waited for his friend to get into position. The lights were off, the door of the shed nothing but a pitch black rectangle. Denny and Bo were nowhere to be seen.

"You sad son of a bitch. So much for covering us." The asshole probably planned to send him to his death, all over an accusation so false it offended Mitch to the core. Sleeping with Joy wouldn't just be adultery on her end; it would be too much like cheating on Allie.

Overhead, the flare began to gutter, creating an unpleasant strobe effect. When he turned back, JD had reached Claude's opposite side and stood waiting.

Mitch started forward. JD did the same. Claude continued to stare straight ahead, and Mitch wished he'd kept the flashlight. With the flare gone, he couldn't see the man's face at all. As they closed the distance on either side of him to ten yards, Mitch watched the movement of his waving arm, back and forth, back and forth, and marveled at how stilted it looked, jerky and sort of...

Mechanical, he thought, still moving forward. *Like that automated billboard out on Bear Creek for Honest Jake's used car lot, with a giant version of Jake himself waving at you as you drive past.*

The answer hit him then, as he reached the prone figure, that one detail that made the scene look so wrong:

Claude's breath didn't condense when he shouted for help.

At the same time, JD switched on the flashlight, pointed it down at the figure on the ground, and they both saw the truth.

Claude Dunn was undeniably dead. His body had been badly mangled, throat torn open and left arm chewed off, leaving a stump of gleaming bone where his elbow should be. At first, Mitch thought his lower half was buried in the ground, until he realized the man's torso ended at the hips, the rest of him propped up by the sloping mound of his beer gut, turning him into a bizarre human bean bag chair. A tangled clot of organs trailed from the bottom of his waist, the intestines spread out in a bloody fan around him. His face, which looked so frightened from a distance, was now clearly frozen in a terrified grimace of agony.

Mitch stared down at him, trying to understand how this dead man still moved, when that waving arm went limp and fell to his side. The front of Claude's broad stomach bulged even further before splitting open in a gush of blood and viscera. From within that gruesome hole, a spindly monstrosity emerged and leapt straight up at Mitch's face.

TWENTY FOUR

Joy stepped into the yard on the south side of the Whitaker's house and took in the scene.

The structure she'd seen through the window was actually three separate iron crosses. She recognized the huge monstrosities from the Whitaker's kitchen, each one showcasing enough ornate metalwork to weigh at least fifty or sixty pounds. They'd been hastily planted in the ground just a few feet from the tree line in a semicircle, their bases surrounded by small piles of fresh earth to hold them in place. Samuel stood beside them, with the rifle in one hand and a roll of duct tape in the other.

"Wait...you're gonna crucify us?" Joy asked. "With *duct tape?*" A shrill laugh clawed its way up her throat, one that, if given voice, would most likely never stop.

"No," Samuel answered, and raised one arm solemnly toward the woods. Joy squinted but saw nothing for several seconds, not until her eyes adjusted to the darkness. Then she realized that a dim glow filtered through the trees, the same sort of illumination she'd seen just before Helen plunged her arm into that shimmering hole in reality. It reminded her of the crackling way television static lights up a room. "We're gonna tie you to them and let the devil's minions set you free from this world."

"No, please, you can't!" Conrad begged.

"We didn't do anything wrong!" Shirley added.

"If that's true, then you have nothing to fear," Deborah told them, placing a hand on her own chest. It was such an effete, self-aggrandizing gesture that Joy wanted to pull her hair again, only this time she wouldn't stop until the cunt looked as bald as her husband. "Those creatures may kill you, but they can never destroy your soul. If you're as innocent as you claim, you will go straight to the Lord."

Joy snorted. "You better go first then. Cause I'm gonna have some interesting things to tell *the Lord* about your little plan here."

Deborah scowled at her. "We are performing a mercy to you all. Sparing you from what's to come. Besides...I don't think I have to worry about seeing you in the afterlife."

From behind Joy, Madeline whispered, "Say hello to your boyfriend in hell, bitch."

"C'mon, let's go." Samuel beckoned to Conrad and Shirley, still shivering in each other's arms.

When neither moved, Deborah came forward, seized Shirley's arm, and hauled at her. The woman screamed and thrashed and tried to pull free. Conrad came at Deborah with both fists and murder in his eyes, but Samuel stepped between them. He smashed the rifle's stock into the middle of the other man's face. It cracked so loudly in the otherwise quiet night that, for a heartbeat, Joy thought he'd accidentally pulled the trigger at the same time. Shirley gave a hoarse sob as her husband fell to his hands and knees with blood spewing from a split lip. When she tried to go to him, Samuel and Deborah each took one of her arms and dragged her away.

They took her to the cross on the left, then forced her up against it so that Joy could see her in profile. She pleaded with them, but Deborah showed no emotion or mercy, just held her in place while Samuel taped her wrists to the arms of the cross, then her ankles to the base. When they finished, she looked like a redneck version of the crucifixion, but the metal stood firm in the ground as she wiggled and bucked her hips. The glimmer coming through the trees painted a pale shadow of her on the cold ground.

Conrad had climbed drunkenly to his feet by the time they returned for him. He was so disoriented that Samuel just led him to the cross on the opposite end from his wife, then put the rifle on the ground while they attached him to it. The urge to bolt forward and grab the weapon itched in Joy's brain, but, besides the fact that she wouldn't make it half the distance, Madeline jabbed the revolver into her back again and growled, "Don't even think about it." A minute later, Conrad hung from the bindings, all but unconscious, blood running down his chin and throat that steamed in the freezing air.

Deborah and Samuel stepped back from the human sacrifices to admire their handiwork just as a high-pitched roar exploded from the trees behind them.

Everyone froze. Goosebumps spread across Joy's arms and neck. She could see nothing in the woods, but the angry, squealing bellow sounded a lot bigger than the tree gators or dino-bats.

Then came the sound of branches crashing together. Shirley shrieked in terror and renewed her struggles.

"They're here!" Samuel hissed. For someone who believed heaven waited for him, his eyes held plenty of fear. He beckoned frantically to Madeline. "Bring her!"

"Go! *Move!*" Madeline sounded equally unsettled as she squeezed Joy's neck and drove her toward the empty cross in the middle.

It's all over once they string you up, sweetheart.

With no real plan in mind, Joy planted her feet. Madeline walked into her back a heartbeat later. As she recovered, Joy spun, pulled the scissors from her waistband, and stabbed blindly outward.

The blades sank into Madeline's stomach all the way to the handles. It both amazed and disgusted Joy how easily they parted the flesh. The other woman staggered back a step, a look of shock on her face as a red inkblot spread across her belly.

Then the surprise turned to fury.

"You fucking *bitch!*" she screeched, and raised the revolver.

Joy grabbed her arm and forced it down. The weapon barked. A hole appeared in the ground just inches from Joy's foot. She wrenched the gun out of Madeline's grasp and stepped behind her before turning to face the others.

Samuel snatched up the rifle and aimed it in their direction. "Stop!" he shouted. Beside him, Deborah slowly advanced, her mouth twisted into an ugly snarl.

Joy backed toward the house, pulling Madeline along with one hand locked around her throat. The woman went slack in her arms as the life bled out of her. She pointed the revolver around her human shield, switching targets between Samuel and Deborah, but her hand shook so much she couldn't steady the weapon. "Get back! I will fucking shoot you lunatics!"

"Just kill them both," Deborah snarled at her husband.

That unearthly squeal blasted again, the sound of pigs screwing in hell. Over Samuel's shoulder, Joy saw the branches and undergrowth at the tree line part as something stepped into the yard.

Her breath caught in her throat.

If the creature had backed into view, Joy might have confused it with a rhinoceros, except for the disfigured brown shell that made up its flesh. Its body, a broad, segmented barrel, stood on four stout, crooked legs that ended in spindly digits, like foot-long toes. They dug into the earth as it walked, making it appear to tiptoe with each step. The gait would've been oddly graceful for something so large, if its misshapen legs didn't cause it to lumber from side to side.

But all of this registered only in the back of her mind, because the thing's head drew all her attention.

Or its lack of one.

Between its massive shoulders, a hollow cavity descended deep into its body. It reminded Joy of a stuffed dog she had as a kid, who could be turned inside out by shoving its head down inside its cloth body. The mouth of this opening—wide enough to fit a basketball in—was covered in fine white threads several inches long that wiggled and wagged like gigantic sperm tails.

Samuel and Deborah saw her attention shift. They looked at each other like characters in a comedy before turning around, the standoff forgotten.

Everyone watched as the creature approached Conrad. Even Shirley remained silent, her jaw hanging open as the thing entered the semicircle of crosses. When it got within a few yards away of him, the hairs around that opening began to jitter even faster. Something stirred inside that cavity, and then a host of scabby tentacles emerged.

There were seven of them, each as thick as Joy's wrist and colored an obscene shade of pink. They looked dry and brittle, more like rough bone than malleable flesh. The tentacles slid out of the creature's body, growing longer and longer as they quested through the air toward the unconscious man. They'd reached ten feet in length when they began to explore Conrad, feeling him up and down. Joy's throat clenched in a disgusted gag.

In a lightning-quick burst of movement, the tentacles latched onto the bare skin of Conrad's arms, face, and neck. They shuddered.

Conrad's entire body crumpled. It looked like an optical illusion from a demented magician: one second, the man was thick and heavy and alive in his duct tape bindings, the next his skin began to wrinkle and deflate until he looked like an Egyptian mummy, a skeleton shrink-wrapped in flesh and dressed in clothes ten sizes too big.

Every drop of moisture had been sucked from his body, like a kid with a juice pouch.

Shirley renewed her screams and thrashed on her cross.

It released the husk of her husband and turned to her. Those tentacles whipped around. Instead of latching on to her, they slid behind her waist. She continued to shriek and buck as they coiled around her hips.

They squeezed.

Blood gushed from Shirley's mouth, nose and ears. Her eyeballs bulged from their sockets. She fell silent, and the thing released her, leaving the crushed body to dangle from the cross.

Samuel doubled over and vomited onto his lawn. Joy's gut lurched as her own dinner attempted escape.

But Deborah cried, "*Yes, yes, free them!*" She walked toward the crosses and dropped to her knees with hands in the air, like an actor in a musical at the end of the big number. "*Take us all to the Lord!*"

"Deb. Deb, get up." Samuel wiped the back of one hand across his puke-stained lips, then put it on his wife's shoulder and shook her gently. He sounded ready to be done with human sacrifices once and for all, yet he didn't take his eyes off the creature as he urged his wife to stop testifying.

When it started toward the Whitakers, Samuel raised the rifle and fired twice.

Both shots punctured the pitted carapace around the thing's chest. It reared on its thick back legs and gave an indignant bellow that came from deep inside the hole where the tentacles originated.

"*WHAT ARE YOU DOING?*" Deborah reached up from the ground to grab at her husband's weapon.

The creature charged forward, narrowing the fifteen yards that separated it from the couple. Those tentacles slashed through the air ahead of it. One of them struck Samuel in the side, sending him airborne. He somersaulted twenty feet before slamming against the base of a tree.

Deborah shrieked. She fell back on her ass and scooted through the grass, away from the alien beast that now loomed over her.

Joy let go of Madeline. The woman was either dead or unconscious when she hit the ground. Joy turned toward the house, only ten short steps away, but paused when Deborah squealed, "*No! No, I don't want this!*"

The other woman crawled after her, sobbing with her mouth open and eyes rolling, lost to terror. A small pang of sympathy surprised Joy. Behind Deborah, two of the creature's tentacles lashed out and caught her by the ankles. Joy leapt toward her without thinking, dropping the gun to seize the other woman's wrists. She pulled as hard as she could.

They stared into each other's faces for a heartbeat before the tendrils yanked Deborah out of her grasp as easily as a flower plucked from its stem. They lifted her completely off the ground. She dangled upside down in the air for a moment, screaming, before the tentacles twitched in opposite directions.

Deborah Whitaker split in half like a gore-filled piñata, raining blood and organs down upon the lawn.

As the creature tossed the pieces aside, Joy got up and sprinted for the house. Fear narrowed her vision to a pinhole. She expected to feel one of the tentacles snare her at any moment, but she made it through the door unmolested. Joy kept moving, back down the hall and into the living room, where the door to the basement waited.

Samuel's keys waited on the kitchen bar. She grabbed them and tried each until she found the right one, then sprinted down the stairs.

Roberta looked up at her from the floor as Joy hurried into the basement. "What happened? What was all that screaming?"

"W-where are the others?" Barry asked.

"We have to go," Joy told them around gasps. She couldn't breathe. The world seemed to be made of crooked angles. Is this what it felt like when your sanity came unraveled? "Help me get Helen and Arthur up." When neither of them moved, she sucked in enough air to shout, "*C'mon, move!*"

"Joy," Roberta said softly. "Arthur's dead."

The words calmed her burgeoning hysteria as sharply as a slap to the face. Arthur's body still lay by the base of the steps. Joy squatted beside him. She touched the man's arm and stood up again, now calm and focused. "Then help me carry Helen."

Roberta and Joy each grabbed one of the old woman's arms and lifted her out of the chair, careful not to touch her burns. She stirred and murmured, "Where am I? What's... what's happening?"

"We're getting you out of here," Joy said, as they carried her up the stairs.

"Wait, just hold on a minute!" Barry stood standing by the wall. "What happened to Conrad and Shirley? I'm not going out there until you tell me what's—"

One of the narrow windows above him burst, spraying glass. Those horrible tentacles boiled into the room. In the light, Joy could see puckered dimples at the tip of each one. They fastened onto Barry before the man could react and leeched him dry.

"*What is that?*" Roberta screamed. "*Oh god, what* is *that?*"

"*Keep going!*" Joy urged, turning away from Barry's shriveled corpse.

They carried Helen through the house, down the hallway, to the interior garage door. The BMW that Samuel mentioned earlier sat inside. Joy used the key remote on the ring to unlock the doors and the two of them laid Helen in the back seat.

She got behind the wheel, found the garage remote above the sun visor, and started the big bay door rolling upward. Time raced by, but she knew it couldn't be more than two minutes since she reentered the house. Joy gunned the engine. They shot out of the garage in a squeal of tires, knocking the door off its track.

The Whitaker's gravel driveway curved toward the back of the house, away from the woods and the crosses. Joy flipped on the headlights and careened down it so fast that every bump bounced them in their seats. As they reached the north side of the property, the creature bounded around the corner of the house and into their path.

Joy swerved, barely missing the monster. In the rearview mirror, she saw it swivel and waddle after them on its prehensile toes. The driveway ended at 407 just ahead, and Joy narrowly avoided rolling the BMW as she turned onto the road at forty miles per hour.

She straightened the vehicle out on the gravel. Coaxed speed from the engine. The creature appeared alongside the passenger window and easily paced them. Roberta screamed as those tentacles shattered the glass and whipped into the car.

Joy yanked the wheel on pure instinct, smashing the car against the beast's flank. The impact rocked them. The monster squealed again and backed off, reeling in its scaly appendages. For a moment, they pulled ahead, and Joy watched the mirror so intently that Roberta caught her off guard when she shouted, "*Look out!*"

She brought her eyes back to the road in time to see it take a hard curve to the left. Joy stomped the brakes and tried to make the turn, but could feel control slipping away. The BWM skidded on the gravel, performing a dizzy 180 at the curve before slamming to a stop with its rear end in the ditch.

They faced the opposite direction now. The creature stood in the middle of road just twenty yards away. Its shadow from the car's headlights looked like a moose with an invisible head, the knot of tentacles giving the impression of floating antlers. Joy waited for it to charge, but instead, it abruptly wheeled around, took a few unstable steps back toward the house, and collapsed. She felt the thud of it hitting the ground in her bones.

"Is...is it dead?" Roberta whispered.

"I don't know how it can be. We didn't hit it that hard."

"Just go. Drive away."

Joy wanted nothing more. She just didn't know which way to go. The creature lay in the path that would take them to Bear Creek Parkway and possible help, if they dared to get closer. Turning right would only lead them back to the burnt remains of the community center and the eventual dead end of the road.

And her own house along the way, of course.

"We have to find them," Roberta told her from the passenger seat, as if reading her mind.

If she knew for sure that it was only Denny back there, she might've left without a second thought. This is what her husband had been preparing for, so let him have his war. But she couldn't go as long as a chance existed that anyone else was still alive with him.

Any*one, dear?*

Joy revved the engine until they climbed out of the ditch, then drove further north on 407.

TWENTY FIVE

The horror that tore out of Claude Dunn's corpse was a squirming bundle of countless, insectile legs about the size of a Saint Bernard puppy. It sprang a full six feet into the air, directly at Mitch's head. He recoiled, causing the damn thing to smash into his chest instead. It hit with the force of a miniature wrecking ball, bowling him over backward and riding him all the way to the ground.

His numb ass took the brunt of the fall, but he still hit his back hard enough to wallop the air from his lungs. The tall grass closed in around him. He couldn't see the thing sitting on his torso, but felt it scrabble toward his face. Mitch grabbed blindly, chest burning from lack of oxygen. His hands closed around those chitinous appendages, like a bundle of crab legs against his palm. He heard a sharp *clack!* as something snapped at his cheek. The thing thrashed in his grip.

"*Mitch!*" JD's voice, calling from somewhere nearby.

"*O-over here!*" he sputtered, finding his breath at last. "*Get this goddamn thing off me!*"

A moment later, the bright beam of the flashlight illuminated the monster on his chest. Its structure resembled a spider, but that was like saying a fly had wings so it must be a bird. That brown, plated flesh covered its oblong body, hard knots and lumps stretching the surface. A ridiculous number of legs sprouted in all directions, connected by swollen joints and sporting barbed hooks. On the front of its bloated body, pincer-like mandibles strained toward his throat. As Mitch struggled to keep them away, he saw them open and a gravelly imitation of his own voice drifted out, moaning, "*Geeet thiiis goddaaamn thing off meee!*"

Then JD grabbed hold of the ugly little sucker and hauled it away from Mitch's face. It hissed and snapped at the air with the frenzy of a shark. As Mitch tried to get out from under it, one of his hands lost its grip.

The creature used the freedom to twist to the side and latch onto JD's forearm. He howled and dropped the flashlight as those mandibles sank into his flesh.

Mitch sat up, ripped the creature off JD, and slammed it against the ground. It tried to flip back over, but he leapt atop it this time and pinned its legs with his knees.

The heavy flashlight lay in the grass to his left. He raised it above his head and brought it whistling down on the thing's blind, putrid face. It squealed in pain or rage. Mitch bludgeoned it again, over and over, until its hard outer shell fractured. Chunks of clotted goo splattered him, reminding him of the bile that Morgan puked on his shirt. This thing smelled just as chargrilled as that poor son of a bitch.

"C'mon, get up man, it's dead!" JD grabbed his arm. Blood poured down his wrist from the fresh bite wound.

Mitch left the creature on the ground with its countless legs still twitching. He barely had the energy to stand, breath irregular, blood thundering at his already sore temples. "You all right?"

"I can still move my fingers, so I guess that's all that matters." JD grimaced. "Stings like a motherfucker though."

"That's what you get for not running to the house like I told you." Mitch gave a sigh of relief and clapped his friend on the shoulder. "But Jesus, am I glad you stayed."

"Yeah, well, thank me later. Where there's one of these things, there's usually more."

"*Hey!*"

Mitch looked up to find Denny and Bo jogging across the field toward them. They lugged heavy camping packs strapped with weapons on their backs, and held huge semi-auto rifles.

"You guys okay?" Denny asked as he came to stop.

"No thanks to you," Mitch said through clenched teeth. "What the hell happened to you covering us?"

"I couldn't see what to shoot with you in the way, jackass. What was it, anyway? Is Claude okay?"

"See for yourself."

He handed the goo-covered flashlight to Denny and watched as the two men approached their friend. A moment later, Bo exclaimed, "Oh Christ!" and then stepped away, gagging.

Denny took off the camping pack and knelt to examine the creature's remains. "What the fuck's this one do?"

Mitch leaned down beside him. "Near as I can tell, it burrowed up inside Claude, used him like a ventriloquist dummy to draw us out." He looked at all those legs again and thought he could at least understand their purpose now: they would all be needed to manipulate muscles and yank tendons to work their host's limbs. Some old cartoon popped into his head, of an organ player who grew extra hands to play a frantic tune. "It could even do an impression of our voices. These things are damn crafty."

Denny looked up at him, eyes glittering in the darkness. "Then we'll just have to be craftier." He held out the rifle in his hands, a scoped AR-15 painted in camouflage. "Fully loaded. And feel free to fire away, cause I got plenty of ammo."

Mitch glared at him for another second until his anger evaporated. He accepted the weapon. "Thanks."

Denny seemed on the verge of saying more. Then he nodded, jutted his bruised jaw, and turned to dig in the pack beside him. He fished out a flat black pistol and handed it to Mitch also. "Here's one for your butt buddy. Guess he earned it. When we get inside I wanna arm everybody else and then start settin some traps. Crafty or not, we can kill these fuckers, which means we can defend ourselves."

A few hours ago, Mitch would've laughed at such gross exaggeration. But, as he moved toward JD with the pistol, he was again glad to have somebody like Denny in this with him, even if he hated the guy's guts.

"Hey man, take this and let's..." Mitch trailed as he looked at his friend.

JD stood ramrod straight, arms stiff at his sides. As Mitch got closer, he could see the cords in the other man's neck standing out like steel bands beneath the skin.

"Denny, bring the flashlight!"

With the light on him, JD looked like a very realistic statue. Every muscle in his body remained bunched and tense, joints locked into place, like the Tin Man at the beginning of *The Wizard of Oz*. His jaw was locked up hard enough to make his tongue muscle bulge from the underside, the lips pulled back into a terrible grimace that put every tooth in his head on display.

"Oh shit." For the first time tonight, panic threatened to overtake all of Mitch's rational thought. "He's having some kind of seizure, we have to do something!"

"If that's a seizure, it's the calmest one I've ever seen."

"He could be dying!"

"Relax. He's still breathin. If he's still breathin, he ain't dyin."

Relief made Mitch's legs watery. His friend's chest was the only part of him still moving. No, not true, actually. Mitch also noticed that JD's eyes remained laser-focused on their faces, following them wherever they moved.

"JD, can you hear me? Move your eyes if you understand me."

His eyes moved up and then down, up and down.

"Can you move the rest of your body?"

Left to right this time. Even with his face frozen in a death rictus, Mitch could see the terror in his eyes. He stuck the pistol in his pocket, then grabbed his friend's bicep and tried to haul his arm away from his side. It remained locked in place, the muscles rigidly flexed. They felt as hard as granite beneath the flesh.

"What the hell happened to 'im?" Denny asked.

The blood leaking down JD's wrist caught Mitch's attention. "That thing bit him. It must've...injected him with something. Paralyzed him." The implication of this—that Claude might've been alive and unable to move when the monster hollowed him out and climbed inside like a suit of armor—made Mitch's blood run cold.

"Uh, Denny?" Bo interrupted. He still stood a few yards away, looking back toward the survival shed and the rest of the field to the northeast of the house. "I...I think I see somethin..."

Mitch squinted into the night and thought he saw a flicker of movement, followed by several more. An odd clacking sound reached his ears.

"Fire a flare," Denny said, his voice oddly flat.

Bo raised the orange gun skyward and let off another phosphorus round. When that red sun burst into existence overhead, Mitch's heart plummeted into his stomach.

The entire far end of the field was alive with more of the puppet masters, hundreds of them, all bounding across the high grass toward the house like an army of giant fleas. Their legs rattled and clacked each time they soared through the air. With the amount of ground they covered in each hop, Mitch estimated they would be upon the four of them in thirty seconds.

"There's always more," he whispered.

"Get to the house." Denny sounded remarkably calm as he shouldered his pack.

"What about JD?"

Denny swore under his breath, then shouted, "Bo, start tossin some of them bangers! Maybe it'll discourage the bastards long enough for us to get Sleeping Beauty inside!"

Mitch wrapped his arms around JD's waist and lifted. The man weighed a good two hundred pounds, only ten or so more than Mitch himself. If he'd been limp, Mitch could've thrown him over one shoulder; the weight would've been just as dead, but at least it would be manageable. But JD stayed perfectly stiff and upright, a true statue, making it impossible to get him far enough off the ground to take a step, much less run.

"Here, tilt 'im over!" Denny commanded. He gave JD's shoulder a hard shove, rocking him back on his heels, then caught him before he could hit the ground. "Grab his feet and let's go, goddamn it!"

Mitch slung the rifle strap over his head and hoisted his best friend up like a stack of lumber. Denny led the way toward the house as they ran with JD slung awkwardly between them. Mitch would've laughed if not for the the fact that death was literally at their heels.

He looked back to see Bo pull one of the round metal bulbs from the shed out of his own backpack. He twisted something on the top, then reared back and lobbed it across the field. Mitch lost track of it in the darkness, but a second later a brilliant orange and yellow explosion blossomed. The sound of it was a deep bass rumble, surprisingly subdued, but heat washed over them even from twenty yards away.

"What are those?" he asked between panting breaths.

"Homemade grenades," Denny answered, then glanced at him sheepishly over the length of JD's body. "I use 'em when we go fishin."

"There is definitely a reason your neighbors hate you."

Another boom went off behind them. The tremor vibrated the soles of Mitch's feet. He twisted around again to look.

Denny's 'bangers' left smoking craters in the field. As Bo threw another one, Mitch saw the swarm scatter to avoid the explosion. The blast incinerated a handful, but, on the whole, they kept coming, bouncing through the grass toward the house.

And Bo stood right in their path.

He realized the danger at the last second. Bo raised the rifle to his shoulder and fired off a few ineffective rounds, then spun and sprinted away. Mitch saw one of the things come leaping up out of the grass to his right. With its legs tucked in, the creature looked like a cannonball. It smashed into Bo's hip from behind. He stumbled but managed to stay on his feet, until two more of the creatures soared down on his shoulder and back, driving him to his knees. Bo screamed as their mandibles chewed into his neck from both sides.

"Goddamn it," Denny huffed, turning to look back for only a second. "God-fuckin-damn it. Move your pansy ass, El Presidente or I'm leavin you both."

Mitch faced forward again and concentrated only on running. The clacking of the crablike legs came from right behind them.

Thankfully, the back door of the house opened when they were still a few yards away. Doc and Eli stepped outside and held out their hands to offer help, but Denny just bellowed, "*Gangwaaaaay!*" He didn't slow down as he plowed into the two men with JD's head as a battering ram. Mitch came through the door last, and entered the kitchen in time to see Doc stumble backward, rebound off Gladys, and crash into the rocking chair to which Lena was tied with the tail of his robe flapping like a cape. Both chair and vet toppled and spilled into the floor.

Denny dropped JD on the kitchen tile, dumped his camping pack, and ran back to slam the door. "*Get somethin to cover the windows!*" he barked.

The words were barely out of his mouth before the first of the creatures struck the outside of the house with a thud, followed by more in an unending succession that made Mitch think of a hail storm. Except this hail would turn them all into a gory version of the Muppets if it got inside.

Carla burst into the room and proceeded to scream her head off in the entry. Doc and Eli lifted the wooden dining table and pushed past her into the kitchen just as the room's only window shattered. One of the puppeteers rolled onto the floor with legs flailing. It skittered at JD's prone form. Mitch unslung the rifle and tried to get a bead on it, but before he could fire, Gladys raised a foot and stomped on the thing until its rotted insides splattered across the tile.

"Mitchy, you sure know how to run an HOA meeting," she proclaimed.

Denny helped Doc and Eli get the table positioned over the broken window before any more got in. They could hear them out there though, crawling over the exterior of the lodge and even clambering onto the roof as they searched for a way in.

"We have to get the rest of the windows boarded up before they get to the other side!" Denny told them.

"Don't you have any more grenades?" Mitch asked.

"Yeah, but we'd have to chuck 'em pretty far out to make sure they don't blow a hole in the house! And that's not gonna do much good if the fuckin things are crawlin up our ass!"

The four men started out to the living room. Gladys grabbed Mitch's arm as he went by. "What should I do?"

"There's not much you can do, sweetheart. Just keep JD out of trouble."

Denny's home didn't have many windows to cover. They worked in two teams, using whatever they could find to seal up the weak spots and close off doors as the creatures bashed away at the exterior. An infestation gained a foothold in the gun room, but Denny and Mitch fired the ARs into the bottleneck until they were all dead and then drilled a thick piece of sheet metal across the window.

"*These aren't gonna hold forever!*" Doc shouted from the living room, where he and Eli were putting their weight against a barrier made of dining chairs that jumped and rattled constantly.

"*Then grab a gun and blast 'em as they come through!*" Denny yelled back, then grumbled to Mitch, "Fuck it all, I *told* Joy these windows were a defensive nightmare when we built the house, but oh no, she wanted to see actual sunlight."

The sheet metal on the window was already dented and bent out of shape from the bodies repeatedly bashing into it from the other side. The entire house filled with the racket of the monsters attacking from all sides.

Mitch raised the rifle. "We're in real trouble here." Fear numbed him to the point that he could no longer feel the trigger against his fingertip.

They were going to die.

And, even though he supposed that his blackout trances were a subconscious desire to do just that, now that the prospect stared him in the face, he discovered that he very much wanted the opposite.

From elsewhere in the house came the sound of a door slamming. A second later, the siege abruptly cut off. The uncertain silence that followed was somehow worse.

"What the hell...?" Denny frowned and ran for the living room with Mitch right behind him.

As soon as she saw them, Carla pointed at the front door and screamed, "It's Gladys, she went outside!"

All five of them gathered around the window that looked out on the front of Denny's property and peered through chinks in the makeshift barricade.

Gladys walked calmly but quickly away from the house with her good arm held awkwardly away from her body. The creatures began leaping off the house and bouncing toward her.

"Jesus, what's that old bird doing?" Doc asked.

"We have to go after her!" Mitch started toward the door, but Denny grabbed his shoulder.

"I don't wanna stop you from playin hero again, but you might wanna take a look at what she's got in her hand first."

Mitch looked. Gladys stood fifteen yards out from the house now, and the leggy monsters swarmed her. Hundreds of them bounced around in a rough circle like excited dogs, hung from her blouse, sank their mandibles into her legs. But in the hand that she held away from her body were several familiar metal bulbs, and, as the creatures finally bore her to the ground, Gladys used her thumb to activate whatever catalyst set off Denny's bangers.

Both she and her attackers disappeared in a ball of flame so big and bright it left Mitch momentarily blind. The entire house shook with the concussion.

"Looks like that vaporized a good chunk of 'em," Denny said solemnly.

Doc rubbed at his eyes behind his glasses. "What about the rest? Are they coming back?"

"No, they're leavin. Jumpin back across the field in a big goddamn hurry. Maybe the blast spooked 'em."

"It didn't before," Mitch said. With his vision cleared, he could see Gladys' flaming remains outside. Razor blades of grief sliced the back of his throat as he swallowed. Twice this lady saved his life tonight, and he would never have a chance to return the favor.

"Maybe we should turn off the lights," Eli suggested. "Like we did at the community center."

"I www-would advise against that," a rough, slurred voice said behind them. They spun to find Morgan, T struggling to sit up on the couch. He coughed long and hard, a sound more from his chest than his throat, then rasped, "Not if you want to...live through tonight."

TWENTY SIX

Doc insisted on a thorough examination before he would let any of them so much as speak to Morgan. He'd injected the man with a potent cocktail of adrenaline and other medicines from Denny's home pharmacy just before the explosions, and wanted to monitor the man's vitals to see how much damage the forced awakening might've caused. Impatience ate away at Mitch, but he and the others used the time to refortify the lodge and turn on every light in the place. Surprisingly, his headache ebbed during the defense of the house, so at least he could focus on the tasks at hand.

Lena was still tied to the overturned rocking chair in the dining room, slumped over in her bonds so that the side of her head rested on the floor. Mitch managed to pull her upright again and found the woman still listless and unresponsive, staring right through him when he asked if she was all right. Deep cracks carved through the wood backing of the chair and one armrest wobbled, either from the fall or Doc's weight landing on it. He made a mental note to move her somewhere more secure as soon as he got the chance and then hurried to check on JD.

His friend still lay on the tile in the kitchen, every muscle tight as drum skin. Mitch leaned in to hover over his face and asked, "You all right, buddy?"

JD's eyes bounced frantically from side to side in his otherwise frozen face. The perpetual snarl on his lips made Mitch's skin crawl.

"Does it...does it hurt? Are you in pain?"

The man stared at Mitch as he considered this, then his eyes moved side to side again, more reluctantly this time.

"Okay, good. Just...don't worry, we'll figure something out. Let's at least get you up so you can hear whatever this guy has to say."

With Eli's help, they carried JD into the living room and stood him in the corner like another of Denny's stuffed hunting trophies. His eyes flicked past Mitch to the couch just as that rough, mangled voice inquired, "Sss-spider? Lots of... crab legs?"

Mitch turned. Morgan sat up higher on the couch, watching them and drinking water from a glass as Doc held two fingers against the blistered flesh of his neck. Seeing him conscious for the first time—without screaming and thrashing in pain—somehow made the burns horrible all over again, a mottled carpet of deep reds and charcoal black that covered half his face. The line where they began was so defined—starting just below the hairline of his left temple, stretching down to the point of his chin on a slight diagonal, and then down his neck to disappear beneath the collar of his singed shirt—that they looked fake, like trick-or-treat makeup. If this was the result of radiation, as Doc figured, it did a much neater job than an open flame would have. A good surgeon might be able to salvage the blistered sections, but the black parts were just too charred, including a dead patch of flesh that ringed his cheek and eye. The unmarred skin on the right looked clammy and pale, with sweat beads growing from every pore; even with whatever medication Doc put him on, he must be in incredible pain. One eye remained permanently hidden beneath the crispy flap of its lid, but the other burned feverishly bright in its socket.

"Yeah. One of them bit him on the arm."

Morgan gave a slow, that's-what-I-figured kind of nod. "Poison causes noo...noo..." He stopped, forced himself to swallow so hard that his Adam's apple bobbed. "Neural paralysis," he finished, tiptoeing through each syllable. His slurred speech impediment sounded drunken. The medication might be compounding it, but the burns were the real problem. The left third of his lips were cooked and stiff, making him look like a stroke victim when he spoke. His tongue appeared to be fighting just to form each syllable. "Should wear off in...couple hours."

Mitch came closer, kneeling down beside the couch next to Doc while being careful not to hunker on his injured ass cheek. "My name's Mitch Flynn."

"D-Doctor Thomas Morgan. PhD."

One mystery solved, at least. Mitch went around the room and introduced the others. Carla and Eli stood together in front of JD, still frozen with his rictus grin. As he finished, Denny stepped into the doorway of the gun room with his rifle and asked, "Can we speak to His Royal Highness yet, Doc?"

The vet directed his answer to Mitch. "He's stable, but that's really just a guess on my part. The adrenaline got him conscious and I gave him just enough morphine to take the edge off his pain without making him too dopey. Don't even want to know where Denny came by medication of that caliber. Anyway, I'd like to keep Dr. Morgan here away from any stress for a few more hours, but I have a feeling you'd veto me on that, wouldn't you Mitch?"

"Need..." Morgan gave another of those deep coughs that sounded like a chainsaw in his chest. Each breath took an effort to draw in, interrupting the flow of his words. When he spoke again, he kept his rogue tongue carefully under control. "Need to talk. Time is a factor."

"We agree," Mitch told him gently. "We've seen a lot of strange things tonight that all have something to do with you. So please, tell us what you know."

Morgan shook his head slowly, dislodging an avalanche of black flakes from his chin that drifted down on to his chest. "*You* tell *me*. Where am I?"

"My house," Denny said. "Towards the tail end of 407. If you know Bear Creek, it's about—"

The burned man waved his good hand to cut off the details. Frustration brought back out the slur in his words. "I mmm-mean...where *am* I? This is still...America, right?"

Mitch glanced at Doc, then back at Denny, who came further into the room with one eyebrow halfway up his forehead. "Uh, yeah, this is America. Texas, to be exact. About a hundred or so miles east of Waco."

A strangled, gurgled sound came from deep in Morgan's throat that Mitch at first took to be another cough, before realizing it was laughter. The man leaned his head back on the couch, closed his good eye, and mumbled, "Perfect. Just perfect. Could be worse. Could also be a whole h-helluva lot better."

"That fire fucked up more'n his face," Denny muttered as he sank into the recliner to Mitch's left and propped his weapon against the handle.

Morgan's head sprang back up again, his good eye spinning crazily for a moment until it focused on Mitch. "I can stop this. Just need…phone. If cells are down, a landline w-will work."

"We don't have one," Mitch told him. The casual mention of the cell outage made him want to crack this man's head open like a piñata to get the answers they needed. "At least, not here. We've been trying to get to one all night to call for help, but those…those *things* outside keep cutting us off at every turn."

Horror stole into Morgan's eye. His mouth worked like a fish, a blister on the left corner breaking open and oozing watery brown fluid. "Have…have they…*killed* anyone?"

"Yes. Quite a few people, in fact."

"Oh dear god." A tear slipped from his good eye, mingled immediately with sweat on the bridge of his nose, and cascaded down his cheek. "Anyone aware of the situation? Anyone in…authority?"

"Not that we know of. We're just a small, unincorporated neighborhood. The nearest town is seventy miles away. Like I said, we've been too busy running for our lives to even call the sheriff."

"Shit." Morgan's voice dropped to a mumble again. "Just got w-worse after all."

"Okay." Mitch snapped his fingers to bring the man back to the conversation. "That's where you're at and we can't do anything to change the circumstances. Look, why don't you tell us what's going on, and we can go from there."

"Can't do that."

"Why not?"

"C-classified."

"*What?*" Denny jumped to the edge of the recliner, nearly slipping off the seat in the process. "What the hell're you talkin about, 'classified?'"

"All of this, everything going on...a highly sensitive g-governmental concern."

"Who the fuck do you work for?" Denny demanded. "NSA? The CIA? Fuckin Halliburton?"

"You don't have c-clearance for—"

"*Here's my fuckin clearance!*" Denny roared. He leapt toward the couch, both hands held out in front of him to throttle the life from the charbroiled man on his sofa. Mitch and Doc scrambled to grab his arms and kept his wrath from falling upon Morgan. "*My wife and all my friends died tonight because of those motherfuckers! That gives me all the goddamn clearance I need, you classified government shithead!*"

Mitch was genuinely surprised to see tears in the man's eyes.

On the couch, Morgan gasped and sputtered as he tried to keep out of Denny's reach. "I'm sss-sorry...not mmm-my fault...!"

Denny suddenly went limp and stood with head bowed. Mitch turned him around and led him back to the recliner with a hand on his shoulder, then forced him to sit. He considered taking the rifle beside him, but instead, he turned and leveled his own finger at Morgan. "You wouldn't even be alive right now if we didn't haul your unconscious body around with us all night. I don't care how classified it is, we're already part of this. You *made* us part of it when you stumbled onto our doorstep and brought this shit—whatever it is—down on our heads. So if you want a phone so bad, you need to tell us what these things are and how to get away from them, or we're all gonna die right here."

Morgan's mouth trembled; at least, the right half did. His head bobbled, and Mitch waited for him to slip under again. "Don't know what they are," he finally whispered. "No one d-does. We just opened the door...and there they were..."

"What does that even mean?" Mitch approached him again, sinking back to his knees in the floor. "Just...give us *something* we can understand! We already know it has to do with doors and a quarantine and someone named Cybil; hell, you told us that much last time you woke up."

The rapid list of information made Morgan's good eye stretch open in shock. He obviously had no memory of his spell at the community center. "W-what does it matter now? Never be able to...contain this." His shoulders slumped as something in him broke. He spoke slowly and methodically, working hard to enunciate and keep the breathing pauses from his voice. "I...I don't work for the government. I'm a team leader at a lab...*contracted* by the government. That's *SIPPL*, not *Cybil*: Seahill Incorporated P-Particle Physics Laboratory."

"And where is this lab?"

Morgan shook his head, still looking reluctant. "Offices are...outside Albany."

"*New York?*" Doc whistled through his front teeth. "You're a long way from home, Doctor. How did you end up in the middle of rural Texas?"

"Pure chance." Morgan's bloated tongue poked out and wet his lips nervously. "But...m-might be easier for you to understand when I tell you...for the last three years...my division has been w-working on...a reliable method of teleportation."

An uncomfortable silence filled the room. From the corner of his eye, Mitch could see Denny leaning forward again in his chair, and Carla and Eli frowning at one another, but he didn't look away from Morgan as he asked, "Are we talking 'Beam me up, Scotty' here, Doctor Morgan?"

The ghost of a smile played around the good corner of the man's mouth. "Fiction. Not feasible. Our focus was more on...s-stable wormholes." Denny gave a confused grunt, to which Morgan explained, "Like opening a d-door. One side is point A, step through to point B."

"And you succeeded?"

"Oh yes. Two years ago." The pride in Morgan's voice was unmistakable. "Sent hunk of wood...one side of room to the other. T-ten feet. But...with enough power...this sort of bridge could go anywhere."

"Christ on a cracker," Doc murmured. His hand didn't know whether to rub at his triple chins or his ample bosom. "How far is 'anywhere?' Could this thing let a person just walk right on to another *planet?*"

"With precise enough coordinates. The math is...s-staggering. But energy is key. That bridge across the room used...t-*terawatts* of electricity. Government built a separate electric grid just to keep the power companies from noticing the d-draw."

To Mitch's left, Denny began a slow, sarcastic clap. "All right, yay, good for you," he said, his voice much softer but just as caustic. "How the hell does that explain those fuckin things out there?"

The smile fell off Morgan's face in a hurry. "The bridges... don't go from point A to point B. Not directly. There's...a space between the doors we can't account for. That's what we took to calling it: the Between."

A deep, protracted chill skated along Mitch's spine, along with a pulse of pain between his temples. Morgan continued, but the scientist looked just as spooked. "Whatever it is...it's lightless and f-filled with...a new element. We named it Arthenon."

Doc frowned. "It's radioactive, isn't it?"

"Yes, but the energy is c-corrosive. Eats through just about anything given enough time. Animal test subjects...

well, they l-looked like me. On the other side of the doors, it acts like a liquid, but when it crosses over it's a harmless gas. One that disrupts all known forms of w-wireless communications." He paused, gave another phlegmy, wet cough. "The military...took over the lab. Wanted some way to harness it. So, to keep the most important p-project in human history from being turned into another weapon...we t-told them we would need to explore the Between."

"Hang on," Denny interrupted. "I thought you said this stuff would burn you up if you went in there."

"Caustic. Needs direct contact. Depending on the covering, a human could stay inside for up to an hour. Then we... we realized the space w-wasn't empty."

"Those creatures live in there," Mitch murmured.

"Yes. Don't know what they are, either. Cellular makeup is...strange. Not even carbon-based." Morgan coughed and shook his head. Now that they'd pried open the floodgates, he couldn't stop talking. He looked through them now, into memory. "Exploratory team disappeared. Then these awful things that look like giant stick b-bugs came through. Breached containment and killed three techs." Morgan came back to himself suddenly, grabbed Mitch's arm with his good hand, and looked around at all of them. "Listen to me, those things are incredibly dangerous!"

Denny snorted. "Yeah, we got that."

"No, yyy-you don't understand!" He tongue began to slip again in his urgency. "After the b-breach, we started l-*luring* them out for study! Over one hundred catalogued species so far! All p-predators, highly intelligent! They don't even seem to have a biologic need to fff-feed! They just maul and kill, like they enjoy it!"

"Trust me, we know, we've seen it," Mitch told him.

He gently took the man's hand off his arm and held it to calm him down. The skin felt smooth and soft compared to his own callused palm. "Cut to the chase, Doctor Morgan. What went wrong? How did you end up here?"

Morgan made an effort to get himself and his speech back under control. "An explosion. Two other techs and myself... running end-of-day shutdown. S-stabilizer hit a power surge. Created a door at random. Tried to shut it down and something blew. Blast must've pushed me right through. I had on a containment suit, or I'd be dead." He grimaced, an expression which looked especially awful on his face. "C-came to in a field. Suit must've ripped while I was inside. Arthenon burned me."

"But that doesn't make sense. Why did it bring you *here?*"

Morgan's jaw clenched, resulting in another rain of charred skin flakes. "Told you, sheer ch-chance. Bridge had no target. Could've ended up at the b-bottom of the ocean. Or in a volcano. With enough power, I could've been shot halfway to...Alpha Centauri."

Mitch would never have followed any of this with his headache flaring. And if he hadn't seen most of what this man was describing with his own eyes, he certainly wouldn't have believed it. He opened his mouth to ask one of the other thousand questions that sprang to mind, but Doc silenced him with a look and jumped in with, "Yes, we get it, we won the cosmic bad luck lottery tonight. But you said you can stop it with a phone call. How?"

Morgan coughed again, this time unleashing dribbles of brown fluid down his chin that looked like watery chewing tobacco. Eli came forward and offered the man a handkerchief, which he used to wipe at the liquid. Talking had taken a toll on him, but not even Doc appeared ready to make him stop. "The stabilizer must still be running, back in Albany. If the other techs are dead...no one knows it. Just need to c-contact someone to kill the stabilizer. Until we do...new portals will just k-keep opening."

"We've seen several of them," Mitch confirmed. "Shimmery curtains that just sort of float in the air?"

Morgan nodded. "No s-specified coordinate means the stabilizer must be generating new connections at random. Think of it like...a shotgun blast aimed at your entire neighborhood."

"And every new connection is another way those things can get out?"

A loud crash from the dining room stopped Morgan before he could answer.

TWENTY SEVEN

Across the room, Carla let out a tiny shriek. Denny jumped to his feet, snatching back up the rifle beside his recliner, but Doc Fatso and El Presidente froze up so hard, you couldn't tell much difference between them and the JD statue in the corner.

And of course they did. Even after everything they'd been through tonight, everything this deep-fried quack told them in the last ten minutes, none of these people possessed the slightest survival instinct. They would stick their heads in an alligator's mouth if someone told them there was a McDonald's inside. Hell, Flynn didn't even have the AR anymore.

The only way they would make it through this is if Denny carried them.

So he marched toward the dining room without hesitation, rifle held up and ready, ignoring the nagging fear that tried to lock up his knees. At the entry, he took a breath, held it, and peered around the corner to see what new monstrosity had broken into his home.

Instead of brown-shelled aliens from Dimension X, he found the splintered remains of his rocking chair.

Lena was gone.

"*Shit!*" Denny raced into the kitchen, the only direction the crazy bitch could've gone.

The back door of the house hung open to the night.

He stood in the doorway, scanning the overgrown field around his house through the rifle scope, ready in case one of the spider-crabs should come leaping out at him. Still pitch black out there, no sign of their fugitive, which made him think she'd probably run around either corner of the house, toward the road. Or else she was lying out there in the grass, waiting to spring up like the Vietcong as soon as one of them got close to her. She was already dressed for the part.

A moment later, Flynn appeared beside him. "Anything?"

"Don't see her. Goddamn it, how the hell'd she get loose?"

After an uncomfortable pause, Flynn admitted hesitantly, "The chair broke earlier when it fell. I was gonna move her somewhere else, but with everything that happened..."

"Way to go, retard. Maybe you wanna cut off our hands and feet next, just to give us a little more of a challenge." Denny shook his head in disgust. He shouldn't have expected anything more from the man that might've fucked his wife, and yet he did. "I knew that crazy lez was fakin the whole shock routine."

To his utter amazement, Flynn cupped his hands around his mouth and shouted, "LENA! COME BACK!"

Denny smacked the man's hands away from his face. "Jesus Christ, man, I was just jokin about the give-us-a-challenge thing! Those creepy-crawlies don't need any help findin the buffet line!"

"We can't let her go out there by herself."

"Goddamn, you are *such* a Boy Scout. You wanna go after her, be my guest. I'm guessin it didn't work out too well for ol' Porter when you sent him to chase her down. Personally, I just hope those things get to her before *she* gets to *us*."

Flynn said nothing, but from the way his eyes cut away, Denny could tell that he agreed, at least to some degree. Maybe the guy wasn't such a lost cause. You know, for a wife-fucker.

A roar drifted up from somewhere in the distance.

It came from the direction of the Corps land, beyond the boundaries of his property, a blast of pure noise that, even from so far away, rattled his bones.

"You may've just got your wish," Flynn whispered.

Denny studied the night. "What the hell was that?"

"I don't know. And I don't wanna find out."

They closed and locked the door, then retreated back to the living room. When he saw them, Morgan tried to sit up and failed, flopping back against the leather and coughing up a little more of that chewing tobacco fluid that splattered in all directions. That couch would be a lost cause if they survived this. "What is it, what happened?"

Denny flapped a dismissive hand. "Woman we had tied up escaped."

Morgan stared at him, eye wide and mouth hanging open.

"She was...mentally unbalanced," Flynn explained.

"That's a polite way of sayin she's a fuckin psychopath." Denny paced around the far side of the room and stopped next to JD, whose frozen snarl seriously creeped him out. "And she's prob'ly just about tied with your monsters for kill count tonight."

Doc made a sympathetic clucking sound with his tongue against the roof of his mouth. "I wouldn't say her chances of surviving out there are very good."

Morgan's mouth twisted in two directions; Denny suspected it was an attempt at a frown. "They g-get worse with every passing second."

An odd mewling sound floated through the living room. It took Denny a moment to realize it came through JD's clenched teeth right beside him. "Hey Flynn, I think your sidekick is gettin some feeling back."

Flynn ignored him and perched on the opposite arm of the couch from Morgan. "You mentioned keeping the lights on before. Does it keep these monsters away?"

"They sure didn't seem fazed by it when they attacked my house," Doc added.

"No. Not them. But they need Arthenon to live. Like oxygen. They can only go without for a short time."

Denny used one finger to poke at JD's stiff cheek muscles as he listened. The man's eyes glared at him while inarticulate but angry gargling came from deep in his throat. "Like they're scuba divers or something."

"That's a g-good analogy."

Flynn frowned and held up a hand. "Then why did you have us turn on the lights?"

"Because the *d-doors* are light sensitive," Morgan answered impatiently, and Denny couldn't help smirking a bit. He may only understand about three out of every five words this mad scientist said, but at least he'd gotten a gold star. "Too much light…they dissipate."

Doc nodded along. "So light keeps these doorways from opening near you. And if there are no doorways near you—"

"—it forces those things to go further from the energy they need if they want to get to you," Flynn finished.

Morgan nodded quickly, eyelids fluttering.

"Then we don't have to do jack shit!" Denny exclaimed.

He turned away from JD and pointed at the nearest boarded up window. "We're makin this out to be harder than it has to be, people! Sunrise is in, what? Another four hours? If we can just survive till it gets bright outside, these portals go away, your lab opens up, and someone turns off your machine. Right?"

On the couch, Morgan drew in a ragged breath and held it for a moment. His chin trembled. Denny got the sudden sinking feeling that, out of everything this guy had told them, they would like this part the least. "The longest…we've ever kept a portal stabilized is thirty minutes," he said slowly. "Arthenon is so c-corrosive…it's more like *burning* a hole in reality. It leaves a trace behind. Like an echo. We theorized that, if one was left open long enough…it might become irreversible. Maybe even grow on its own." He lifted his bad arm, turning his hand so they could see the partially melted silver Rolex strapped to his barbecued wrist. The time showed as 4:23 AM in the Eastern time zone, where he'd come from. "These bridges…they've been in place for close to eight hours. Need to g-get them shut off now, as soon as possible." He swallowed. "Or those creatures might have a permanent gateway."

"You know, you really should've led with that," Flynn said quietly.

Morgan looked sheepish. "Didn't think f-finding a phone would be so hard."

Doc put both of his thick hands over his eyes, like a kid trying to shut out the image of a scary movie. "What you're saying is that these things will be able to come out every night, into our world, to hunt. Doctor Morgan, humanity has spent thousands of years conquering our fear of the dark, and you people are about to give us a whole new reason to be afraid."

"Nnn-no!" Morgan slurred. A bit *too* defensively, Denny thought. "It www-won't be that bad, we'll find the holes and c-contain them, keep light on them —!"

"Yeah, until you decide to turn back on your machine and, whoops, do it all over again!" Doc dropped his hands. An angry red color crept up all of his chins and onto his hound dog jowls. "Because this won't be enough to show you that there are some things you shouldn't meddle with, will it? No, no, why should you care? All you did here was kill a bunch of backwoods retirees! I'm sure you people won't rest until you've turned the entire planet into Swiss cheese!"

Another roar came from outside, this one close enough to shake the windows in their frames. It reminded Denny of the big construction machinery he used to oversee, the bass rumble of a multi-cylinder engine overlaid with the screeching whine of stressed hydraulics.

Eli summed it up a little neater by whispering, "That sounded like a dinosaur." His wife trembled against him while the rest of the room looked around uncomfortably and JD gargled frantically in the corner.

"Whatever it is, it's gettin closer." Denny twirled his hands around each other in a move-it-along gesture. "Maybe we oughta wrap up the science lesson and decide what we're gonna do."

"You have any idea what that sound was?" Flynn asked.

Morgan shook his head, still looking cowed and chastised from Doc's tirade. "The specimens we've catalogued could only be a fraction. There…there could be bigger ones in the Between. Much bigger." His good hand gripped the back of the couch hard enough to dig furrows. "W-we need light. A lot of light. Not a guarantee they won't get to us, but it skews the odds. Is there s-s-someplace like that?"

Flynn's eyes met Denny's across the room. "Don't you even fuckin say it."

"Yeah, I can think of one," Flynn told Morgan.

"Does she have a landline?" Doc asked.

"Honestly, I don't know."

"Then what's the point of goin?" Denny demanded.

"Because it's worth the chance to find out."

"And if she doesn't, we're even worse off!" Denny opened his arms wide to indicate the entire house. "I still say we could defend ourselves right here and wait it out 'til morning. Then we could walk into town if we had to."

"Denny," Doc began, in a soft, patient tone that sounded too much like patronizing, "we wouldn't have lasted another five minutes against those spider things."

"That's only cause we weren't *prepared!*" Denny pounded a fist against the wall beside him hard enough to make Carla flinch. How could these people be so blind, so insistent on taking the stupidest, most dangerous course of action? The alligator's gullet waited just ahead, and these morons were all looking for those golden arches inside. "I'm tellin you, we can do it!"

"Did you not hear what he just said?" Flynn asked. "There's more than just our lives at stake here. We have a responsibility to—"

"I don't give a shit about that!" Denny gritted his teeth. "Whatever happens is *his* problem! We're not the ones that caused this mess, so why should we risk our lives just to find him a goddamn phone!"

"There's...another option." Morgan's interruption was soft, but still enough to silence them all. "W-we could always try...crossing back over the b-bridge to turn off the stabilizer ourselves."

They all stared at him for a moment, digesting this, before Denny said, "You mean go into this...whatever, other dimension...where those things *live?* Oh yeah, that sounds much safer!"

"How would we even do that?" Flynn asked. "Won't we get burned?"

"Just need a way to c-cover our skin long enough to get through. Would have to be watertight, though."

"I think a scuba suit would be harder to come by than a phone," Doc said.

"But if we *could* do it," Flynn pressed, sliding down onto the couch to sit closer to Morgan, "what happens when we walk through one of these portals? What's on the other side?"

"Absolute d-darkness." Morgan's good eye clouded with dread. "A deeper darkness than you've ever imagined. There's something...something w-wrong with the light spectrum. You won't be able to see anything, not even with a f-flashlight. The only thing visible would be the doorways, and there'll probably be a lot scattered around. But, if I'm right, only *one* will take you b-back to my lab. You just have to find it, go through...and t-turn off the equipment."

"Couldn't help but notice it's suddenly us doin all the work in that little story," Denny muttered.

"What about the creatures?" Flynn asked.

"J-just move fast...and get out before they find you."

"Now Mitch, you can't be considering this," Doc said, then immediately shrugged his fleshy shoulders and added, "What am I saying, of course you aren't, you don't have any way to get through this 'Between.'"

Denny closed his eyes, leaned his head back, and sighed loudly. He would regret this, he just knew it. "Would a radiation suit work?"

All eyes turned to him. Morgan said, "Even s-something designed for low level emission would give you...a good five minutes."

Flynn rose from the couch. "Denny...do you *have* a radiation suit?"

"Right out there in the shed," he answered.

And then the ceiling of his goddamn house came crashing down, plunging them into darkness.

TWENTY EIGHT

Mitch thought a bomb had gone off, that Lena had returned with enough ordnance to level a city block and finish the job she'd started at the community center. But there was no explosion, no blast, no noise at all except the splintering thunder of the roof giving way. He looked up to see the thick wooden ceiling beams above his head cracking like toothpicks to release a flood of debris, then threw himself off the couch in an awkward, sideways lurch.

He hit the hardwood floor on his ribcage, a jarring crash that sent hot ice picks jabbing through his chest. A second later, a bowling-ball-sized chunk of fiberglass and camouflage-colored shingles slammed into the side of his left leg, flexing his knee the wrong direction. Mitch grunted and he rolled across the floor to get clear of the avalanche. A high, girlish scream that must be Carla came from elsewhere in the room, impossible to pinpoint in the chaos, but he didn't stop moving until he hit a wall. As he looked up to assess the situation, the electricity in the lodge shorted out, leaving them in the residual glow from Lena's stadium lights next door.

A gaping hole had been torn straight through the ceiling. Shards of timber jutted from the sides and shredded insulation dangled down like thick cobwebs. Stars and the cold October moon were visible beyond. If Mitch hadn't leapt away, he would've been crushed.

Thomas Morgan, on the other hand, was not so lucky.

The cascading debris formed a pile so big it completely engulfed Denny's leather sofa and the doctor along with it. One blackened hand hung out of the heap, the fingers curled into a claw.

"Who's hurt?" Mitch croaked, followed by a hoarse whimper. The words caused a blast of echoing pain through his head. The migraine was back, worse than before, perhaps worse than *ever*, the electric jolts bad enough to nauseate him.

He got muffled replies from Carla and Eli somewhere to his left, along with an indignant gurgle from JD. On the other side of the wreckage, Denny's voice groaned, "Uhhh, somebody owes me a new roof, goddamn it."

"We have to go," Mitch whispered, sitting up. Every movement brought lurching agony.

"Hold on, I gotta find my rifle!"

To Mitch's right, Doc sat up, pushing aside splintered two-by-fours and waving away the thick cloud of dust that hung in the air. He caught sight of the buried couch, but must've come to a very different conclusion than Mitch, because he heaved his bulk up and stumbled through the rubble toward it. "Oh my Lord, someone help me, we have to dig him ou—!"

A shadow appeared above the hole in the ceiling, one that blotted out the moonlight, and then a massive shape forced its way inside, ripping open even more of the roof in the process. In the darkness, Mitch could make out only a swatch of leathery skin and teeth as long as his forearm. With dawning horror, he realized it was a gigantic head, one bigger than Doc's entire car, attached to a neck that didn't look thick enough to support it. The long rectangular head split up the middle as it muscled into the room, revealing a gullet lined with a jagged mountain range of incisors.

Doc came to a halt beneath it. The hefty man's reflexes might be slow, but to Mitch, it didn't look like he even tried to escape. He just stared up in awe as those huge jaws lowered around him and then closed almost delicately on his rotund belly.

The man only began to scream from inside that monstrous mouth when it lifted him off his feet. One of his slippers flew through the air as his legs scissored.

Mitch didn't think, just scrambled up and lunged toward him, something in his knee crying out in protest. He got a grip on the vet's thick ankles as they kicked in midair, then planted his own feet and pulled.

Like playing tug-of-war with a dump truck. Doc continued to wail as the creature lifted higher, and Mitch's toes lost contact with the floor as he went along for the ride.

Then the creature began to chew, its mouth opening and snapping shut again. The vet's screams spiraled higher. A sticky rain fell onto Mitch's head, sluiced down his cheeks. The coppery smell of blood made him gag.

There was an audible pop, the sound of a water-filled balloon breaking. Doc's limbs went slack.

Mitch let go.

He crashed back to the floor, a fall of only a few feet, but his left leg folded and spilled him onto his side amid the debris. Waves of pain crashed over him. Above him, the gargantuan jaws continued to chomp, mangling Doc in that maw like a man with a turkey leg.

Except these nightmares from beyond space didn't need to eat, only destroy.

Another shadow rose up on the far side of the room, this one human-sized.

"*You're trespassin, motherfucker!*" Denny bellowed.

He opened fire with the rifle, a string of quick explosions. Mitch could see him in the burst of each muzzle flash, Denny baring his teeth while he pumped rounds into the monster's irregular head. The thing was an alien nightmare, random antennae and hornlike protuberances jutting from the rough outer shell and fangs shaped like scythes that poked past the boundary of its mouth. The idea of killing such a behemoth with what amounted to a BB gun was laughable, but once the fourth or fifth bullet peppered its face, the creature's mouth sprung back open, spewing out the gnawed remains of Doc's corpse. It let loose another of those godawful roars.

In the confines of the lodge, Mitch could feel the sound waves in his organs, a vibration so intense it threatened to split his aching skull in half. A hot, fetid wind swept through the room, smelling of burnt rot.

Denny never stopped firing. The creature thrashed in a fury, swinging its head back and forth in wild arcs. One of these hit Denny in the chest and sent him hurtling across the room. A moment later, its snout smashed into the back of the house with a cataclysmic crash.

The collision rocked the entire lodge like an earthquake. Everything shifted and slid. Shelves fell over, cabinets spilled. The rest of the ceiling began to disintegrate. Mitch could hear Carla screaming again, but all he could do is cover his head as sheetrock and wood fell across him and wait for it to end.

When it did, and all grew quiet, he opened his eyes and peeked through the layer of debris atop him.

The house looked like a war zone. Rubble lay everywhere. The rear wall had fallen into the grass outside, taking most of the roof with it. The debris formed a junkyard mound at least three yards high. Something in the foundation must have given way also, because the rest of the lodge canted at a drunken angle, like a house of cards just before it collapses. Mitch pushed enough of the ruins away so he could sit up.

A few feet away, something else moved in the wreckage. Eli and Carla's heads poked out. "Is...is it gone?" she whispered.

"I don't know." Mitch worked furiously to dig himself out. "And we can't wait to find out."

It took them a few seconds to get to their feet. Mitch's knee throbbed whenever he put weight on it, but it was nothing compared to the bolts of pain arcing behind his eyeballs. The migraine felt like a tinier set of jaws, devouring him from the inside. Still, as the couple started for the door, Mitch found the strength to say, "Hold on, I need help with JD!"

They found him in the corner where they'd left him, bleeding from a few nicks and scrapes but still intact. He could blink now, and his lips quivered as he gurgled at them. Mitch grabbed his shoulders while Eli got his feet. They started to carry him away, but after a few steps, Mitch stopped and looked around.

He could see no sign of Denny anywhere in the shambles of the house. Still, he would've gone back to look, but the creature loosed another roar from just beyond the pile of rubble at the back of the house. Mitch and Eli moved away from it, toward the front door, which now sat at a twenty degree slant and had to be shoved open in its crooked frame. Carla led the way as they lugged JD through.

"Where do we go?" she squeaked as they ran across the porch.

"Anywhere but here," Mitch said. It sounded good but meant nothing, because he was out of ideas, out of options, and too exhausted and sore to take even another step.

Bright lights blazed in his eyes, momentarily blinding him.

A dark blue BMW raced up the beaten dirt driveway from 409. It slammed to a halt at the base of the steps in a cloud of dust.

Joy leaned out the driver window, waving to them frantically. "*C'mon, get in!*"

Mitch didn't bother to ask questions. He hobbled down the steps, trying not to drop JD's stiff form as the migraine caused a wave of dizziness. Roberta sprang from the passenger side and opened the back door for them, but when she saw JD, she shrieked, "*Oh my sweet baby, what's wrong with him?*"

"He's paralyzed, but he's coming out of it!" Mitch told her. "Just help us get him inside!" Together, they managed to lay JD across the back seat, his head resting on the lap of an elderly lady that Mitch remembered from the HOA meeting. Eli and Carla squeezed in beside her as Roberta dove back in the passenger door and scooted across the seat.

"There's enough room up front!" Joy told him over the roof of the car. Though she spoke to him, her gaze remained fixed on her slumping house. He thought he saw a small, wistful grin touch one corner of her mouth.

Mitch looked as well, but his gaze drew to the metal shed on the far side of the field. "I can't go."

Now her head whipped around to him. "Mitchell Flynn, are you goddamn crazy?"

The use of his full name threw him for a loop. No one had called him that since Allie. He closed the passenger door and limped around the vehicle to her window. "I can stop this. Morgan told us how. Just take everyone else and drive, get to town, and find Sheriff Detwiler. Tell him to contact Seahill Labs in New York. They'll understand what's happening."

She grabbed his hand and squeezed till he thought the bones would break. "We are NOT leaving you."

He wanted to say...well, actually, he didn't know what he wanted to say. His feelings for this woman had changed drastically in the last eight hours, and now wasn't the time to figure them out.

And later won't be either if you don't survive what you're planning to do.

Luckily, Roberta saved him from the dilemma by screaming.

Mitch turned just as the creature that destroyed Casa Carson stepped out from behind its crumbling remains.

Eli came closest with his dinosaur comparison, but, in the end, the goliath in front of them was unlike anything that ever walked this planet. It towered over them, at least 15 feet tall at the highest point, which wasn't even its head. The body resembled a lowercase 'r': a stout torso of pitted brown flesh that looked like the trunk of a redwood, and an elongated giraffe-like neck curving off the top. The gigantic mouth that swallowed Doc whole hung from the end, like a carrot waved in front of a donkey. It had no limbs to speak of except at its base, where four spindly appendages sprouted to give the odd body structure some stability.

Evolution would never have built something so hideous. It was *wrong*, in every sense of the word, a crime against nature, an abomination that should be destroyed down to its very last cell. Mitch could stand to look at it by telling himself it was fake, a bad prop from a laughably horrible sci-fi movie.

Like the rest of its brethren, the creature possessed no visible eyes, but it sensed them somehow. It started toward the car, the bottom half of its huge body swiveling back and forth. Not only was it faster than Mitch would've believed possible, but so light on its feet that it barely made a sound.

He couldn't stop staring at it, not even as the thing ducked its hideous face and cranked open its jaws in preparation to scoop him up.

A streak of tremendous, world-shattering pain shot through his forehead, jerking him out of the trance.

"*Go!*" he shouted at Joy, tearing his hand out of hers and limping away from the vehicle. Mitch moved toward the far side of the lodge, trying to keep the house between him and the giant. He heard the squeal of tires, but didn't look back until he'd reached the corner of the house.

The BMW roared backward up the long driveway. Either the noise or vibration kept the creature's attention, because it gave chase, cutting across the field at an angle to intersect. Joy bounced onto the road and slung the car around hard enough to throw dirt and gravel. It took her only a moment to shift gears and floor the gas, but, by that point, the thing loomed over her. The wheels spun uselessly as its mouth clamped around the back corner of the vehicle, holding it in place. From this distance, the size ratios made the Beamer look like a toy car being bitten by a hideously disfigured dog.

Mitch could hear the metal and plastic being crushed, along with terrified screams from inside the car. He watched helplessly, mind racing, blood thundering painfully between his ears.

The monster opened and closed its jaws, chomping, trying to get a better grip on its prey. The BMW's tires found enough traction to tear free, but one of the rear wheels wobbled. As it picked up speed, the front end began to whiplash back and forth.

The giant started toward them again.

"*Hey!*" Mitch shouted, stepping into the open. His voice didn't carry far, but who knew if this thing could hear it anyway? He waved his arms over his head. "*Hey, you big, goofy-looking bastard! Come on back this way!*"

The creature paused. Its pendulous neck swung back and forth between him and the car as it crawled away, swerving all over the road.

Then it opted for the easier kill, and came galloping back at Mitch.

TWENTY NINE

Joy yanked the steering wheel back and forth in an attempt to control the swerving BMW. Every time she got it straightened out, the vehicle jerked toward the opposite side of the road until she could wrestle it back to center. A terrible squealing drifted up from the undercarriage; she suspected it came from a bent axle. The motion coupled with her shot nerves quickly made her queasy.

"Go go go go go," Roberta chanted, in a breathless, wheezing voice.

"I'm trying," Joy growled, hauling at the wheel. The image of that monstrosity wouldn't leave her head, scuttling behind them like one of Lovecraft's Elder Gods and then lowering its gaping jaws to clamp on to the car. She thought they probably could outrun it in a working vehicle, but they were barely doing 20 miles an hour and she was afraid to give the car any more gas.

The woman that had gotten into the car in front of Joy's house twisted around in her seat to look out the back window. She called out, "It's going away! It's not chasing us!"

Joy checked the rearview mirror in time to see the towering creature turn and start back across the field. The thing's silence as it moved only added to its creepiness; you expected thundering, earthquake-inducing footfalls from something that big. Then the trees crowded in on either side of the road, blocking it from view. *Good luck, Mitch*, she thought, and let out a breath she didn't realize she'd been holding. When she pressed harder on the accelerator, the car surged to the left again. "Uh, I hate to say it, but we're not gonna get very far like this."

"*We have to!*" Roberta screamed and clutched at Joy's arm. "*We have to leave, I'm done with this bullshit, I don't wanna be here anymore!*"

Joy gave a tired chuckle. Either that, or let frustration drive her to the same hysterics. "You're preaching to the choir sweetheart, but there's no way we're gonna be able to drive this thing all the way into town."

From the backseat came a liquidy gurgling just barely discernible as human speech. "Liiights," JD burbled.

"He's right," the other man in the back confirmed. "Dr. Morgan said we have a better chance at surviving around bright lights. We were talking about going to Lena's place just before that thing tore through your house."

The property next door to Joy's came up on their left, the lights in the yard making the trees look like they were on fire. They'd made it a paltry hundred yards, but she didn't want to risk going on and having the car break down, not if this place offered some chance at safety.

"If anyone's got a better idea, now's the time." Joy slowed enough to manhandle the BMW onto the gravel driveway leading down to the immaculate cabin.

Roberta turned in her seat and looked at the couple in the back. "Will the light keep that big one away?"

The man shrugged and gave a confused grimace. "I...I don't think so. It just makes the portals go away."

"Then what's to stop it from just comin over here when it gets finished with Mitch and doin the same thing to *this* house?"

"Doesn't matter," Joy said. "Lena didn't bring her car to the meeting, remember? If we can get to it, we'll roll right back outta here."

A few seconds later they wobbled to a stop in front of the house, parking beneath one of the light poles. Even from here, Joy could see that the door had been battered down.

"We should be careful," the man in the back said.

"Now there's an understatement."

"No, I mean, Lena's out here somewhere."

"Great." Joy sighed. Her hands shook when she took them off the steering wheel, from a potent combination of exhaustion and fear. If her heart didn't slow soon, she thought it might explode in her chest. "Let's just worry about getting inside and we'll go from there."

Joy got out cautiously, ready to bolt back inside at the slightest sign of danger. She peered through the trees, back toward her house, but could see nothing. They pulled JD's weirdly stiff body from the car and carried him toward the door while Roberta helped Helen. Along the way, Eli introduced himself and his wife, and gave Joy a condensed, thirty second rundown of everything the man named Thomas Morgan told them about their present situation before his demise. The story was too insane for her wrung-out mind to grasp, much less believe. But one pertinent fact stood out from the others.

"So Mitch is gonna put on Denny's stupid nuclear suit and go through one of those glowing doors?" Joy looked over her shoulder, at the burned sleeve of flesh on Helen's arm. She didn't see how anyone could survive exposure to something like that, even encased in steel and concrete, much less a thin layer of rubber protection. "He really is goddamn crazy." *Or suicidal.*

"You think that's why the thing back at Deborah's house fell over dead when it chased us?" Roberta asked. "It got too far away from one of these...portal-whatevers?"

"Sure sounds like it."

"There's something else." Eli sounded uncomfortable as they stepped on to the porch. "I thought you might want to know...your husband...he—"

"Nope," Joy cut him off. No way could she sort through that trainwreck right now. For now, it was enough to know that Casa Carson had fallen to ruin, and that she would never be going back. "Plenty of time for that later."

They carried JD over the threshold—where the pieces of the door lay scattered—and into the dim foyer of the house, where several lamps burned. The Hennings' place was much nicer than Joy's, the layout and decorations warm and homey, but the furniture all looked like something from a turn-of-the-century British parlor. They passed by a narrow, closed door then her foot squelched into a tacky puddle on the floor. "Look out, there's something..."

She spotted the form stretched across the base of the stairs just ahead and halted. Roberta and Carla followed her gaze and screamed in unison, like a couple of schoolgirls watching a horror movie rather than living one. Joy held up a hand to silence them.

They laid JD across a gorgeous Victorian couch upholstered in pea-green crushed velvet, and then Joy approached the body. And that's really all it was: a body. The torso ended at the shoulders, but the gore splattered on the stairs and landing quickly provided an identity.

"That's Porter Staubs," Roberta whispered. "I'd recognize that suit anywhere. Did those things do that to him?"

Joy shook her head. "No. Lena did this. He helped her get home, and the bitch murdered him for it. I *really* hope she gets what's coming to her." She looked around, at the rest of the house. Every light in the house appeared to be on. Through the archway into the den ahead, she spotted a phone sitting on the edge of an antique end table in the corner. "Make sure her car is in the garage, then look around and see if you can find the keys," she told Eli. "I'll call the Sheriff."

As Eli and Carla hurried off, Joy went to the phone and picked it up. A dial tone greeted her. She dialed 911, waited while it rang three times, and then an automated voice said, "You have reached the Bear Creek County Sheriff's Department. We are unable to take your call. Please leave your name, number, address, and a brief description of the situation, and someone will contact you shortly."

She hung up the phone, slamming it down on the cradle. "Since when do they not have people answering the goddamn phones all night at the sheriff's station?"

Across the room, Roberta put Helen down in another recliner. "What if...what if it's happening there, too? What if that scientist was wrong, and it's happening *everywhere?*"

"Then we sit tight until morning and come up with a new plan. Like he said, our best chance is to stay near the light."

As soon as these words were out, Joy wanted to kick herself for saying them. A statement like that only invited disaster, and the universe had done everything it could to foil her tonight.

So she wasn't too surprised when all the lights in the house snapped off a moment later.

THIRTY

Mitch limped back toward the shattered lodge, even though he knew it would offer no protection from the humongous creature. Part of him—most of him—wanted to wait for the thing to descend, to let it grind him to paste, but he found he still had a little fight left, even after the world stole his wife, his child and his dog, even after watching most of his neighbors be torn to pieces over the last few hours, even with this eternal migraine reaching new heights of pain, like a chainsaw held against the inside his skull. His only real consolation was that he'd bought enough time for Joy, JD and the others to escape.

He worked his way along the canted side of the house, unsure where to go. Through a broken window, he saw the giant's head appear above the missing roof and weave back and forth, searching for him like a girl with a dollhouse. Mitch ducked lower and kept moving toward the attached carport, which offered the only cover for fifty yards around.

The shadows beneath the aluminum awning were deep. He took a few steps and bumped into a blocky, waist-high shape and grabbed hold to keep from toppling over it. A tarp covered the object, but he could feel protruding cylinders through the vinyl that could only be handlebars.

Denny's ATV. Mitch worked his way around it, intending to cram himself into the small space between the vehicle and the wall and hide until the thing went away.

Something already in the crevice sprang out at him. A scream boiled up his throat, but a hand covered his mouth to stop it.

"It's me, dumbass," Denny hissed in his ear before removing the hand. Even in the dark, Mitch could see that blood cascaded down one side of his face from a long cut on his forehead.

"Jesus, we thought you were dead!"

"Yeah, sure. Not like my wife showin up out there gave you any *other* reason to leave me behind."

Before Mitch could apologize, a crash came from inside the house, followed by a piggish snuffling right on the other side of the wall.

"We have to make a run for it," he whispered.

Denny held up his hand. A set of keys jangled between his fingers. "Why should I run when I can ride?" He reached over and pulled the tarp away from the vehicle beside them, revealing a camouflaged four-wheeler with deep-tread tires that looked like they might be more comfortable on a monster truck.

"You think that's fast enough to outrun it?"

"Don't concern you, cause you ain't gettin on it."

Mitch's jaw squeezed shut so hard it felt like his teeth cracked. *Now?* This white trash son of a bitch wanted to measure dicks again *now?* The rush of anger sent another white hot knife through his brain. "Oh c'mon, you can't—!"

"Here's what's gonna happen." Denny slung a leg over the seat. The action caused him to grunt in pain and grab his midsection; Mitch realized the creature must've caused some serious internal damage when it headbutted him across the room. "You're gonna get to my shed, put on my nuke suit, and go turn off that goddamn machine. I'm gonna ride this baby outta here and lead that giant turd-sicle away so you got time to do it."

Mitch stared at him and wondered if the man had a brain injury as well. "I-I can't let you do that. Why don't you get the suit and I'll distract it?"

Denny snorted. "Shit, no. You think I wanna go into this other dimension? Trust me, I'm gettin the better end of this deal. You just handle your bidness and I'll handle mine."

"But…even if I get the suit, there's no guarantee I can find one of these portals."

"That ain't gonna be a problem no more, slick." Denny swept a hand across the open end of the carport.

Mitch looked out, across the field and toward the woods beyond. His stomach sank. That dim glow he'd seen back at the community center came from *everywhere* now. Shimmering portals of all sizes spread across the panorama, floating in the tall grass or between the trees or even high up in the air. They crackled and pulsed with energy, as if feeding off one another. There were too many to count, and, as he watched, another one suddenly popped into existence thirty or forty yards to their left, spilling out that shifting glow.

"I'm guessing those are the good doctor's 'doorways,'" Denny said.

"Yeah," Mitch murmured, unable to tear his eyes from the sight. "It's happening faster now. God, if these become permanent…"

Denny nodded. "So let's not waste time arguin. The suit's in a cabinet at the rear of the shed. Everything just zips on under a Velcro flap." He slipped the key in the ignition, then looked at Mitch. His eyes burned in the darkness. "If you make it back, just...just take care of her, all right?"

His earnestness took Mitch so much by surprise, he could only blink and nod.

"Also, you remember one thing...she really likes her asshole played with while she's comin."

"Oh for Christ's sake, Denny!"

The other man brayed obnoxious laughter, then twisted the key and fired up the ATV's ignition. "*Good luck, dipshit!*" He roared out of the carport and turned the handlebars to steer the vehicle east, away from the shed. Mitch watched him zoom across the field of glimmering portals. A heartbeat later, one of the creature's enormous feet smashed through the wall above his head, peppering him with chunks of wood. He ducked as the entire carport awning tore free and tumbled across the field like a punted football. The monster passed directly over Mitch's head—he looked up in time to see some puckered orifice as big as a manhole cover that cropdusted him with burnt sour stink—then it scurried after Denny with its eerily silent steps.

Mitch gave it time to move away, then sprinted toward the shed as fast as his injured knee would allow.

He'd crossed this same stretch of land an hour before with the spider-crabs in hot pursuit. If something like that came leaping out of the portals now, there would be no escape. But considering he planned to go through one himself in the next few minutes, worrying about it seemed moot. In any case, Mitch ran wide circles around the glowing doorways and arrived at the shed door a minute later.

The overhead lights switched on automatically when he pulled open the door. He moved toward the back, weaving through racks of weapons, stacks of gallon water bottles, shelves of non-perishables and tools and more of Denny's homemade grenades, all the way to a black wood cabinet against the metal wall. Mitch pulled it open.

A bright yellow bundle of glossy material sat inside, next to a black mask with a full face shield. He took out the former and shook it open to a reveal a one-piece garment that looked a few sizes too big for him. The fabric was stiff, heavy duty rubber, but couldn't be more than a quarter of an inch thick.

"Five minutes," he muttered. "You better be right about this, Morgan."

It took a moment to find the zipper running from the shoulder down to the hip, but once he got it open, Mitch stepped inside the boots, moved his hands into the heavy gloves sewn into the ends of the arms, and zipped the bodysuit back up. A heavy hood with tight elastic around the opening flipped over his head, leaving only a small circle around his forehead, cheeks, and chin exposed.

The mask had a long, sloping faceplate with two orange protrusions on the inside which he hoped were rebreathers, otherwise he would suffocate long before the caustic element in the Between could burn him up. Mitch slid it on, and tightened the straps until the pressure around his head became painful. He took a few experimental breaths. The air coming through the mask tasted metallic and stale.

He turned and strode back toward the entrance of the shed in his bulky outfit. The guns tempted him from either side, but he didn't know if they would be able to survive the trip. The last thing he wanted was a bunch of gunpowder exploding in his hand if Morgan's Arthenon ate through the plastic parts and got to the bullets.

Outside, one of the glowing portals had appeared just a few feet from the shed, as though waiting for him. The idea made him shudder. Mitch approached it and stopped in front of the shimmering wall, which was only a little taller and wider than him. He could feel the energy discharge even through the radiation suit, making the hair all over his body stand up stiff.

Blood thumped inside his skull, loud enough for him to hear the rush. And the migraine roared, just about tearing his head off with every heartbeat. His courage fled, replaced by a fear as great as the one that swept over him when the police showed up on his doorstep and told him that his wife had died. He wanted to turn around, lock himself in the shed, and retreat into his thoughtless, empty-headed fugue until morning.

Over the past year, when thoughts of suicide danced briefly through his mind like leaves skittering along a sidewalk in the breeze, the thought of Allie and his forever unborn child kept him moving, kept him breathing, if only to hold on to their memory a little longer. This time, however, he found Joy front and center, with that final squeeze of his hand, and the way she'd used his full name.

Maybe what scares you most is the idea that there might still be some happiness left for you in the world.

The idea cut through his burgeoning panic, squashed the throb at his temples more thoroughly than even his trances could.

He raised a hand to touch the glowing portal and then lowered it again. No sense dipping a toe into the pool; this was all or nothing.

Mitch took a deep breath, closed his eyes, and stepped forward into another dimension.

THIRTY ONE

Denny suspected his ribs were broken when he woke up in the wreckage of his home, but it took only a few seconds of sitting astride the four-wheeler for him to be certain. Every bounce and jolt caused fire to consume his torso, but he hunched low over the handlebars anyway and revved the engine as hard as it could go.

He never looked over his shoulder to see if the giant ballsack was following him. Couldn't, really, not unless he wanted to drive straight into one of the glowing portals scattered across the field like landmines, which grew more intense and vivid by the second. Denny knew it was back there though; his hunter's intuition could feel the fucker breathing down his neck.

The ATV's huge tires chewed through the grass as he sped toward the Corps of Engineer land that bordered the back of his property. He'd gotten this baby up to sixty-five miles per hour on a straight track of level ground before, but every dozen yards the shimmering curtains forced him to swerve, sacrificing speed for maneuverability. He'd planned to head to the gate and down onto the trail he and Claude had blazed through the thick woods, except now that seemed like a bad idea. If any of the good doctor's doorways blocked the narrow path, there wouldn't be anyplace to dodge.

That only left driving across whatever open ground he could find until his luck eventually ran out.

And then it did, when one of the floating doorways sprang into existence just a few yards in front of him, growing like a tumor in midair. Denny twisted the handlebars hard, narrowly missing the edge, and caught a strong whiff of burning ozone. But the turn proved far too tight for his speed. The ATV went up on its two left wheels, tilting his seat to a forty degree angle. Denny leaned against the turn and clung to the vehicle, but denied the urge to brake. For just a moment, he thought it might tip all the way over. Then the tires pounded back to the earth, grinding his shattered ribs together.

Through a glaze of tears, his eyes landed on the switch for the ATV's halogen headlights.

"Oh, fuck me..."

He flipped the switch. Twin cones of glaring light stabbed out in front of him for a good twenty yards. The portals they struck dissipated like smoke in a strong wind. With a grin, Denny pointed the four-wheeler back at the gate and hit the gas.

Now that he didn't have to concentrate so hard on driving, he chanced a look back.

And squawked in surprise.

The thing was right *there*, hurtling after him with its awkward waddling gait. Its head strained forward at the end of that long, curved neck, jaws stretched open in anticipation of snatching him up. He faced forward and coaxed a little more speed from the engine.

A five-foot high chain link fence topped with razor wire

separated his property from the Corps land. The gate, thank Jesus, was just splintery old wood that he'd been meaning to replace for years. He struck it doing fifty, the impact bars on the four-wheeler's grill disintegrating the obstruction. The ATV went airborne for a few seconds before coming down hard on the winding downhill trail through the woods, another jolt that made him whimper.

Behind him, the creature roared. Denny looked back and saw that its spindly legs were tangled in the fence. The barricade slowed it for only a moment before it tore free, ripping a ten-yard long section of the chain link right out of the ground. It scuttled onto the path, snapping tree trunks like matchsticks, and Denny noticed something interesting.

The behemoth's sides worked like a bellows, the tube of its torso expanding and contracting with great effort. It reminded him of his father's chronic emphysema near the end of his life, as the man struggled to draw each new breath. Denny never touched a cigarette in his life because of his dear old dad, and had harangued Joy until she quit as well.

"*Ah, are you feelin homesick?*" Denny taunted. Despite the pain it caused, he stood up on the footholds of the four-wheeler and jubilantly waved his arm in the air like he was riding a rodeo bull. "*C'mon fuckhead, I wanna mount your head over the gate when I rebuild my house!*"

In response, the creature twisted its neck sideways, ripped an entire tree out of the ground with its massive jaws, then reared back and launched it through the air like a javelin.

The aim was impeccable. Denny saw the missile incoming and hit the brakes just in time to avoid having his skull turned into a pancake. The tree exploded as it hit the trail in front of him, splintering in all directions, and he smashed into the stump a heartbeat later.

The ATV flipped, catapulting him from the seat. Denny flew through the air before plowing into the ground feet first and rolling another three yards through the dirt. His vision blacked out as the shock caused his brain to reboot, but he clung to a thin thread of consciousness.

A dreary haze coated the entire world. His right arm flopped uselessly when he sat up, but the pain felt very far away. He could see the creature at the top of the hill, plodding toward him as though each step took monumental effort. Blackish foam leaked from its mouth. It reached the pulverized four-wheeler, gave a full body shudder, and then fell over with an earth-shattering crash. Something that looked like a huge brown slug lolled out of its mouth just inches from Denny's boot sole.

"Don't seem...so smart...to me," Denny declared, and collapsed to the dirt.

THIRTY TWO

Roberta uttered a small shriek in the dark living room.

"Stay calm," Joy said, though her own heart took the express elevator right up her throat. Through the window beside her, she could see that the spotlights on the lawn were off as well. "With all the wattage going through this house, it probably happens all the time. Could be a breaker."

"Then what're we gonna do?"

"You have a phone? I lost mine in the woods."

"No, but JD does."

Roberta dug through her husband's pockets where he lay on the high-backed antique couch and handed her the device. Joy scanned through apps until she found his flashlight, then swept the glow across Roberta, the unconscious Helen, and JD's stiff form. "You stay here with them and keep trying to reach someone in town. I'll go take a look around, see if it's the breaker."

"Okay, just…hurry."

Joy grabbed a fireplace poker and moved around the corner and down a short hallway. She intended to start her search in the kitchen, wherever that might be, but ran into Eli and Carla coming the other direction.

"Did you find their car?"

Eli shook his head. "Garage is empty. She must've driven it back to the community center when she firebombed the place. What happened to the lights?"

"They just went off. I'm on my way to find the breaker."

"While we looked for the garage, we found another set of stairs that led down. House like this, it's gotta be in the basement."

Joy sighed heavily. "Of course it would be. I'll be able to write a book about other people's basements after tonight. All right, show me where."

The door stood a little further on, and the stairway beyond it led down into soupy darkness. On a shelf just inside the door sat a big, high intensity flashlight bright enough to burn a retina. Joy took it instead and dropped JD's phone into her pocket.

"You guys don't have to come," she said, although the idea of going down there alone made her feel like someone dropped a brick on her stomach. "Roberta and the others are still in the den."

Carla shook her head quickly. "No offense to her, but, uh...you're kinda the only competent one here."

"And if that big thing comes to trash this house, the basement might be the only safe place," Eli added. "If it looks okay down there, maybe we should all go in."

Joy shrugged and took the lead as they descended, with the poker in one hand and the wide beam carving through the darkness in front of them.

Lena's basement was much longer than the Whitakers, stretching the entire length of the house, and reminded her of the dusty, hole-in-the-wall fabric stores her grandmother took her to as a child. Various workstations sat everywhere, topped with sewing machines and crafting elements. Narrow aisles lined by cardboard boxes squeezed between shelves packed with fabric bolts and plastic-wrapped packages of foam padding. More Victorian furniture was piled everywhere, sofas and tables and chairs, some of them disassembled down to bare wood. It smelled clean though, to an antiseptic degree, and the walls were the same plaster and wood paneling as upstairs rather than dirt.

"What is this place, a sweatshop?" she whispered.

"They restore antique furniture," Carla answered. "This must be their work studio."

Eli tapped her shoulder and pointed to get her to direct the flashlight beam upward, where cables ran across the underside of the ground floor. "Electric lines. Breaker panel has to be down here somewhere."

They ventured further into the basement, past a workstation fitted with an industrial fabric cutter, and into the nearest cluttered supply aisle.

If the couple used a system for their storage, Joy certainly didn't see it. They passed boxes overflowing with fabric swatches and stacked cans of wood lacquer. Some of the passages became so narrow, Joy had to suck in her gut to get through. She alternated between sweeping the flashlight around and using it to follow the cables snaking across the ceiling, which all seemed to be leading to a spot on the easternmost wall. If they could just find a way through this maze to get to it.

Joy skirted around the edge of a beaten chaise longue, then turned into another aisle crowded by shelves on one side and waist-high plastic storage bins on the other. The trail of electric lines led down to a huge steel box mounted on the wall at the opposite end. "Let's just do this fast. If it's anything more complicated than a flipped circuit, we go back upstairs to the others and figure our next move."

"Agreed," Eli said. "Hold the flashlight over my shoulder so I can take a look."

Joy trained the beam on the breaker box as Eli moved forward. Carla stayed even closer to her than the claustrophobic space warranted until they reached the wall, then finally stood aside to watch. Eli undid the latch and opened the metal door.

The interior looked like the victim of a sledgehammer. The metal plating was bent, revealing torn wires. Joy realized two things simultaneously, that there would be no fixing this to get the lights back on without a professional electrician, and that they'd been fools to come down here.

A dark shape rose up from the wall of bins behind Carla.

Joy shouted a warning as she swung the flashlight around. The beam illuminated Lena's snarling, swollen, demented face, but it caught only the barest gleam of the hatchet in her hands because it was already in motion. The square blade buried itself in the side of Carla's neck, cleaving through the flesh like tissue paper.

Eli yelled his wife's name as he lunged toward her. At the same time, Lena yanked the weapon free. A single spurt of arterial blood sprayed across the wall. Carla stumbled forward to meet her husband, gurgling deep in her throat, eyes uncomprehending. She fell into his arms, dragging him into the floor with her.

Lena shoved through the wall of bins like a football player through a paper banner, still dressed in the tattered, bloodstained remains of her Rambo outfit. A huge swollen lump on the side of her head made her look as disfigured as the creatures outside. Her eyes were wild, more animal than human. The madwoman stood over Eli as he held his dying wife and raised the hatchet.

Joy leapt forward, instinct driving her, and brought the fireplace poker up. Lena's blade caromed off the thin metal bar with a discordant spang! The impact rattled up Joy's arm.

The other woman screeched in anger and backhanded the hatchet at her head. Joy threw herself backward away from it. The blade whistled through the air an inch from her nose. She stumbled into a stack of fabric bolts that toppled beneath her weight. The flashlight beam bounced around the room until she could get it under control.

Eli had been holding his hands over his wife's hacked throat to stop the bleeding. Now he looked up at last and made a feeble grab at Lena's legs. She brought a bony knee into his jaw hard enough to make his teeth clack, then chopped downward with the weapon. This time, Joy could do nothing to save him. The man's skull split down the middle when the blade hit him in the forehead. Joy's stomach clenched as a froth of brains and blood leaked out of the wound.

With her victim still dangling from the hatchet, Lena looked up at Joy.

"*How DARE you!*" she roared. "*How dare you people invade my home after you murdered my Cynthia!*"

"You're the only person murdering people, you crazy bitch!"

Lena shrieked and lurched toward her with the hatchet held over her head. Joy, still lying on a pile of satin and crushed velvet, waited until it descended before swinging up and across with the fireplace poker. This time she hit the other woman on her stick-thin forearm. Lena howled in pain as the hatchet sailed away across the basement.

Joy pulled back, meaning to hit her again, but the lunatic fell upon her. Even though Lena weighed thirty pounds less than her, she was a formidable fighter. Her hands were a whirlwind as she thrashed and clawed. Joy let the fireplace poker and flashlight clatter to the floor so she could try to capture her flailing arms. The two of them grappled in the darkness, grunting and straining. And, just when Joy came close to subduing her, Lena lowered her head and closed her teeth around a chunk of Joy's cheek.

The pain was searing. Joy screamed as Lena shook her head back and forth, like a dog with a hank of meat. She could feel the skin tear when the other woman pulled away, a sensation much worse than the bat creature biting her in the community center parking lot. The savagery of the act broke something inside Joy. Lena cackled triumphantly through a mouthful of flesh and wrapped her hand around Joy's throat, squeezing until her windpipe clamped shut.

Panic overrode all other thought and instinct. Joy bucked, twisted her hips, and rolled the smaller woman off of her, breaking the chokehold.

Behind her, barely visible in the backwash of the flashlight, a set of backless shelves formed a narrow tunnel that led beneath a workbench on the other side. Joy shoved bric-a-brac out of her way and crawled into the dark space on hands and knees, her only thought escape. A hand grabbed her foot but she kicked it away and kept moving, into another pitch black aisle and under a long wooden table, burrowing deeper into the clutter, losing herself in the maze of crafting supplies. She finally stopped in the hollow beneath a beaten settee, curling up in a miserable ball while the hole in her cheek pulsed fire. Her mind felt like a bridge with too many snapped cables, swaying violently in the wind just before it collapses entirely.

From elsewhere in the basement, she could hear Lena panting and growling in frustration as she knocked over shelves and blundered through the wreckage, searching for Joy in the dark.

"All right then, dearie!" the woman called, voice echoing in the tomblike space. "I'll just start with your friends upstairs and come back for you when I'm finished!"

Joy held her breath and listened as the crashes and bangs receded, leaving her alone in the dark.

THIRTY THREE

Something had happened to Mitch's eyes.

They'd been plucked from his skull by some new nightmarish specimen. Or maybe his migraine finally turned into the stroke he'd always feared and blinded him. Because the darkness on the other side of the doorway was too complete and total to exist outside of his own mind, a velvety, rich black that pressed in at him from all sides. His feet rested atop a squishy, spongy surface, but he couldn't see it or even his own body when he looked down, just that constant, unending murk in all directions.

He let out an involuntary gasp and flailed his rubber-coated arms in front of him, seeking some sort of sensational input to replace the loss of his sight. Not only did the darkness of the Between *look* tangible, it *felt* like it, too. His invisible limbs encountered the slightest bit of a resistance, not much different from moving at the bottom of a swimming pool. Morgan's voice floated through his head, explaining how Arthenon acted like a liquid on the other side of the portals.

His lungs constricted, squeezing out the last of his oxygen. A deep, abiding hysteria began to overtake him. This place Morgan and his scientist buddies had discovered wasn't just a void, it was *null* and void, an absence, a vacuum where not even rational thought could survive. Here was his nirvana, his limbo, the negative headspace he'd been trying to achieve for months now, ever since he'd watched Allie put in the ground. He'd imagined it as a dark sea, pretended that he might find her again somewhere in it, but now that he'd arrived, everything that made up Mitchell Flynn had been annihilated to such a degree that not even his base components existed.

He was nothingness. He was oblivion.

He was *between*.

And if anything remained of his deceased wife somewhere out there, he prayed her new existence was nothing like this.

The anxiety attack might have continued until it reduced him to no more than a quivering mess if a strange sizzling noise hadn't reached his ears, a sound that reminded him of greasy bacon cooking. It came from all around him, and, after a moment, he understood.

The acidic element that filled this dimension was dissolving his radiation suit, eating right through the rubber to get at him.

If he didn't find a way out soon, he would receive the Thomas Morgan third degree burn makeover in just a few very short minutes.

The image brought him back from the raw edge of panic, enough that he could at least breathe again. Instead of focusing on the unending darkness, he concentrated instead on the sensations he could still detect: the feel of the slick material against his skin, the smell of the metallic air flowing into his nostrils through the rebreather, that yielding surface beneath his feet. They all proved that he was still real, still existed, and squashed the last of his fear so that his brain could start working again.

For the first time, Mitch thought to turn around.

Suddenly, his eyes found something to look at again. An oval-shaped picture floated in the darkness, one with jagged edges that depicted the moonlit field he'd just come from, with Denny's wrecked lodge in the background. It *had* to be a picture, because the dim illumination didn't reach beyond the borders of its frame, the way light through a window would. But, as he watched the tall grasses sway in the breeze, Mitch understood he was seeing the portal he'd come through from the other side. No shimmering curtain blocked the view from this end. The nighttime meadow—which seemed so dark as he ran through it—now looked like a sunny beach compared to Morgan's hellish Between, yet none of that radiance spilled past the doorway. The optical impossibility made Mitch's head hurt all over again.

A lot more than your head is gonna hurt if you don't get moving NOW!

Mitch turned away from the exit and moved deeper into the Between, an action as difficult as a drowning man giving up a life preserver. That resistance dragged at him, made each of his limbs feel coated in molasses. He pushed against it, ignoring his sore knee so he could gain enough speed to jog through the darkness.

From Morgan's story, Mitch envisioned this place as an empty, featureless plane, nothing more than a big, black shoebox, but now that he'd gotten over the blindness, he knew how wrong that was. The ground wobbled beneath his foot with each step, and he could hear other noises over the hiss of his suit being cooked away, strange cracklings and rustlings and chirps, and a distant, monotone roar that sounded like rushing water. An entire world existed here, one that could never be seen by human eyes. He just hoped to god he didn't fall off a cliff while he explored it.

Without warning, another tear in the darkness appeared ahead and to his right. He angled toward it. The doorway's distance and size were impossible to judge without anything to compare it to; only when he got closer could he tell that it was half his height and looked out on a swath of dense woods.

Mitch turned away and kept moving. He panted now, the effort of having to move through the dense atmosphere beginning to exhaust him. That sizzling filled his ears, a constant reminder of time slipping away. How long had he been here? Two minutes? *Three?* Or did it only feel that long in his frantic mind?

Doorways of all sizes and shapes swam out of the gloom around him, like some bizarre art gallery with different perspectives of the same subject. He hurried to each in turn, peering through to see where they went.

Most of them opened onto more unidentifiable tracts of field and forest, somewhere along 407. One led back to the burned ruins of the community center. One only a handbreadth in diameter sat in the back seat of someone's car; Mitch could've reached through and touched the steering wheel if he'd wanted. In one he actually saw Denny, trudging across the landscape with his right arm hanging awkwardly against his side. Another that loomed over him appeared to go nowhere at all until he got closer and saw that it hovered thirty or forty feet in the air above someone's house, a fall that would surely kill him. The dizzying view allowed him to look above the trees at a long, rolling section of dark Corps land.

Jesus, how big is this place? Morgan said he should have plenty of time to find the exit, but the doctor hadn't seen all the new portals popping into existence. If Mitch had to check them all, he would never make it. Fresh panic caused him to pant as he braced for the unimaginable pain that would come as soon as his suit breached.

The doorways surrounded him now, everywhere he turned, a jumble of images made even more confusing by the fact that his faceplate was melting. He only glanced at them as he ran by, his heart hammering. Mitch caught snippets of trees, trees, the back of his own cabin, trees, an aerial view of Bear Creek Parkway, trees, a black granite countertop island covered with wires and equipment beneath a ceiling that looked metallic, more trees, a—

He came to a stumbling halt.

That countertop. It looked like the kind you'd find in every high school science classroom in the country, cluttered with beakers and Bunsen burners. Not only that, but the weird metallic ceiling above it looked partially scorched.

From somewhere in front of him, a wild, angry howl rose up.

One of the creatures who lived in this terrible place had found him.

Mitch wheeled around and ran through the thicket of portals, looking for the one with the black countertop. He could hear quick, scampering footsteps. Whatever chased him gave another furious cry.

The doorway appeared ahead in the midst of several others. It must be Morgan's lab, unless someone on 407 had installed an office building in their garage. Which, he couldn't help noting, would be a huge bylaw violation. Mitch ran toward as fast as he could go on his tender knee, but was still a few steps away when the thing behind him raked claws across his back.

THIRTY FOUR

"My poor darling," Roberta cooed, stroking JD's hair. "My hurt little baby hubby."

"I'm fine, Berta, really," JD told her. He usually hated it when his wife fussed over him, but the fact that she was alive—not to mention that he could speak and move his head again—overjoyed him too much to stop her. Besides, the rest of him remained as rigid as a slab of concrete, so he was pretty much at her mercy. "Look, I think I can move my little finger again."

He lay stretched across the fancy couch in Lena Henning's living room, lit only by the moon through the windows. When Joy left to find the breakers, Roberta slipped under him, so she could cradle his head in her lap. Across the room, the old woman with the burned arm lay in the recliner, completely unconscious.

Roberta leaned forward eagerly to look at his hands. "Which one?"

"Uh, the right one. I think."

"JD...it's not moving."

"Are you sure?"

"Pretty certain."

"Oh. Well, it probably will soon." He took a deep breath and prepared to say what had been going through his head the entire time he was locked up inside his own body. "Berta, listen...in the fire...I looked everywhere, but I couldn't find you. I...I thought I'd lost you. And if so, I just...I'd never have been able to forgive myself."

"But you didn't lose me, sweetheart." She hunched over to kiss his forehead. "I know what my big, brave man needs." To his complete surprise, Roberta slid her fingers down his neck, over his chest, and began tickling him below the belt. "Would it help if I milked Mr. Chubbers?" she whispered, before playfully biting his ear lobe.

The last time she'd made such an offer was sometime before the birth of their son, so it killed him to say, "Thanks babe, but I really don't think I need to be any stiffer than I already am."

She giggled girlishly. "Then can I do anything at all for you?"

"Actually, I *am* pretty hungry. Everyone else ate sandwiches over at Denny's but...I was too sick about you."

"I'll see if there's anything in the kitchen." Roberta slid out from under him and started into the den. JD stared up at the ceiling, ignoring a sudden itch on his cheek. He tried to move for the thousandth time, but his limbs still wouldn't obey him. They weren't numb, just frozen in place. JD went to the Petrified Forest as a kid, and kept imagining his body as one of those trees turned to stone. Being unable to move and defend himself was one of the most terrifying, frustrating, and humiliating experiences of his life.

Right now though, he worried more about Mitch. His best

friend was out there, and JD should be watching his back. If only his body would finish thawing out, maybe he could—

His wife gave a short cry from the other room, followed by a thump and a crash.

"Berta?" he called. The paralysis ended at his shoulders, so he twisted his head around as far as it would go. He couldn't see past the arm of the couch. "You okay?"

Footsteps crossed the room toward him, but stopped before entering his field of vision. He could sense someone standing beside the couch, just a foot away.

"Who's there?" JD demanded.

A face slid into view above him; an insane, deformed, terrible visage so twisted with hate that drool leaked from its thin lips and dripped onto his chin.

"The owner of the house is supposed to ask that question," Lena said, in a mocking parody of Roberta's coddling tone.

"Oh, you fuckin loony tune! What'd you do to my wife?"

Without warning, Lena hammered the bottom of one balled-up fist down onto his nose; the pain caused a burst of light behind his eyeballs. "Have some respect," she spat. "You're a guest in my home. An uninvited one, at that."

JD snuffled around the blood filling up his nostrils and repeated, "What'd you do to Roberta?"

Her snarl turned into a grin, which looked even more horrible on her gaunt, bloodstained face. Her own nose was swollen up so big, it must be interfering with her vision. "Oh, she's fine. Lying in the hallway. I was going to kill her like I did those trespassers in the basement...but then I realized that was too good for the likes of you two."

"*HELP!*" JD bellowed. Terror slammed through his stony body. He looked at the unconscious woman in the recliner. "*Ma'am, wake up, please!*"

The old lady didn't stir. Lena gave a mean-spirited laugh and walked out of his field of vision again. He heard a metallic rattling before she reappeared with a furniture-moving dolly.

"Let's get you up," she snarled.

JD continued to scream as she dragged him off the couch and manhandled his stiff body into an upright position. Then she worked the dolly under his shoe soles and leaned him backward until she could roll him around like a stack of boxes, an act even more degrading than being paralyzed in the first place. He struggled, desperate to make his limbs work, then, when that failed, tried to bite her fingers on the handles as she wheeled him through the living room.

"I shoulda killed you back there at Denny's house!" he shouted over his shoulder. "What the hell is wrong with you? I mean, Jesus Christ, lady!"

She grabbed one of his ears and twisted until something tore. His shrieks filled the entire house. Lena set him back upright on the dolly and came to stand in front of him. "Was it you?"

"Me *what?*" JD's voice cracked on the last word. He could feel blood streaming down the side of his neck.

Lena studied him, her eyes like two glittering chunks of flint in the dark living room. "I didn't think about it until I saw you and your chubby little wife cozied up on *my* couch, but...you showed up to the meeting late. Is that because the two of you were here...in this house...murdering my dear, sweet Cynthia?"

"*No! That's fuckin ridiculous!*"

"Don't deny it! I know Flynn wanted us dead for daring to defy him, and you are his right hand!"

"Would you stop and think for just a minute?" JD pleaded.

"Why would we kill Cynthia? Over some goddamn *lights?* Those things out there, *they* did it, not us!"

For a split second, indecision flickered in her cruel eyes. Somewhere deep inside she knew the truth, but she'd lived with hatred for so long—cherished it, cultivated it, used it as a weapon—she just couldn't let go. Lena shook her head stubbornly as she walked behind him and began rolling the dolly again. "No. No, I refuse to believe that. You people had it in for us since day one."

Reasoning with her was useless. Instead he asked, "Where are you takin me?"

"Once I escaped from that barbarian's house next door, I stood outside and listened to a little more of what that doctor said. When you all started talking about coming here, I came home to prepare for you. And found something very interesting in my bathroom."

She wheeled him back the way they'd come in, past Porter's beheaded corpse at the base of the stairs, to the narrow door just a few steps from the busted entrance of the house. Lena stopped the dolly directly in front of it. A very familiar, shimmering light came through the crack at the bottom.

"Oh shit no," JD moaned.

Lena reached around him, twisted the door knob, and threw open the door, revealing a tiny half-bathroom, the kind with only a sink and toilet.

But JD could barely see them through the glimmering portal that floated in the darkness just beyond the door.

"I kept the lights on to make sure nothing came through," she told him. "But now...I think I'll send something the *other* way."

"Oh god, please don't."

"Burn in hell, killer. Your wife will be right behind you."

She gripped the handles and started to roll him toward the portal, but a polite cough from the missing front door stopped her.

"Jesus," Denny moaned. "Do I have to do everything around here?"

THIRTY FIVE

Even with a dislocated shoulder, broken ribs and probable concussion, Denny figured himself more than a match for his elderly, rail-thin, lesbian neighbor. He'd survived much worse than her tonight, then navigated back through the field of portals to find her on the verge of giving Miller an acid bath in Dimension X. Miller himself must've agreed with this assessment, as he immediately started shouting, "*C'mon Denny, knock her on her ass!*"

But all that confidence went right out the window when she ran at Denny with her bony hands outstretched, wailing like a banshee. The snarling, crazed look on her face actually terrified him more than being chased by the gigantic monstrosity.

He fell back a step and raised his good arm to defend himself. She hit him with the force of a linebacker, hard enough to drive his much larger mass into the doorframe. His dizzy head reeled from the impact; the soothing black of unconsciousness crept into the periphery of his vision. He almost let it take him, until her hands began clawing at his face. Denny tried to knock them away, but she was as quick and vicious as a Tasmanian devil.

One thumb plunged into his left eye socket. He could feel it in there, putting pressure against his nasal cavity. He heard a gritty crunch, and something wet and slimy flowed down his cheek.

Denny didn't recognize the anguished sound that came out of his mouth. He screamed high and long, then grabbed a handful of her short hair and ripped the woman off him like a yowling cat. She tumbled backward into Miller. The entire dolly crashed over on its side, spilling them both into the floor, but Lena was back up in a heartbeat, squatting in the floor and growling at Denny, all traces of humanity gone.

"*Oh you bitch*," he sobbed, blinking away tears from his remaining eye. Denny started forward, intending to bury his boot heel in her pinched little face. "*You fuckin cunt, you've had this comin a long t—*"

She caught him off guard yet again, scrambling toward him on all fours and latching onto his leg like a pole at a stripper joint. Teeth bit through his pants leg and into the meat of his calf. Denny tried to shake her off, but his dislocated arm threw him off balance. He twisted awkwardly as he fell, landing hard on his shattered chest.

Pain sapped the last of his fight. He could only lay there and think, *this wacko bulldyke actually* beat *me.*

Denny looked up. Lena stood over him, hands held above her head in triumph, laughing hysterically at the ceiling. The sparking glow from the portal in her bathroom fell across the crone in undulating sheets, somehow completing the picture of lunacy. Both he and Miller lay at her feet, neither of them in any shape to get up.

So he was very relieved when Joy walked out of the shadows of the den behind Lena holding a huge wooden table leg like a caveman's club.

His wife didn't make a sound, just reared back over her shoulder and swung the club directly into the side of Lena Henning's temple. A low, hollow *thok!* cut off her shrieky laughter mid-peal. She reeled away from the blow and, for one heart-stopping moment, it looked like she might stay on her feet, but then she tripped over Miller's prone body and went sprawling.

Through her bathroom doorway and straight into the portal.

That shimmering glow disappeared, replaced by ultimate darkness. Lena screamed from the other side, one long fire whistle of agony that sounded like it came from miles away. Her legs were the only part of her visible; they stuck out of the portal and drummed against the tile floor of her bathroom for several seconds before finally going still.

Joy dropped the table leg, trudged forward, and sank into the floor beside Denny. Blood streamed down her face from a hole in her cheek that would probably leave a nasty scar. But he supposed he didn't look much better at the moment.

She glanced over at him and croaked, "You okay?"

He grunted. "My goddamn eyeball is egg yolk, woman. Whatta *you* think?"

Joy nodded slowly, then said, "I want a divorce."

"Yeah," Denny agreed with a sigh. "Me too."

THIRTY SIX

Mitch felt the claws of the creature behind him rip through the back of his radiation suit, followed by an unbearable burning sensation as the Arthenon began eating at his flesh. The pain consumed him, blotted out all thought with a red haze of agony.

Then he hurtled through the portal and back into his own world.

Even though the lighting in the room he entered was dim, the illumination still blinded him after the unending blackness. The drag on his limbs vanished and he careened out of control across a short stretch of sterile white tile and barreled into the lab workstation before he could slow down. Mitch rolled across the tabletop, smashing a complicated apparatus festooned with wires, then fell into a smoking heap on the other side, facedown amid the wreckage.

He could've happily laid there for a week, but claws clicked against the tile floor he'd just run across. Whatever was chasing him had come through the portal as well. Mitch ignored the searing pain across his upper back as he scrambled to his knees and peeked over the top of the counter.

The portal he'd come through floated just a few yards away, in what looked like the crater of a bomb blast. A clear tube jutted from the polished silver ceiling, held in place by gears and rotors. It looked retractable, made to lower down and seal in place around the portal to a circular metal platform beneath, obviously some kind of containment protocol. The entire setup was blackened and coated with soot. Mitch thought the origination point for the fire was a huge panel of circuitry and electrical conduits built into the cinderblock wall on the other side, most of which were melted to slag. If he'd understood Morgan's story, something in this array had exploded and pushed the scientist right through the portal.

The other men Morgan mentioned lay against the far wall, where the explosion must have thrown them, two partially incinerated corpses wearing suits very much like Mitch's.

Motion to the left caught his eye. A dark, sinewy form darted between several rows of freestanding cabinets and clothing racks that held more containment suits.

Mitch tore at the zipper of the radiation hood, desperate to be free of the constricting outfit. He didn't know if the creature had lost track of him or if it was merely toying with him, but he wanted to be ready to defend himself. The outer layer of the rubber still sizzled in a few places, and smelled like a burnt tire. His back burned and throbbed bad enough to bring tears to his eyes; he wondered how much of his flesh had been dissolved in the split second of contact. Once he got the hood and rebreather off, he became aware of a droning, irregular buzz in the air, a sound like an inconstant electrical current. As he pulled the body suit off, Mitch took in the rest of the room.

He was in some kind of big rectangular observation cell. Concrete made up three of the walls—one of which, at the opposite end from where he crouched, had a huge steel vault door set into it—and the fourth was made of either thick glass or plastic. It all looked like ordinary lab space converted to contain the portal, a backup to the retractable tube, a hasty solution to a problem they didn't anticipate. These people had been woefully unprepared to deal with the power they'd discovered. Around the periphery of the room were those freestanding cabinets and racks filled with scientific equipment, along with shelves that held rows upon rows of what looked like empty aquariums. He saw nothing that looked like a machine he could shut off, and realized they probably wouldn't have kept it inside this cell anyway.

That misfiring electric buzz came from the other side of the glass wall. Through the clear partition, he could see the rest of the lab, a cavernous room that housed rows of desks and workstations. They reminded Mitch of the way NASA mission control looked in the movies. Overhead fluorescents provided only weak illumination, no more than a glow. There were no windows at all, but he wondered if he would see the New York skyline if there had been.

Something crashed inside the cell, close to where the creature disappeared.

Mitch quietly slid his boot free of the radiation suit and crawled behind a row of cabinets and past more workstations toward the door of the cell. It was a solid slab of square steel a yard wide and several high, anchored into the wall with geared hinges as big as his bicep. A small screen beside it glowed dull green. From the floor, he reached up with both hands and pushed against the latch bar across the middle. Not only did it stay firmly in place, the screen beside it gave an angry screech and turned from green to red. A calm female voice intoned, "Please scan security pass."

Mitch jumped and glanced over his shoulder. Still no sign of the creature, but it had plenty of places to hide while it stalked him. Fear made his bowels crawl as he searched in vain for a way to open it.

He was trapped. Morgan either forgot to give him the laminated badge attached to his coat or just didn't get around to it before being crushed by one of the hellish monsters his experiments unleashed upon the world. Either way, Mitch couldn't get out of this room unless he grabbed a new suit and went back through the portal.

Then he remembered the two dead men.

Mitch turned around and slunk back the way he came. Once he reached the last workstation, he paused. There was nothing else to use for cover in this corner of the room, where the portal floated. But he could see another ID badge clipped to the breast of one of the bodies on the floor. He just prayed it wasn't too burned for the scanner.

Rather than draw the procedure out by sneaking, Mitch skittered out onto the scorched tile on hands and knees. He gave the shimmering portal a wide berth, and reached the corpse a second later. Mitch unclipped the ID badge just as a low hiss came from his left. He turned his head to look...

And felt his heart squeeze into a hard knot.

A brown-plated skull poked between the legs of one of the hanging containment suits on the other side of the portal, just a few feet away, an eyeless, lopsided cranium with crooked devil horns on top, and several long, waving antennae along a ridge where its nose should've been. A sizeable mouth hung open just below these, filled only with yellow incisors that grew out of the lipless hole in a tangled mess.

Those antennae swept across the room before honing in on him. A twitch shook the corners of its gaping mouth.

Warm horror oozed over Mitch as he realized the creature had just grinned.

And then it exploded into motion, shoving over the entire rack of suits to get to him. Mitch caught a brief glimpse of an elongated, humanoid body and sickle-like claws before he rolled in the opposite direction. He sensed the creature lunge, but it got tangled in the clothing rack. One of its arms swiped out as he jumped to his feet and limped past. The long claws at the end of its hand missed Mitch's leg by inches.

He ran back to the cell door. The creature roared in fury as it paced him through the aisles of cabinets and lockers on the opposite side of the room. With as fast as it moved, Mitch knew the footrace would've been lost already if not for his head start.

Mitch held the badge ready and swiped it across the scanner, which considered the authorization for a handful of agonizing heartbeats before giving a congenial beep. Something in the door clicked. This time, when he pushed the latch, the slab of heavy steel swung open on its mechanized hinges.

He rushed through and came to a flailing halt.

Another creature stood in his path, this one as big as a black bear, with multiple appendages and the head of a mantis.

Except this one was behind a sheet of glass, and suspended in amber-hued fluid.

Specimens lined the narrow corridor beyond the cell door, hideous creatures sealed into liquid vats that sported a host of readouts. Mitch collected his wits and turned to force the door shut.

A scaly brown arm snaked through, preventing the cell from closing. It whipped around in mad circles, slashing blindly. Razor-sharp claws tore Mitch's forearm down to the bone. With blood gushing down his arm, Mitch moved out of range of the claws, put his back against the cold steel, and pushed.

"*Go back to hell!*" he shouted, surprised at the raw desperation in his own voice. The thing on the other side of the door was winning the shoving contest, slowly overcoming him an inch at a time. Those claws would be able to reach him again in seconds. Mitch stared at them, then noticed the small handle on the wall just past them labeled with the words "EMERGENCY CONTAINMENT LOCKDOWN." Mitch leapt away from the door, skirted around the claws, and pulled the handle.

Klaxons blared. The door, which swung open without his weight, slammed all the way closed again with a deep, resounding *thoom!* The heavy steel ripped through the creature's arm with hundreds of pounds of pressure. Black oil sprayed across the wall in a fan. The appendage fell to the floor at Mitch's feet, clawed digits still wriggling. The sirens cut off a moment later.

When he was sure the door couldn't open, Mitch limped away, squeezing the gaping wound in his arm with his free hand to staunch the blood flow. He followed the hallway of specimen tanks, which made two right turns before depositing him in the control room just outside the observation cell.

The creature waited for him on the other side of the clear wall, giving Mitch a chance to study it for the first time. It was far more human than anything else that had crawled out of the Between, a head, two legs, and two arms—well, *one* arm now—but the similarities ended there. The proportions of its body were far longer, stretched out like taffy, giving it an extra two feet over Mitch's five-ten height. It looked just as crudely made as the others though, with a twisted spine and swollen joints beneath the rocky outer shell. Even without eyes, its rudimentary face followed him as he crossed through the sea of desks and hesitantly approached the glass. Black fluid dribbled onto the floor from the stump of its arm. The grievous injury didn't seem to bother it as much as Mitch's savaged appendage.

That twitch tugged at its mouth as he approached. Mitch stood on the other side of the glass, looking up at that horrible visage, and cringed as its jaw opened and those gnarled teeth separated. A noise rose from the depths of its gullet, perfectly audible through the transparent barrier, but it still took Mitch a moment to understand that it was speaking to him in perfect English.

In a guttural, screechy voice that sounded like someone gargling a mouthful of angry bees, it said, "*Your world...will be ours.*"

Then it turned away and bounded across the cell, hurtling over counters and leaping back into the portal. Mitch saw the blackness of the other side one more time before the shimmering curtain closed.

"Not if I have anything to say about it." Mitch turned and limped deeper into the laboratory, leaving a trail of blood as he followed the buzzing sound to another door across the room. Freezing cold air buffeted him when he opened it to reveal a bank of computer servers stretching from floor to ceiling, and a squat, glossy white box the size of a coffin on the floor. Cables snaked out of it in all directions. The sputtering drone came from somewhere beneath the gleaming cover.

"So you're the thing that caused all this," he said, swaying on his feet as he spoke. The blood loss made him a little dizzy, but no way would he allow himself to pass out until he'd seen this through to the bitter end. "You know, I could just unplug you, but if Doc was right, they'd have you back up and running by the end of the day. And that *cannot* happen."

He looked around the control room. A toolbox sat beneath one of the workstations. Mitch walked over and dug out a good, solid hammer and hefted it as he trudged back to the stabilizer.

For the first time in months, his head didn't hurt even the tiniest bit.

THIRTY SEVEN

Joy was the only able-bodied person left in the group. She managed to help Denny, Helen, Roberta, and JD down into Lena's basement, away from the glittering portal in the bathroom and the multiple others forming outside. She bandaged Denny's missing eye and then they sat in the dark without talking until an electronic beep sounded in Joy's pocket. The sudden noise in the silence caused them all to jump.

Joy put her hand in her pocket, clueless as to what it could be, and pulled out JD's ringing cell phone. She'd completely forgotten that she had it.

"Holy shit," JD murmured. "The phones're workin again."

"Answer it!" Roberta urged.

The device lit up with the incoming call, and a picture of Mitch displayed on the screen. Joy's stomach clenched as she pushed the answer button. "H-hello?"

"I was looking for JD, but I'm just as happy to hear your voice."

"Mitch," she said in relief, and JD gave a jubilant howl. "Are you all right?"

"Well, I seem to be stuck in New York, but other than that..." He gave a tired chuckle. "Did you make it to town?"

"Not exactly. We're in Lena's basement."

"Good. Stay there. The portals should all be closed, but don't leave until daylight. Just in case."

Joy smiled. The action made the hole in her cheek throb and she was very aware of Denny's brooding glare, but she was too ecstatic to care about either. "It's over? It's really over?"

"No. It's not. And I don't know if it ever will be."

The smile dropped off her face. "What does that mean?"

She heard hesitation on the other end of the line. "Morgan and his scientist buddies, I don't think they have any idea what they really discovered. Those monsters didn't just stumble into our dimension when the door opened. One of them...it talked to me." She could hear him take a shuddering breath. "I destroyed their machine, but that's just not enough."

The room performed a lurching spin around Joy. "What are you going to do?" she asked numbly.

He didn't hesitate with his answer, which told her how futile it would be to try talking him out of it. "Burn this whole place to the ground. They probably have all their work backed up offsite somewhere, but maybe it'll set them back. Long enough for you and the others to get the word out about this to anyone who'll listen. Promise me you'll do that."

"We will!" she said desperately. "But what about you, you could still—!"

"*If* I make it out of here alive," he began. "I can't see the government letting me walk away. Not after what I've seen. I'll probably just end up in a gulag somewhere." His voice became a gruff whisper as he added, "But trust me, there are *much* worse places to be. I've seen them firsthand. And compared to that, a secret government torture facility would be a five-star resort."

"This isn't your responsibility," she told him. "You've done enough. *Lost* enough. You don't have to do this."

"Yeah, well, I don't see anybody else here." Mitch gave that worn-out laugh again. "And the best part is, my head doesn't hurt at all anymore. But, to tell you the truth, I'm pretty sure I have you to thank for that."

She looked at Denny now, met his fiery gaze with one of her own until he finally relented and looked away. "I think you've more than repaid me."

"Take care of yourself, Carson. And tell JD to do the same."

The phone went dead in her hands. She sat there and thought about how sucker-punchingly unfair life could be.

"So what's El Presidente up to?" Denny asked.

Joy forced herself to smile, something she'd done often since marrying Denny. She suspected that, in the future, those smiles would be much more genuine. "Playing hero."

Her soon-to-be-ex-husband sighed and shook his head. "Sounds about right."

Like this novel?

YOUR REVIEWS HELP!

In the modern world, customer reviews are essential for any product. The artists who create the work you enjoy need your help growing their audience. Please visit Goodreads or the website of the company that sold you this novel to leave a review, or even just a star rating. Posting about the book on social media is also appreciated.

About the Author

Russell C. Connor has been writing horror since the age of five, and is the author of two short story collections, five eNovellas, and fourteen novels. His books have won two Independent Publisher Awards and a Readers' Favorite Award. He has been a member of the DFW Writers' Workshop since 2006, and served as president for two years. He lives in Fort Worth, Texas with his rabid dog, demented film collection, mistress of the dark, and demonspawn daughter.

His next novel—*The Halls of Moambati*, Volume IV of *The Dark Filament Ephemeris*—will be available in 2021.

Made in the USA
Coppell, TX
12 March 2021